P9-DDY-758

" Go to Washington and save my father's life."—Act III.

*Frontispiece.*

# THE LION AND THE MOUSE

BY
### CHARLES KLEIN

## A Story *of* American Life

NOVELIZED FROM THE PLAY BY
### ARTHUR HORNBLOW

"Judges and Senators have been bought for gold;
Love and esteem have never been sold."—Pope

---

ILLUSTRATED BY
### STUART TRAVIS
AND
SCENES FROM THE PLAY

---

## GROSSET & DUNLAP
PUBLISHERS - NEW YORK

# CONTENTS

# The Lion and the Mouse

## CHAPTER I

THERE was unwonted bustle in the usually
sleepy and dignified New York offices of
the Southern and Transcontinental Railroad Company in lower Broadway. The supercilious,
well-groomed clerks who, on ordinary days, are far
too preoccupied with their own personal affairs to
betray the slightest interest in anything not immediately concerning them, now condescended to bestir
themselves and, gathered in little groups, conversed in
subdued, eager tones. The slim, nervous fingers of
half a dozen haughty stenographers, representing as
many different types of business femininity, were busily rattling the keys of clicking typewriters, each of
their owners intent on reducing with all possible
despatch the mass of letters which lay piled up in
front of her. Through the heavy plate-glass swinging doors, leading to the elevators and thence to the
street, came and went an army of messengers and
telegraph boys, noisy and insolent.

Through the open windows the hoarse shouting of news-venders, the rushing of elevated trains, the clanging of street cars, with the occasional feverish dash of an ambulance—all these familiar noises of a great city had the far-away sound peculiar to top floors of the modern sky-scraper. The day was warm and sticky, as is not uncommon in early May, and the overcast sky and a distant rumbling of thunder promised rain before night.

The big express elevators, running smoothly and swiftly, unloaded every few moments a number of prosperous-looking men who, chatting volubly and affably, made their way immediately through the outer offices towards another and larger inner office on the glass door of which was the legend "Directors Room. Private." Each comer gave a patronizing nod in recognition of the deferential salutation of the clerks. Earlier arrivals had preceded them, and as they opened the door there issued from the Directors Room a confused murmur of voices, each different in pitch and tone, some deep and deliberate, others shrill and nervous, but all talking earnestly and with animation as men do when the subject under discussion is of common interest. Now and again a voice was heard high above the others, denoting anger in the speaker, followed by the pleading accents of the peace-maker, who was arguing his irate colleague into calmness. At intervals the door opened to admit other arrivals, and through the crack was caught a glimpse of a dozen directors, some seated, some standing near a long table covered with green baize.

It was the regular quarterly meeting of the directors of the Southern and Transcontinental Railroad Company, but it was something more than mere routine that had called out a quorum of such strength and which made to-day's gathering one of extraordinary importance in the history of the road. That the business on hand was of the greatest significance was easily to be inferred from the concerned and anxious expression on the directors' faces and the eagerness of the employés as they plied each other with questions.

"Suppose the injunction is sustained?" asked a clerk in a whisper. "Is not the road rich enough to bear the loss?"

The man he addressed turned impatiently to the questioner:

"That's all you know about railroading. Don't you understand that this suit we have lost will be the entering wedge for hundreds of others. The very existence of the road may be at stake. And between

you and me," he added in a lower key, " with Judge
Rossmore on the bench we never stood much show.
It's Judge Rossmore that scares 'em, not the injunction. They've found it easy to corrupt most of the
Supreme Court judges, but Judge Rossmore is one
too many for them. You could no more bribe him
than you could have bribed Abraham Lincoln."

" But the newspapers say that he, too, has been
caught accepting $50,000 worth of stock for that de-
cision he rendered in the Great Northwestern case."

" Lies! All those stories are lies," replied the other
emphatically. Then looking cautiously around to make
sure no one overheard he added contemptuously, " The
big interests fear him, and they're inventing these lies
to try and injure him. They might as well try to blow
up Gibraltar. The fact is the public is seriously
aroused this time and the railroads are in a panic."

It was true. The railroad, which heretofore had
considered itself superior to law, had found itself
checked in its career of outlawry and oppression.
The railroad, this modern octopus of steam and steel
which stretches its greedy tentacles out over the land,
had at last been brought to book.

At first, when the country was in the earlier stages
of its development, the railroad appeared in the guise
of a public benefactor. It brought to the markets of

the East the produce of the South and West. It opened up new and inaccessible territory and made oases of waste places. It brought to the city coal, lumber, food and other prime necessaries of life, taking back to the farmer and the woodsman in exchange, clothes and other manufactured goods. Thus, little by little, the railroad wormed itself into the affections of the people and gradually became an indispensable part of the life it had itself created. Tear up the railroad and life itself is extinguished.

So when the railroad found it could not be dispensed with, it grew dissatisfied with the size of its earnings. Legitimate profits were not enough. Its directors cried out for bigger dividends, and from then on the railroad became a conscienceless tyrant, fawning on those it feared and crushing without mercy those who were defenceless. It raised its rates for hauling freight, discriminating against certain localities without reason or justice, and favouring other points where its own interests lay. By corrupting government officials and other unlawful methods it appropriated lands, and there was no escape from its exactions and brigandage. Other roads were built, and for a brief period there was held out the hope of relief that invariably comes from honest competition. But the railroad either absorbed its rivals or pooled interests with them, and thereafter there were several masters instead of one.

Soon the railroads began to war among themselves, and in a mad scramble to secure business at any price they cut each other's rates and unlawfully entered into secret compacts with certain big shippers, permitting the latter to enjoy lower freight rates than their competitors. The smaller shippers were soon crushed out of existence in this way. Competition was throttled and prices went up, making the railroad barons richer and the people poorer. That was the beginning of the giant Trusts, the greatest evil American civilization has yet produced, and one which, unless checked, will inevitably drag this country into the throes of civil strife.

From out this quagmire of corruption and rascality emerged the Colossus, a man so stupendously rich and with such unlimited powers for evil that the world has never looked upon his like. The famous Crœsus, whose fortune was estimated at only eight millions in our money, was a pauper compared with John Burkett Ryder, whose holdings no man could count, but which were approximately estimated at a thousand millions of dollars. The railroads had created the Trust, the ogre of corporate greed, of which Ryder was the incarnation, and in time the Trust became master of the railroads, which after all seemed but retributive justice.

John Burkett Ryder, the richest man in the world—the man whose name had spread to the farthest corners of the earth because of his wealth, and whose money, instead of being a blessing, promised to become not only a curse to himself but a source of dire peril to all mankind—was a genius born of the railroad age. No other age could have brought him forth; his peculiar talents fitted exactly the conditions of his time. Attracted early in life to the newly discovered oil fields of Pennsylvania, he became a dealer in the raw product and later a refiner, acquiring with capital, laboriously saved, first one refinery, then another. The railroads were cutting each other's throats to secure the freight business of the oil men, and John Burkett Ryder saw his opportunity. He made secret overtures to the road, guaranteeing a vast amount of business if he could get exceptionally low rates, and the illegal compact was made. His competitors, undersold in the market, stood no chance, and one by one they were crushed out of existence. Ryder called these manœuvres " business "; the world called them brigandage. But the Colossus prospered and slowly built up the foundations of the extraordinary fortune which is the talk and the wonder of the world to-day.

Master now of the oil situation, Ryder succeeded in his ambition of organizing the Empire Trading Company, the most powerful, the most secretive, and the most wealthy business institution the commercial world has yet known.

Yet with all this success John Burkett Ryder was still not content. He was now a rich man, richer by many millions that he had dreamed he could ever be, but still he was unsatisfied. He became money mad. He wanted to be richer still, to be the richest man in the world, the richest man the world had ever known. And the richer he got the stronger the idea grew upon him with all the force of a morbid obsession. He thought of money by day, he dreamt of it at night. No matter by what questionable device it was to be procured, more gold and more must flow into his already overflowing coffers. So each day, instead of spending the rest of his years in peace, in the enjoyment of the wealth he had accumulated, he went downtown like any twenty-dollar-a-week clerk to the tall building in lower Broadway and, closeted with his associates, toiled and plotted to make more money.

He acquired vast copper mines and secured control of this and that railroad. He had invested heavily in the Southern and Transcontinental road and was chairman of its board of directors. Then he and his fellow-conspirators planned a great financial coup. The millions were not coming in fast enough. They must make a hundred millions at one stroke. They floated a great mining company to which the public was invited to subscribe. The scheme having the endorsement of the Empire Trading Company no one suspected a snare, and such was the magic of John Ryder's name that gold flowed in from every point of the compass. The stock sold away above par the day it was issued. Men deemed themselves fortunate if they were even granted an allotment. What matter if, a few days later, the house of cards came tumbling down, and a dozen suicides were strewn along Wall Street, that sinister thoroughfare which, as a wit has said, has a graveyard at one end and the river at the other! Had Ryder any twinges of conscience? Hardly. Had he not made a cool twenty millions by the deal?

Yet this commercial pirate, this Napoleon of finance, was not a wholly bad man. He had his redeeming qualities, like most bad men. His most pronounced weakness, and the one that had made him the most conspicuous man of his time, was an entire lack of moral principle. No honest or honourable man could have amassed such stupendous wealth. In other words, John Ryder had not been equipped by Nature with a conscience. He had no sense of right, or wrong, or justice where his own interests were concerned. He was the prince of egoists. On the other hand, he possessed qualities which, with some people, count as virtues. He was pious and regular in his attendance at church and, while he had done but little for charity, he was known to have encouraged the giving of alms by the members of his family, which consisted of a wife, whose timid voice was rarely heard, and a son Jefferson, who was the destined successor to his gigantic estate.

Such was the man who was the real power behind the Southern and Transcontinental Railroad. More than anyone else Ryder had been aroused by the present legal action, not so much for the money interest at stake as that any one should dare to thwart his will. It had been a pet scheme of his, this purchase for a song, when the land was cheap, of some thousand acres along the line, and it is true that at the time of the purchase there had been some idea of laying the land out as a park. But real estate values had increased in astonishing fashion, the road could no longer afford to carry out the original scheme, and had attempted to dispose of the property for building purposes, including a right of way for a branch road. The news, made public in the newspapers, had raised a storm of protest. The people in the vicinity claimed that the railroad secured the land on the express condition of a park being laid out, and in order to make a legal test they had secured an injunction, which had been sustained by Judge Rossmore of the United States Circuit Court.

These details were hastily told and re-told by one clerk to another as the babel of voices in the inner room grew louder, and more directors kept arriving from the ever-busy elevators. The meeting was called for three o'clock. Another five minutes and the chairman would rap for order. A tall, strongly built man with white moustache and kindly smile emerged from the directors room and, addressing one of the clerks, asked:

" Has Mr. Ryder arrived yet? "

The alacrity with which the employé hastened forward to reply would indicate that his interlocutor was a person of more than ordinary importance.

" No, Senator, not yet. We expect him any minute." Then with a deferential smile he added: " Mr. Ryder usually arrives on the stroke, sir."

The senator gave a nod of acquiescence and, turning on his heel, greeted with a grasp of the hand and affable smile his fellow-directors as they passed in by twos and threes.

Senator Roberts was in the world of politics what his friend John Burkett Ryder was in the world of finance—a leader of men. He started life in Wisconsin as an errand boy, was educated in the public schools, and later became clerk in a dry-goods store, finally going into business for his own account on a large scale. He was elected to the Legislature, where his ability as an organizer soon gained the friendship of the men in power, and later was sent to Congress, where he was quickly initiated in the game of corrupt politics. In 1885 he entered the United States Senate. He soon became the acknowledged leader of a considerable majority of the Republican senators, and from then on he was a figure to be reckoned with. A very ambitious man, with a great love of power and few scruples, it is little wonder that only the practical or dishonest side of politics appealed to him. He was in politics for all there was in it, and he saw in his lofty position only a splendid opportunity for easy graft.

He did not hesitate to make such alliances with corporate interests seeking influence at Washington as would enable him to accomplish this purpose, and in this way he had met and formed a strong friendship with John Burkett Ryder. Each being a master in his own field was useful to the other.

# THE MOUSE

Neither was troubled with qualms of conscience, so they never quarrelled. If the Ryder interests needed anything in the Senate, Roberts and his followers were there to attend to it. Just now the cohort was marshalled in defence of the railroads against the attacks of the new Rebate bill. In fact, Ryder managed to keep the Senate busy all the time. When, on the other hand, the senators wanted anything—and they often did—Ryder saw that they got it, lower rates for this one, a fat job for that one, not forgetting themselves. Senator Roberts was already a very rich man, and although the world often wondered where he got it, no one had the courage to ask him.

But the Republican leader was stirred with an ambition greater than that of controlling a majority in the Senate. He had a daughter, a marriageable young woman who, at least in her father's opinion, would make a desirable wife for any man. His friend Ryder had a son, and this son was the only heir to the greatest fortune ever amassed by one man, a fortune which, at its present rate of increase, by the time the father died and the young couple were ready to inherit, would probably amount to over *six billions of dollars*. Could the human mind grasp the possibilities of such a colossal fortune? It staggered the imagination. Its owner, or the man who controlled it, would be master of the world! Was not this a prize any man might well set himself out to win? The senator was thinking of it now as he stood exchanging banal remarks with the men who accosted him. If he could only bring off that marriage he would be content. The ambition of his life would be attained. There was no difficulty as far as John Ryder was concerned. He favoured the match and had often spoken of it. Indeed, Ryder desired it, for such an alliance would naturally further his business interests in every way. Roberts knew that his daughter Kate had more than a liking for Ryder's handsome young son. Moreover, Kate was practical, like her father, and had sense enough to realize what it would mean to be the mistress of the Ryder fortune. No, Kate was all right, but there was young Ryder to reckon with. It would take two in this case to make a bargain.

Jefferson Ryder was, in truth, an entirely different man from his father. It was difficult to realize that both had sprung from the same stock. A college-bred boy with all the advantages his father's wealth could give him, he had inherited from the parent only those characteristics which would have made him successful even if born poor—activity, pluck, application, dogged obstinacy, alert mentality. To these qualities he added what his father sorely lacked—a high notion of honour, a keen sense of right and wrong. He had the honest man's contempt for meanness of any description, and he had little patience with the lax so-called business morals of the day. For him a dishonourable or dishonest action could have no apologist, and he could see no difference between the crime of the hungry wretch who stole a loaf of bread and the coal baron who systematically robbed both his employés and the public. In fact, had he been on the bench he would probably have acquitted the human derelict who, in despair, had appropriated the prime necessary of life, and sent the over-fed conscienceless coal baron to jail.

" Do unto others as you would have others do unto you." This simple and fundamental axiom Jefferson Ryder had adopted early in life, and it had become his religion—the only one, in fact, that he had. He was never pious like his father, a fact much regretted by his mother, who could see nothing but eternal damnation in store for her son because he never went to church and professed no orthodox creed. She knew him to be a good lad, but to her simple mind a conduct of life based merely on a system of moral philosophy was the worst kind of paganism. There could, she argued, be no religion, and assuredly no salvation, outside the

dogmatic teachings of the Church. But otherwise
Jefferson was a model son and, with the exception
of this bad habit of thinking for himself on religious
matters, really gave her no anxiety. When Jefferson
left college, his father took him into the Empire Trading Company with the idea of his eventually succeed-
ing him as head of the concern, but the different views
held by father and son on almost every subject soon
led to stormy scenes that made the continuation of the
arrangement impossible. Senator Roberts was well
aware of these unfortunate independent tendencies in
John Ryder's son, and while he devoutly desired the
consummation of Jefferson's union with his daughter,
he quite realized that the young man was a nut which
was going to be exceedingly hard to crack.

"Hello, senator, you're always on time!"

Disturbed in his reflections, Senator Roberts looked
up and saw the extended hand of a red-faced, cor-
pulent man, one of the directors. He was no favourite
with the senator, but the latter was too keen a man
of the world to make enemies uselessly, so he condescended to place two fingers in the outstretched
fat palm.

"How are you, Mr. Grimsby? Well, what are we
going to do about this injunction? The case has
gone against us. I knew Judge Rossmore's decision

would be for the other side. Public opinion is aroused. The press——"

Mr. Grimsby's red face grew more apoplectic as he blurted out:

"Public opinion and the press be d——d. Who cares for public opinion? What is public opinion, anyhow? This road can manage its own affairs or it can't. If it can't I for one quit railroading. The press! Pshaw! It's all graft, I tell you. It's nothing but a strike! I never knew one of these virtuous outbursts that wasn't. First the newspapers bark ferociously to advertise themselves; then they crawl round and whine like a cur. And it usually costs something to fix matters."

The senator smiled grimly.

"No, no, Grimsby—not this time. It's more serious than that. Hitherto the road has been unusually lucky in its bench decisions——"

The senator gave a covert glance round to see if any long ears were listening. Then he added:

"We can't expect always to get a favourable decision like that in the Cartwright case, when franchise rights valued at nearly five millions were at stake. Judge Stollmann proved himself a true friend in that affair."

Grimsby made a wry grimace as he retorted:

**Yes,** and it was worth it to him. A Supreme Court judge don't get a cheque for $20,000 every day. That represents two years' pay."

"It might represent two years in jail if it were found out," said the senator with a forced laugh.

Grimsby saw an opportunity, and he could not resist the temptation. Bluntly he said:

"As far as jail's concerned, others might be getting their deserts there too."

The senator looked keenly at Grimsby from under his white eyebrows. Then in a calm, decisive tone he replied:

"It's no question of a cheque this time. The road could not buy Judge Rossmore with $200,000. He is absolutely unapproachable in that way."

The apoplectic face of Mr. Grimsby looked incredulous.

It was hard for these men who plotted in the dark, and cheated the widow and the orphan for love of the dollar, to understand that there were in the world, breathing the same air as they, men who put honour, truth and justice above mere money-getting. With a slight tinge of sarcasm he asked:

"Is there any man in our public life who is unapproachable from some direction or other?"

"Yes, Judge Rossmore is such a man. He is one

of the few men in American public life who takes his duties seriously. In the strictest sense of the term, he serves his country instead of serving himself. I am no friend of his, but I must do him that justice."

He spoke sharply, in an irritated tone, as if resenting the insinuation of this vulgarian that every man in public life had his price. Roberts knew that the charge was true as far as he and the men he consorted with were concerned, but sometimes the truth hurts. That was why he had for a moment seemed to champion Judge Rossmore, which, seeing that the judge himself was at that very moment under a cloud, was an absurd thing for him to do.

He had known Rossmore years before when the latter was a city magistrate in New York. That was before he, Roberts, had become a political grafter and when the decent things in life still appealed to him. The two men, although having few interests in common, had seen a good deal of one another until Roberts went to Washington when their relations were completely severed. But he had always watched Rossmore's career, and when he was made a judge of the Supreme Court at a comparatively early age he was sincerely glad. If anything could have convinced Roberts that success can come in public life to a man who pursues it by honest methods it was the success of James Rossmore.  He could never help feeling that Rossmore had been endowed by Nature with certain qualities which had been denied to him, above all that ability to walk straight through life with skirts clean which he had found impossible himself.  To-day Judge Rossmore was one of the most celebrated judges in the country.  He was a brilliant jurist and a splendid after-dinner speaker.  He was considered the most learned and able of all the members of the judiciary, and his decisions were noted as much for their fearlessness as for their wisdom.  But what was far more, he enjoyed a reputation for absolute integrity.  Until now no breath of slander, no suspicion of corruption, had ever touched him.  Even his enemies acknowledged that.  And that is why there was a panic to-day among the directors of the Southern and Transcontinental Railroad.  This honest, upright man had been called upon in the course of his duty to decide matters of vital importance to the road, and the directors were ready to stampede because, in their hearts, they knew the weakness of their case and the strength of the judge.

Grimsby, unconvinced, returned to the charge.

" What about these newspaper charges?  Did Judge Rossmore take a bribe from the Great Northwestern or didn't he?  You ought to know."

"I do know," answered the senator cautiously and somewhat curtly, "but until Mr. Ryder arrives I can say nothing. I believe he has been inquiring into the matter. He will tell us when he comes."

The hands of the large clock in the outer room pointed to three. An active, dapper little man with glasses and with books under his arm passed hurriedly from another office into the directors room.

"There goes Mr. Lane with the minutes. The meeting is called. Where's Mr. Ryder?"

There was a general move of the scattered groups of directors toward the committee room. The clock overhead began to strike. The last stroke had not quite died away when the big swinging doors from the street were thrown open and there entered a tall, thin man, gray-headed, and with a slight stoop, but keen eyed and alert. He was carefully dressed in a well-fitting frock coat, white waistcoat, black tie and silk hat.

It was John Burkett Ryder, the Colossus.

## CHAPTER II

AT fifty-six, John Burkett Ryder was surprisingly well preserved. With the exception of the slight stoop, already noted, and the rapidly thinning snow-white hair, his step was as light and elastic, and his brain as vigorous and alert, as in a man of forty. Of old English stock, his physical make-up presented all those strongly marked characteristics of our race which, sprung from Anglo-Saxon ancestry, but modified by nearly 300 years of different climate and customs, has gradually produced the distinct and true American type, as easily recognizable among the family of nations as any other of the earth's children. Tall and distinguished-looking, Ryder would have attracted attention anywhere. Men who have accomplished much in life usually bear plainly upon their persons the indefinable stamp of achievement, whether of good or evil, which renders them conspicuous among their fellows. We turn after a man in the street and ask, Who is he? And nine times out of ten the object of our curiosity is a man who has made his mark—a successful soldier, a famous sailor, a celebrated author, a distinguished lawyer, or even a notorious crook.

There was certainly nothing in John Ryder's outward appearance to justify Lombroso's sensational description of him : " A social and physiological freak, a degenerate and a prodigy of turpitude who, in the pursuit of money, crushes with the insensibility of a steel machine everyone who stands in his way." On the contrary, Ryder, outwardly at least, was a prepossessing-looking man. His head was well-shaped, and he had an intellectual brow, while power was expressed in every gesture of his hands and body. Every inch of him suggested strength and resourcefulness. His face, when in good humour, frequently expanded in a pleasant smile, and he had even been known to laugh boisterously, usually at his own stories, which he rightly considered very droll, and of which he possessed a goodly stock. But in repose his face grew stern and forbidding, and when his prognathous jaw, indicative of will-power and bull-dog tenacity, snapped to with a click-like sound, those who heard it knew that squalls were coming.

But it was John Ryder's eyes that were regarded as the most reliable barometer of his mental condition. Wonderful eyes they were, strangely eloquent and expressive, and their most singular feature was that they possessed the uncanny power of changing colour like a cat's. When their owner was at peace with the world, and had temporarily shaken off the cares of business, his eyes were of the most restful, beautiful blue, like the sky after sunrise on a Spring morning, and looking into their serene depths it seemed absurd to think that this man could ever harm a fly. His face, while under the spell of this kindly mood, was so benevolent and gentle, so frank and honest that you felt there was nothing in the world—purse, honour, wife, child—that, if needs be, you would not entrust to his keeping.

When this period of truce was ended, when the plutocrat was once more absorbed in controlling the political as well as the commercial machinery of the nation, then his eyes took on a snakish, greenish hue, and one could plainly read in them the cunning, the avariciousness, the meanness, the insatiable thirst for gain that had made this man the most unscrupulous money-getter of his time. But his eyes had still another colour, and when this last transformation took place those dependent on him, and even his friends, quaked with fear. For they were his eyes of anger. On these dreaded occasions his eyes grew black as darkest night and flashed fire as lightning rends the thundercloud. Almost ungovernable fury was, indeed, the weakest spot in John Ryder's armour, for in these moments of appalling wrath he was reckless of what he said or did, friendship, self-interest, prudence—all were sacrificed.

Such was the Colossus on whom all eyes were turned as he entered. Instantly the conversations stopped as by magic. The directors nudged each other and whispered. Instinctively, Ryder singled out his crony, Senator Roberts, who advanced with effusive gesture:

"Hello, Senator!"

"You're punctual as usual, Mr. Ryder. I never knew you to be late!"

The great man chuckled, and the little men standing around, listening breathlessly, chuckled in respectful sympathy, and they elbowed and pushed one another in their efforts to attract Ryder's notice, like so many cowardly hyenas not daring to approach the lordly wolf. Senator Roberts made a remark in a low tone to Ryder, whereupon the latter laughed. The bystanders congratulated each other silently. The great man was pleased to be in a good humour. And as Ryder turned with the senator to enter the Directors Room the light from the big windows fell full on his face, and they noticed that his eyes were of the softest blue.

" No squalls to-day," whispered one.

" Wait and see," retorted a more experienced colleague. " Those eyes are more fickle than the weather."

Outside the sky was darkening, and drops of rain were already falling. A flash of lightning presaged the coming storm.

Ryder passed on and into the Directors Room followed by Senator Roberts and the other directors, the procession being brought up by the dapper little secretary bearing the minutes.

The long room with its narrow centre table covered with green baize was filled with directors scattered in little groups and all talking at once with excited gesture. At the sight of Ryder the chattering stopped as if by common consent, and the only sound audible was of the shuffling of feet and the moving of chairs as the directors took their places around the long table.

With a nod here and there Ryder took his place in the chairman's seat and rapped for order. Then at a sign from the chair the dapper little secretary began in a monotonous voice to read the minutes of the previous meeting. No one listened, a few directors yawned. Others had their eyes riveted on Ryder's face, trying to read there if he had devised some plan to offset the crushing blow of this adverse decision,

34

which meant a serious loss to them all. He, the
master mind, had served them in many a like crisis in
the past. Could he do so again? But John Ryder
gave no sign. His eyes, still of the same restful blue,
were fixed on the ceiling watching a spider marching
with diabolical intent on a wretched fly that had become entangled in its web. And as the secretary
ambled monotonously on, Ryder watched and watched
until he saw the spider seize its helpless prey and
devour it. Fascinated by the spectacle, which doubtless suggested to him some analogy to his own
methods, Ryder sat motionless, his eyes fastened on
the ceiling, until the sudden stopping of the secretary's
reading aroused him and told him that the minutes
were finished. Quickly they were approved, and the
chairman proceeded as rapidly as possible with the
regular business routine. That disposed of, the meeting was ready for the chief business of the day. Ryder then calmly proceeded to present the facts in
the case.

Some years back the road had acquired as an investment some thousands of acres of land located
in the outskirts of Auburndale, on the line of their
road. The land was bought cheap, and there had been
some talk of laying part of it out as a public park.
This promise had been made at the time in good faith,

but it was no condition of the sale. If, afterwards, owing to the rise in the value of real estate, the road found it impossible to carry out the original idea, surely they were masters of their own property! The people of Auburndale thought differently and, goaded on by the local newspapers, had begun action in the courts to restrain the road from diverting the land from its alleged original purpose. They had succeeded in getting the injunction, but the road had fought it tooth and nail, and finally carried it to the Supreme Court, where Judge Rossmore, after reserving his opinion, had finally sustained the injunction and decided against the railroad. That was the situation, and he would now like to hear from the members of the board.

Mr. Grimsby rose. Self-confident and noisily loquacious, as most men of his class are in simple conversation, he was plainly intimidated at speaking before such a crowd. / He did not know where to look nor what to do with his hands, and he shuffled uneasily on his feet, while streams of nervous perspiration ran down his fat face, which he mopped repeatedly with a big coloured handkerchief. At last, taking courage, he began:

" Mr. Chairman, for the past ten years this road has made bigger earnings in proportion to its carrying capacity than any other railroad in the United States. We have had fewer accidents, less injury to rolling stock, less litigation and bigger dividends. The road has been well managed and "—here he looked significantly in Ryder's direction—" there has been a big brain behind the manager. We owe you that credit, Mr. Ryder!"

Cries of "Hear! Hear!" came from all round the table.

Ryder bowed coldly, and Mr. Grimsby continued:

"But during the last year or two things have gone wrong. There has been a lot of litigation, most of which has gone against us, and it has cost a heap of money. It reduced the last quarterly dividend very considerably, and the new complication—this Auburndale suit, which also has gone against us—is going to make a still bigger hole in our exchequer. Gentlemen, I don't want to be a prophet of misfortune, but I'll tell you this—unless something is done to stop this hostility in the courts you and I stand to lose every cent we have invested in the road. This suit which we have just lost means a number of others. What I would ask our chairman is what has become of his former good relations with the Supreme Court, what has become of his influence, which never failed us. What are these rumours regarding Judge Rossmore?

He is charged in the newspapers with having accepted a present from a road in whose favour he handed down a very valuable decision. How is it that our road cannot reach Judge Rossmore and make him presents?"

The speaker sat down, flushed and breathless. The expression on every face showed that the anxiety was general. The directors glanced at Ryder, but his face was expressionless as marble. Apparently he took not the slightest interest in this matter which so agitated his colleagues.

Another director rose. He was a better speaker than Mr. Grimsby, but his voice had a hard, rasping quality that smote the ears unpleasantly. He said:

"Mr. Chairman, none of us can deny what Mr. Grimsby has just put before us so vividly. We are threatened not with one, but with a hundred such suits, unless something is done either to placate the public or to render its attacks harmless. Rightly or wrongly, the railroad is hated by the people, yet we are only what railroad conditions compel us to be. With the present fierce competition, no fine question of ethics can enter into our dealings as a business organization. With an irritated public and press on one side, and a hostile judiciary on the other, the outlook certainly is far from bright. But is the judiciary hostile? Is it not true that we have been singularly free from litigation until recently, and that most of the decisions were favourable to the road? Judge Rossmore is the real danger. While he is on the bench the road is not safe. Yet all efforts to reach him have failed and will fail. I do not take any stock in the newspaper stories regarding Judge Rossmore. They are preposterous. Judge Rossmore is too strong a man to be got rid of so easily."

The speaker sat down and another rose, his arguments being merely a reiteration of those already heard. Ryder did not listen to what was being said. Why should he? Was he not familiar with every possible phase of the game? Better than these men who merely talked, he was planning how the railroad and all his other interests could get rid of this troublesome judge.

It was true. He who controlled legislatures and dictated to Supreme Court judges had found himself powerless when each turn of the legal machinery had brought him face to face with Judge Rossmore. Suit after suit had been decided against him and the interests he represented, and each time it was Judge Rossmore who had handed down the decision. So for years these two men had fought a silent but bitter duel in which principle on the one side and attempted corruption on the other were the gauge of battle. Judge

Rossmore fought with the weapons which his oath and the law directed him to use, Ryder with the only weapons he understood—bribery and trickery. And each time it had been Rossmore who had emerged triumphant. Despite every manœuvre Ryder's experience could suggest, notwithstanding every card that could be played to undermine his credit and reputation, Judge Rossmore stood higher in the country's confidence than when he was first appointed.

So when Ryder found he could not corrupt this honest judge with gold, he decided to destroy him with calumny. He realized that the sordid methods which had succeeded with other judges would never prevail with Rossmore, so he plotted to take away from this man the one thing he cherished most—his honour. He would ruin him by defaming his character, and so skilfully would he accomplish his work that the judge himself would realize the hopelessness of resistance. No scruples embarrassed Ryder in arriving at this determinatioin. From his point of view he was fully justified. " Business is business. He hurts my interests ; therefore I remove him." So he argued, and he considered it no more wrong to wreck the happiness of this honourable man than he would to have shot a burglar in self-defence. So having thus tranquillized his conscience he had gone to work in his

usually thorough manner, and his success had sur-
passed the most sanguine expectations.

This is what he had done.

Like many of our public servants whose labours are
compensated only in niggardly fashion by an inconsiderate country, Judge Rossmore was a man of but
moderate means. His income as Justice of the Supreme Court was $12,000 a year, but for a man in his
position, having a certain appearance to keep up, it
little more than kept the wolf from the door. He
lived quietly but comfortably in New York City with
his wife and his daughter Shirley, an attractive young
woman who had graduated from Vassar and had
shown a marked taste for literature. The daughter's
education had cost a good deal of money, and this,
together with life insurance and other incidentals of
keeping house in New York, had about taken all he
had. Yet he had managed to save a little, and those
years when he could put by a fifth of his salary the
judge considered himself lucky. Secretly, he was
proud of his comparative poverty. At least the world
could never ask him " where he got it."

Ryder was well acquainted with Judge Rossmore's
private means. The two men had met at a dinner, and
although Ryder had tried to cultivate the acquaintance,
he never received much encouragement. Ryder's son

Jefferson, too, had met Miss Shirley Rossmore and been much attracted to her, but the father having more ambitious plans for his heir quickly discouraged all attentions in that direction. He himself, however, continued to meet the judge casually, and one evening he contrived to broach the subject of profitable investments. The judge admitted that by careful hoarding and much stinting he had managed to save a few thousand dollars which he was anxious to invest in something good.

Quick as the keen-eyed vulture swoops down on its prey the wily financier seized the opportunity thus presented. And he took so much trouble in answering the judge's inexperienced questions, and generally made himself so agreeable, that the judge found himself regretting that he and Ryder had, by force of circumstances, been opposed to each other in public life so long. Ryder strongly recommended the purchase of Alaskan Mining stock, a new and booming enterprise which had lately become very active in the market. Ryder said he had reasons to believe that the stock would soon advance, and now there was an opportunity to get it cheap.

A few days after he had made the investment the judge was surprised to receive certificates of stock for double the amount he had paid for. At the same

time he received a letter from the secretary of the
company explaining that the additional stock was pool
stock and not to be marketed at the present time. It
was in the nature of a bonus to which he was entitled
as one of the early shareholders. The letter was full
of verbiage and technical details of which the judge
understood nothing, but he thought it very liberal
of the company, and putting the stock away in his
safe soon forgot all about it. Had he been a business
man he would have scented peril. He would have
realized that he had now in his possession $50,000
worth of stock for which he had not paid a cent, and
furthermore had deposited it when a reorganization
came.

But the judge was sincerely grateful for Ryder's
apparently disinterested advice and wrote two letters
to him, one in which he thanked him for the trouble
he had taken, and another in which he asked him
if he was sure the company was financially sound, as
the investment he contemplated making represented
all his savings. He added in the second letter that he
had received stock for double the amount of his investment, and that being a perfect child in business
transactions he had been unable to account for the extra $50,000 worth until the secretary of the company

had written him assuring him that everything was in order. These letters Ryder kept.

From that time on the Alaskan Mining Company underwent mysterious changes. New capitalists gained control and the name was altered to the Great Northwestern Mining Company. Then it became involved in litigation, and one suit, the outcome of which meant millions to the company, was carried to the Supreme Court, where Judge Rossmore was sitting. The judge had by this time forgotten all about the company in which he owned stock. He did not even recall its name. He only knew vaguely that it was a mine and that it was situated in Alaska. Could he dream that the Great Northwestern Mining Company and the company to which he had entrusted his few thousands were one and the same? In deciding on the merits of the case presented to him right seemed to him to be plainly with the Northwestern, and he rendered a decision to that effect. It was an important decision, involving a large sum, and for a day or two it was talked about. But as it was the opinion of the most learned and honest judge on the bench no one dreamed of questioning it.

But very soon ugly paragraphs began to appear in the newspapers. One paper asked if it were true that Judge Rossmore owned stock in the Great Northwest-

ern Mining Company which had recently benefited so
signally by his decision. Interviewed by a reporter,
Judge Rossmore indignantly denied being interested
in any way in the company. Thereupon the same
paper returned to the attack, stating that the judge
must surely be mistaken as the records showed a sale
of stock to him at the time the company was known
as the Alaskan Mining Company. When he read this
the judge was overwhelmed. It was true then! They
had not slandered him. It was he who had lied, but
how innocently—how innocently!

His daughter Shirley, who was his greatest friend
and comfort, was then in Europe. She had gone to
the Continent to rest, after working for months on a
novel which she had just published. His wife, entirely
without experience in business matters and somewhat
of an invalid, was helpless to advise him. But to
his old and tried friend, ex-Judge Stott, Judge
Rossmore explained the facts as they were. Stott
shook his head. "It's a conspiracy!" he cried. "And
John B. Ryder is behind it." Rossmore refused to
believe that any man could so deliberately try to en-
compass another's destruction, but when more newspaper stories came out he began to realize that Stott
was right and that his enemies had indeed dealt him
a deadly blow. One newspaper boldly stated that

Judge Rossmore was down on the mining company's books for $50,000 more stock than he had paid for, and it went on to ask if this were payment for the favourable decision just rendered. Rossmore, helpless, child-like as he was in business matters, now fully realized the seriousness of his position. "My God! My God!" he cried, as he bowed his head down on his desk. And for a whole day he remained closeted in his library, no one venturing near him.

As John Ryder sat there sphinx-like at the head of the directors' table he reviewed all this in his mind. His own part in the work was now done and well done, and he had come to this meeting to-day to tell them of his triumph.

The speaker, to whom he had paid such scant attention, resumed his seat, and there followed a pause and an intense silence which was broken only by the pattering of the rain against the big windows. The directors turned expectantly to Ryder, waiting for him to speak. What could the Colossus do now to save the situation? Cries of "the Chair! the Chair!" arose on every side. Senator Roberts leaned over to Ryder and whispered something in his ear.

With an acquiescent gesture, John Ryder tapped the table with his gavel and rose to address his fellow directors. Instantly the room was silent again as

He had come to this meeting to-day to tell them
of his triumph.—*Page 46.*

the tomb. One might have heard a pin drop, so intense was the attention. All eyes were fixed on the chairman. The air itself seemed charged with electricity, that needed but a spark to set it ablaze.

Speaking deliberately and dispassionately, the Master Dissembler began.

They had all listened carefully, he said, to what had been stated by previous speakers. The situation no doubt was very critical, but they had weathered worse storms and he had every reason to hope they would outlive this storm. It was true that public opinion was greatly incensed against the railroads and, indeed, against all organized capital, and was seeking to injure them through the courts. For a time this agitation would hurt business and lessen the dividends, for it meant not only smaller annual earnings but that a lot of money must be spent in Washington.

The eyes of the listeners, who were hanging on every word, involuntarily turned in the direction of Senator Roberts, but the latter, at that moment busily engaged in rummaging among a lot of papers, seemed to have missed this significant allusion to the road's expenses in the District of Columbia. Ryder continued:

In his experience such waves of reform were periodical and soon wear themselves out, when things go on just as they did before. Much of the agitation, doubtless, was a strike for graft. They would have to go down in their pockets, he supposed, and then these yellow newspapers and these yellow magazines that were barking at their heels would let them go. But in regard to the particular case now at issue—this Auburndale decision—there had been no way of preventing it. Influence had been used, but to no effect. The thing to do now was to prevent any such disasters in future by removing the author of them.

The directors bent eagerly forward. Had Ryder really got some plan up his sleeve after all? The faces around the table looked brighter, and the directors cleared their throats and settled themselves down in their chairs as audiences do in the theatre when the drama is reaching its climax.

The board, continued Ryder with icy calmness, had perhaps heard, and also seen in the newspapers, the stories regarding Judge Rossmore and his alleged connection with the Great Northwestern Company. Perhaps they had not believed these stories. It was only natural. He had not believed them himself. But he had taken the trouble to inquire into the matter very carefully, and he regretted to say that the stories were true. In fact, they were no longer denied by Judge Rossmore himself.

# THE MOUSE

The directors looked at each other in amazement. Gasps of astonishment, incredulity, satisfaction were heard all over the room. The rumours were true, then? Was it possible? Incredible!

Investigation, Ryder went on, had shown that Judge Rossmore was not only interested in the company in whose favour, as Judge of the Supreme Court, he had rendered an important decision, but what was worse, he had accepted from that company a valuable gift—that is, $50,000 worth of stock—for which he had given absolutely nothing in return unless, as some claimed, the weight of his influence on the bench. These facts were very ugly and so unanswerable that Judge Rossmore did not attempt to answer them, and the important news which he, the chairman, had to announce to his fellow-directors that afternoon, was that Judge Rossmore's conduct would be made the subject of an inquiry by Congress.

This was the spark that was needed to ignite the electrically charged air. A wild cry of triumph went up from this band of jackals only too willing to fatten their bellies at the cost of another man's ruin, and one director, in his enthusiasm, rose excitedly from his chair and demanded a vote of thanks for John Ryder.

Ryder coldly opposed the motion. No thanks were due to him, he said deprecatingly, nor did he

49

think the occasion called for congratulations of any kind. It was surely a sad spectacle to see this honoured judge, this devoted father, this blameless citizen threatened with ruin and disgrace on account of one false step. Let them rather sympathize with him and his family in their misfortune. He had little more to tell. The Congressional inquiry would take place immediately, and in all probability a demand would be made upon the Senate for Judge Rossmore's impeachment. It was, he added, almost unnecessary for him to remind the Board that, in the event of impeachment, the adverse decision in the Auburndale case would be annulled and the road would be entitled to a new trial.

Ryder sat down, and pandemonium broke loose, the delighted directors tumbling over each other in their eagerness to shake hands with the man who had saved them. Ryder had given no hint that he had been a factor in the working up of this case against their common enemy, in fact he had appeared to sympathise with him, but the directors knew well that he and he alone had been the master mind which had brought about the happy result.

On a motion to adjourn, the meeting broke up, and everyone began to troop towards the elevators. Outside the rain was now coming down in torrents and the lights that everywhere dotted the great city only paled when every few moments a vivid flash of lightning rent the enveloping gloom.

Ryder and Senator Roberts went down in the elevator together. When they reached the street the senator inquired in a low tone:

"Do you think they really believed Rossmore was influenced in his decision?"

Ryder glanced from the lowering clouds overhead to his electric brougham which awaited him at the curb and replied indifferently:

"Not they. They don't care. All they want to believe is that he is to be impeached. The man was dangerous and had to be removed—no matter by what means. He is our enemy—my enemy—and I never give quarter to my enemies!"

As he spoke his prognathous jaw snapped to with a click-like sound, and in his eyes now coal-black were glints of fire. At the same instant there was a blinding flash, accompanied by a terrific crash, and the splinters of the flag-pole on the building opposite, which had been struck by a bolt, fell at their feet.

"A good or a bad omen?" asked the senator with a nervous laugh. He was secretly afraid of lightning but was ashamed to admit it.

"A bad omen for Judge Rossmore!" rejoined Ryder coolly, as he slammed to the door of the cab, and the two men drove rapidly off in the direction of Fifth Avenue.

*THE MOUSE*

## CHAPTER III

OF all the spots on this fair, broad earth where
the jaded globe wanderer, surfeited with hack-
neyed sight-seeing, may sit in perfect peace
and watch the world go by, there is none more fasci-
nating nor one presenting a more brilliant panorama
of cosmopolitan life than that famous corner on the
Paris boulevards, formed by the angle of the Boulevard des Capucines and the Place de l'Opéra. Here,
on the " terrace " of the Café de la Paix, with its
white and gold façade and long French windows, and
its innumerable little marble-topped tables and rattan
chairs, one may sit for hours at the trifling expense
of a few *sous,* undisturbed even by the tip-seeking
*garçon,* and, if one happens to be a student of human
nature, find keen enjoyment in observing the world-
types, representing every race and nationality under
the sun, that pass and re-pass in a steady, never ceas-
ing, exhaustless stream. The crowd surges to and fro,
past the little tables, occasionally toppling over a chair
or two in the crush, moving up or down the great
boulevards, one procession going to the right, in the

direction of the Church of the Madeleine, the other to the left heading toward the historic Bastille, both really going nowhere in particular, but ambling gently and good humouredly along enjoying the sights—and life!

Paris, queen of cities! Light-hearted, joyous, radiant Paris—the playground of the nations, the Mecca of the pleasure-seekers, the city beautiful! Paris—the siren, frankly immoral, always seductive, ever caressing! City of a thousand political convulsions, city of a million crimes—her streets have run with human blood, horrors unspeakable have stained her history, civil strife has scarred her monuments, the German conqueror insolently has bivouaced within her walls. Yet, like a virgin undefiled, she shows no sign of storm and stress, she offers her dimpled cheek to the rising sun, and when fall the shadows of night and a billion electric bulbs flash in the siren's crown, her resplendent, matchless beauty dazzles the world!

As the supreme reward of virtue, the good American is promised a visit to Paris when he dies. Those, however, of our sagacious fellow countrymen who can afford to make the trip, usually manage to see Lutetia before crossing the river Styx. Most Americans like Paris—some like it so well that they have made it their permanent home—although it must be added that in their admiration they rarely include the Frenchman. For that matter, we are not as a nation particularly fond of any foreigner, largely because we do not understand him, while the foreigner for his part is quite willing to return the compliment. He gives the Yankee credit for commercial smartness, which has built up America's great material prosperity; but he has the utmost contempt for our acquaintance with art, and no profound respect for us as scientists.

Is it not indeed fortunate that every nation finds itself superior to its neighbour? If this were not so each would be jealous of the other, and would cry with envy like a spoiled child who cannot have the moon to play with. Happily, therefore, for the harmony of the world, each nation cordially detests the other and the much exploited " brotherhood of man " is only a figure of speech. The Englishman, confident that he is the last word of creation, despises the Frenchman, who, in turn, laughs at the German, who shows open contempt for the Italian, while the American, conscious of his superiority to the whole family of nations, secretly pities them all.

The most serious fault which the American—whose one god is Mammon and chief characteristic hustle—has to find with his French brother is that he enjoys life too much, is never in a hurry and, what to the

Yankee mind is hardly respectable, has a habit of playing dominoes during business hours. The Frenchman retorts that his American brother, clever person though he be, has one or two things still to learn. He has, he declares, no philosophy of life. It is true that he has learned the trick of making money, but in the things which go to satisfy the soul he is still strangely lacking. He thinks he is enjoying life, when really he is ignorant of what life is. He admits it is not the American's fault, for he has never been taught how to enjoy life. One must be educated to that as everything else. All the American is taught is to be in a perpetual hurry and to make money no matter how. In this mad daily race for wealth, he bolts his food, not stopping to masticate it properly, and consequently suffers all his life from dyspepsia. So he rushes from the cradle to the grave, and what's the good, since he must one day die like all the rest?

And what, asks the foreigner, has the American hustler accomplished that his slower-going Continental brother has not done as well? Are finer cities to be found in America than in Europe, do Americans paint more beautiful pictures, or write more learned or more entertaining books, has America made greater progress in science? Is it not a fact that the greatest inventors and scientists of our time—Marconi, who gave to the world wireless telegraphy, Professor Curie, who discovered radium, Pasteur, who found a cure for rabies, Santos-Dumont, who has almost succeeded in navigating the air, Professor Röntgen who discovered the X-ray—are not all these immortals Europeans? And those two greatest mechanical inventions of our day, the automobile and the submarine boat, were they not first introduced and perfected in France before we in America woke up to appreciate their use? Is it, therefore, not possible to take life easily and still achieve?

The logic of these arguments, set forth in *Le Soir* in an article on the New World, appealed strongly to Jefferson Ryder as he sat in front of the Café de la Paix, sipping a sugared Vermouth. It was five o'clock, the magic hour of the *apéritif*, when the glutton taxes his wits to deceive his stomach and work up an appetite for renewed gorging. The little tables were all occupied with the usual before-dinner crowd. There were a good many foreigners, mostly English and Americans and a few Frenchmen, obviously from the provinces, with only a sprinkling of real Parisians.

Jefferson's acquaintance with the French language was none too profound, and he had to guess at half the words in the article, but he understood enough to follow the writer's arguments. Yes, it was quite true, he thought, the American idea of life was all wrong.

What was the sense of slaving all one's life, piling up
a mass of money one cannot possibly spend, when there
is only one life to live? How much saner the man
who is content with enough and enjoys life while he
is able to. These Frenchmen, and indeed all the Continental nations, had solved the problem. The gaiety
of their cities, and this exuberant joy of life they com-
municated to all about them, were sufficient proofs
of it.

Fascinated by the gay scene around him Jefferson
laid the newspaper aside. To the young American,
fresh from prosaic money-mad New York, the City of
Pleasure presented indeed a novel and beautiful spectacle. How different, he mused, from his own city
with its one fashionable thoroughfare—Fifth Avenue
—monotonously lined for miles with hideous brown-
stone residences, and showing little real animation
except during the Saturday afternoon parade when the
activities of the smart set, male and female, centred
chiefly in such exciting diversions as going to Huyler's
for soda, taking tea at the Waldorf, and trying to outdo
each other in dress and show. New York certainly
was a dull place with all its boasted cosmopolitanism.
There was no denying that. Destitute of any natural
beauty, handicapped by its cramped geographical position between two rivers, made unsightly by gigantic

sky-scrapers and that noisy monstrosity the Elevated Railroad, having no intellectual interests, no art interests, no interest in anything not immediately connected with dollars, it was a city to dwell in and make money in, but hardly a city to *live* in. The millionaires were building white-marble palaces, taxing the ingenuity and the originality of the native architects, and thus to some extent relieving the general ugliness and drab commonplaceness, while the merchant princes had begun to invade the lower end of the avenue with handsome shops. But in spite of all this, in spite of its pretty girls—and Jefferson insisted that in this one important particular New York had no peer—in spite of its comfortable theatres and its wicked Tenderloin, and its Rialto made so brilliant at night by thousands of elaborate electric signs, New York still had the subdued air of a provincial town, compared with the exuberant gaiety, the multiple attractions, the beauties, natural and artificial, of cosmopolitan Paris.

The boulevards were crowded, as usual at that hour, and the crush of both vehicles and pedestrians was so great as to permit of only a snail-like progress. The clumsy three-horse omnibuses—Madeleine-Bastille—crowded inside and out with passengers and with their neatly uniformed drivers and conductors, so different in appearance and manner from our own slovenly street-car rowdies, were endeavouring to breast a perfect sea of *fiacres* which, like a swarm of mosquitoes, appeared to be trying to go in every direction at once, their drivers vociferating torrents of vituperous abuse on every man, woman or beast unfortunate enough to get in their way. As a dispenser of unspeakable profanity, the Paris *cocher* has no equal. He is unique, no one can approach him. He also enjoys the reputation of being the worst driver in the world. If there is any possible way in which he can run down a pedestrian or crash into another vehicle he will do it, probably for the only reason that it gives him another opportunity to display his choice stock of picturesque expletives.

But it was a lively, good-natured crowd and the fashionably gowned women and the well-dressed men, the fakirs hoarsely crying their catch-penny devices, the noble boulevards lined as far as the eye could reach with trees in full foliage, the magnificent Opera House with its gilded dome glistening in the warm sunshine of a June afternoon, the broad avenue directly opposite, leading in a splendid straight line to the famous Palais Royal, the almost dazzling whiteness of the houses and monuments, the remarkable cleanliness and excellent condition of the sidewalks and

streets, the gaiety and richness of the shops and res-
taurants, the picturesque kiosks where they sold newspapers and flowers—all this made up a picture so
utterly unlike anything he was familiar with at home
that Jefferson sat spellbound, delighted.

Yes, it was true, he thought, the foreigner had indeed learned the secret of enjoying life. There was
assuredly something else in the world beyond mere
money-getting. His father was a slave to it, but he
would never be. He was resolved on that. Yet, with
all his ideas of emancipation and progress, Jefferson
was a thoroughly practical young man. He fully
understood the value of money, and the possession of
it was as sweet to him as to other men. Only he would
never soil his soul in acquiring it dishonourably. He
was convinced that society as at present organized
was all wrong and that the feudalism of the middle
ages had simply given place to a worse form of slavery
—capitalistic driven labour—which had resulted in the
actual iniquitous conditions, the enriching of the rich
and the impoverishment of the poor. He was familiar
with the socialistic doctrines of the day and had taken
a keen interest in this momentous question, this dream
of a regenerated mankind. He had read Karl Marx
and other socialistic writers, and while his essentially
practical mind could hardly approve all their pro-

gramme for reorganizing the State, some of which seemed to him utopian, extravagant and even undesirable, he realised that the socialistic movement was growing rapidly all over the world and the day was not far distant when in America, as to-day in Germany and France, it would be a formidable factor to reckon with.

But until the socialistic millennium arrived and society was reorganized, money, he admitted, would remain the lever of the world, the great stimulus to effort. Money supplied not only the necessities of life but also its luxuries, everything the material desire craved for, and so long as money had this magic purchasing power, so long would men lie and cheat and rob and kill for its possession. Was life worth living without money? Could one travel and enjoy the glorious spectacles Nature affords—the rolling ocean, the majestic mountains, the beautiful lakes, the noble rivers—without money? Could the book-lover buy books, the art-lover purchase pictures? Could one have fine houses to live in, or all sorts of modern conveniences to add to one's comfort, without money? The philosophers declared contentment to be happiness, arguing that the hod-carrier was likely to be happier in his hut than the millionaire in his palace; but was not that mere animal contentment, the happiness which knows no higher state, the ignorance of one whose eyes have never been raised to the heights?

No, Jefferson was no fool. He loved money for what pleasure, intellectual or physical, it could give him, but he would never allow money to dominate his life as his father had done. His father, he knew well, was not a happy man, neither happy himself nor respected by the world. He had toiled all his life to make his vast fortune and now he toiled to take care of it. The galley slave led a life of luxurious ease compared with John Burkett Ryder. Baited by the yellow newspapers and magazines, investigated by State committees, dogged by process-servers, haunted by beggars, harassed by blackmailers, threatened by kidnappers, frustrated in his attempts to bestow charity by the cry " tainted money "—certainly the lot of the world's richest man was far from being an enviable one.

That is why Jefferson had resolved to strike out for himself. He had warded off the golden yoke which his father proposed to put on his shoulders, declining the lucrative position made for him in the Empire Trading Company, and he had gone so far as to refuse also the private income his father offered to settle on him. He would earn his own living. A man who has his bread buttered for him seldom accomplishes anything he had said, and while his father had appeared to be angry at this open opposition to his will, he was secretly pleased at his son's grit. Jefferson was thoroughly in earnest. If needs be, he would forego the great fortune that awaited him rather than be forced into questionable business methods against which his whole manhood revolted.

Jefferson Ryder felt strongly about these matters, and gave them more thought than would be expected of most young men with his opportunities. In fact, he was unusually serious for his age. He was not yet thirty, but he had done a great deal of reading, and he took a keen interest in all the political and sociological questions of the hour. In personal appearance, he was the type of man that both men and women like— tall and athletic looking, with smooth face and clean-cut features. He had the steel-blue eyes and the fighting jaw of his father, and when he smiled he displayed two even rows of very white teeth. He was popular with men, being manly, frank and cordial in his relations with them, and women admired him greatly, although they were somewhat intimidated by his grave and serious manner. The truth was that he was rather diffident with women, largely owing to lack of experience with them.

He had never felt the slightest inclination for business. He had the artistic temperament strongly developed, and his personal tastes had little in common with Wall Street and its feverish stock manipulating. When he was younger, he had dreamed of a literary or art career. At one time he had even thought of going on the stage. But it was to art that he turned finally. From an early age he had shown considerable skill as a draughtsman, and later a two years' course at the Academy of Design convinced him that this was his true vocation. He had begun by illustrating for the book publishers and for the magazines, meeting at first with the usual rebuffs and disappointments, but, refusing to be discouraged, he had kept on and soon the tide turned. His drawings began to be accepted. They appeared first in one magazine, then in another, until one day, to his great joy, he received an order from an important firm of publishers for six washdrawings to be used in illustrating a famous novel. This was the beginning of his real success. His illustrations were talked about almost as much as the book, and from that time on everything was easy. He was in great demand by the publishers, and very soon the young artist, who had begun his career of independence on nothing a year so to speak, found himself in a handsomely appointed studio in Bryant Park, with more orders coming in than he could possibly fill, and

enjoying an income of little less than $5,000 a year.
The money was all the sweeter to Jefferson in that he
felt he had himself earned every cent of it. This
summer he was giving himself a well-deserved vaca-
tion, and he had come to Europe partly to see Paris
and the other art centres about which his fellow students at the Academy raved, but principally—although
this he did not acknowledge even to himself—to meet
in Paris a young woman in whom he was more than
ordinarily interested—Shirley Rossmore, daughter of
Judge Rossmore, of the United States Supreme Court,
who had come abroad to recuperate after the labours
on her new novel, " The American Octopus," a book
which was then the talk of two hemispheres.

Jefferson had read half a dozen reviews of it in as
many American papers that afternoon at the *New York
Herald's* reading room in the Avenue de l'Opéra, and
he chuckled with glee as he thought how accurately this
young woman had described his father. The book had
been published under the pseudonym " Shirley Green,"
and he alone had been admitted into the secret of
authorship. The critics all conceded that it was the
book of the year, and that it portrayed with a pitiless
pen the personality of the biggest figure in the commercial life of America. " Although," wrote one reviewer,
" the leading character in the book is given another

name, there can be no doubt that the author intended to give to the world a vivid pen portrait of John Burkett Ryder. She has succeeded in presenting a remarkable character-study of the most remarkable man of his time."

He was particularly pleased with the reviews, not only for Miss Rossmore's sake, but also because his own vanity was gratified. Had he not collaborated on the book to the extent of acquainting the author with details of his father's life, and his characteristics, which no outsider could possibly have learned? There had been no disloyalty to his father in doing this. Jefferson admired his father's smartness, if he could not approve his methods. He did not consider the book an attack on his father, but rather a powerfully written pen picture of an extraordinary man.

Jefferson had met Shirley Rossmore two years before at a meeting of the Schiller Society, a pseudo-literary organization gotten up by a lot of old fogies for no useful purpose, and at whose monthly meetings the poet who gave the society its name was probably the last person to be discussed. He had gone out of curiosity, anxious to take in all the freak shows New York had to offer, and he had been introduced to a tall girl with a pale, thoughtful face and firm mouth. She was a writer, Miss Rossmore told him, and this was

her first visit also to the evening receptions of the
Schiller Society. Half apologetically she added that
it was likely to be her last, for, frankly, she was bored
to death. But she explained that she had to go to these
affairs, as she found them useful in gathering material
for literary use. She studied types and eccentric char-
acters, and this seemed to her a capital hunting ground.
Jefferson, who, as a rule, was timid with girls and
avoided them, found this girl quite unlike the others
he had known. Her quiet, forceful demeanour appealed
to him strongly, and he lingered with her, chatting
about his work, which had so many interests in
common with her own, until refreshments were served,
when the affair broke up. This first meeting had been
followed by a call at the Rossmore residence, and the
acquaintance had kept up until Jefferson, for the first
time since he came to manhood, was surprised and
somewhat alarmed at finding himself strangely and
unduly interested in a person of the opposite sex.

The young artist's courteous manner, his serious
outlook on life, his high moral principles, so rarely met
with nowadays in young men of his age and class,
could hardly fail to appeal to Shirley, whose ideals of
men had been somewhat rudely shattered by those she
had hitherto met. Above all, she demanded in a man
the refinement of the true gentleman, together with

68

strength of character and personal courage. That Jefferson Ryder came up to this standard she was soon convinced. He was certainly a gentleman: his views on a hundred topics of the hour expressed in numerous conversations assured her as to his principles, while a glance at his powerful physique left no doubt possible as to his courage. She rightly guessed that this was no *poseur* trying to make an impression and gain her confidence. There was an unmistakable ring of sincerity in all his words, and his struggle at home with his father, and his subsequent brave and successful fight for his own independence and self-respect, more than substantiated all her theories. And the more Shirley let her mind dwell on Jefferson Ryder and his blue eyes and serious manner, the more conscious she became that the artist was encroaching more upon her thoughts and time than was good either for her work or for herself.

So their casual acquaintance grew into a real friendship and comradeship. Further than that Shirley promised herself it should never go. Not that Jefferson had given her the slightest hint that he entertained the idea of making her his wife one day, only she was sophisticated enough to know the direction in which run the minds of men who are abnormally interested in one girl, and long before this Shirley had made up her mind that she would never marry. Firstly, she was devoted to her father and could not bear the thought of ever leaving him; secondly, she was fascinated by her literary work and she was practical enough to know that matrimony, with its visions of slippers and cradles, would be fatal to any ambition of that kind. She liked Jefferson immensely—more, perhaps, than any man she had yet met—and she did not think any the less of him because of her resolve not to get entangled in the meshes of Cupid. In any case he had not asked her to marry him—perhaps the idea was far from his thoughts. Meantime, she could enjoy his friendship freely without fear of embarracsing entanglements.

When, therefore, she first conceived the idea of portraying in the guise of fiction the personality of John Burkett Ryder, the Colossus of finance whose vast and ever-increasing fortune was fast becoming a public nuisance, she naturally turned to Jefferson for assistance. She wanted to write a book that would be talked about, and which at the same time would open the eyes of the public to this growing peril in their midst —this monster of insensate and unscrupulous greed who, by sheer weight of his ill-gotten gold, was corrupting legislators and judges and trying to enslave the nation. The book, she argued, would perform a

public service in awakening all to the common danger.
Jefferson fully entered into her views and had furnished her with the information regarding his father
that she deemed of value.  The book had proven a success beyond their most sanguine expectations, and
Shirley had come to Europe for a rest after the many
weary months of work that it took to write it.

The acquaintance of his son with the daughter of
Judge Rossmore had not escaped the eagle eye of
Ryder, Sr., and much to the financier's annoyance, and
even consternation, he had ascertained that Jefferson
was a frequent caller at the Rossmore home.  He immediately jumped to the conclusion that this could
mean only one thing, and fearing what he termed " the
consequences of the insanity of immature minds," he
had summoned Jefferson peremptorily to his presence.
He told his son that all idea of marriage in that quarter was out of the question for two reasons:  One was
that Judge Rossmore was his most bitter enemy, the
other was that he had hoped to see his son, his destined successor, marry a woman of whom he, Ryder,
Sr., could approve.  He knew of such a woman, one
who would make a far more desirable mate than Miss
Rossmore.  He alluded, of course, to Kate Roberts,
the pretty daughter of his old friend, the Senator.
The family interests would benefit by this alliance,

which was desirable from every point of view. Jefferson had listened respectfully until his father had finished and then grimly remarked that only one point of view had been overlooked—his own. He did not care for Miss Roberts; he did not think she really cared for him. The marriage was out of the question. Whereupon Ryder, Sr., had fumed and raged, declaring that Jefferson was opposing his will as he always did, and ending with the threat that if his son married Shirley Rossmore without his consent he would disinherit him.

Jefferson was cogitating on these incidents of the last few months when suddenly a feminine voice which he quickly recognised called out in English:

" Hello! Mr. Ryder."

He looked up and saw two ladies, one young, the other middle aged, smiling at him from an open *fiacre* which had drawn up to the curb. Jefferson jumped from his seat, upsetting his chair and startling two nervous Frenchmen in his hurry, and hastened out, hat in hand.

" Why, Miss Rossmore, what are you doing out driving?" he asked. " You know you and Mrs. Blake promised to dine with me to-night. I was coming round to the hotel in a few moments."

Mrs. Blake was a younger sister of Shirley's mother.

# THE MOUSE

Her husband had died a few years previously, leaving her a small income, and when she had heard of her niece's contemplated trip to Europe she had decided to come to Paris to meet her and incidentally to chaperone her. The two women were stopping at the Grand Hotel close by, while Jefferson had found accommodations at the Athénée.

Shirley explained. Her aunt wanted to go to the dressmaker's, and she herself was most anxious to go to the Luxembourg Gardens to hear the music. Would he take her? Then they could meet Mrs. Blake at the hotel at seven o'clock and all go to dinner. Was he willing?

Was he? Jefferson's face fairly glowed. He ran back to his table on the *terrasse* to settle for his Vermouth, astonished the waiter by not stopping to notice the short change he gave him, and rushed back to the carriage.

A dirty little Italian girl, shrewd enough to note the young man's attention to the younger of the American women, wheedled up to the carriage and thrust a bunch of flowers in Jefferson's face.

" *Achetez des fleurs, monsieur, pour la jolie dame?* "

Down went Jefferson's hand in his pocket and, filling the child's hand with small silver, he flung the flowers in the carriage. Then he turned inquiringly to Shirley for instructions so he could direct the *cocher.* Mrs. Blake said she would get out here. Her dressmaker was close by, in the Rue Auber, and she would walk back to the hotel to meet them at seven o'clock. Jefferson assisted her to alight and escorted her as far as the *porte-cochère* of the modiste's, a couple of doors away. When he returned to the carriage, Shirley had already told the coachman where to go. He got in and the *fiacre* started.

"Now," said Shirley, "tell me what you have been doing with yourself all day."

Jefferson was busily arranging the faded carriage rug about Shirley, spending more time in the task perhaps than was absolutely necessary, and she had to repeat the question.

"Doing?" he echoed with a smile, "I've been doing two things—waiting impatiently for seven o'clock and incidentally reading the notices of your book."

## CHAPTER IV

**T**ELL me, what do the papers say?"
Settling herself comfortably back in the
carriage, Shirley questioned Jefferson with
eagerness, even anxiety. She had been impatiently
awaiting the arrival of the newspapers from " home,"
for so much depended on this first effort. She knew
her book had been praised in some quarters, and her
publishers had written her that the sales were bigger
every day, but she was curious to learn how it had
been received by the reviewers.

In truth, it had been no slight achievement for a
young writer of her inexperience, a mere tyro in literature, to attract so much attention with her first book.
The success almost threatened to turn her head, she
had told her aunt laughingly, although she was sure
it could never do that. She fully realized that it was
the subject rather than the skill of the narrator that
counted in the book's success, also the fact that it had
come out at a timely moment, when the whole world
was talking of the Money Peril. Had not President
Roosevelt, in a recent sensational speech, declared that

75

it might be necessary for the State to curb the colossal fortunes of America, and was not her hero, John Burkett Ryder, the richest of them all? Any way they looked at it, the success of the book was most gratifying.

While she was an attractive, aristocratic-looking girl, Shirley Rossmore had no serious claims to academic beauty. Her features were irregular, and the firm and rather thin mouth lines disturbed the harmony indispensable to plastic beauty. Yet there was in her face something far more appealing—soul and character. The face of the merely beautiful woman expresses nothing, promises nothing. It presents absolutely no key to the soul within, and often there is no soul within to have a key to. Perfect in its outlines and coloring, it is a delight to gaze upon, just as is a flawless piece of sculpture, yet the delight is only fleeting. One soon grows satiated, no matter how beautiful the face may be, because it is always the same, expressionless and soulless. "Beauty is only skin deep," said the philosopher, and no truer dictum was ever uttered. The merely beautiful woman, who possesses only beauty and nothing else, is kept so busy thinking of her looks, and is so anxious to observe the impression her beauty makes on others, that she has neither the time nor the inclination for matters of greater importance. Sensible men, as a rule, do not lose their hearts to women whose only assets are their good looks. They enjoy a flirtation with them, but seldom care to make them their wives. The marrying man is shrewd enough to realize that domestic virtues will be more useful in his household economy than all the academic beauty ever chiselled out of block marble.

Shirley was not beautiful, but hers was a face that never failed to attract attention. It was a thoughtful and interesting face, with an intellectual brow and large, expressive eyes, the face of a woman who had both brain power and ideals, and yet who, at the same time, was in perfect sympathy with the world. She was fair in complexion, and her fine brown eyes, alternately reflective and alert, were shaded by long dark lashes. Her eyebrows were delicately arched, and she had a good nose. She wore her hair well off the forehead, which was broader than in the average woman, suggesting good mentality. Her mouth, however, was her strongest feature. It was well shaped, but there were firm lines about it that suggested unusual will power. Yet it smiled readily, and when it did there was an agreeable vision of strong, healthy-looking teeth of dazzling whiteness. She was a little over medium height and slender in figure, and carried herself with that unmistakable air of well-bred independence that bespeaks birth and culture. She dressed stylishly, and while her gowns were of rich material, and of a cut suggesting expensive modistes, she was always so quietly attired and in such perfect taste, that after leaving her one could never recall what she had on.

At the special request of Shirley, who wanted to get a glimpse of the Latin Quarter, the driver took a course down the Avenue de l'Opéra, that magnificent thoroughfare which starts at the Opéra and ends at the Théâtre Français, and which, like many others that go to the beautifying of the capital, the Parisians owe to the much-despised Napoleon III. The cab, Jefferson told her, would skirt the Palais Royal and follow the Rue de Rivoli until it came to the Châtelet, when it would cross the Seine and drive up the Boulevard St. Michel—the students' boulevard—until it reached the Luxembourg Gardens. Like most of his kind, the *cocher* knew less than nothing of the art of driving, and he ran a reckless, zig-zag flight, in and out, forcing his way through a confusing maze of vehicles of every description, pulling first to the right, then to the left, for no good purpose that was apparent, and averting only by the narrowest of margins half a dozen bad collisions. At times the *fiacre* lurched in such alarming fashion that Shirley was visibly perturbed, but when Jefferson assured her that all Paris cabs travelled in this crazy fashion and nothing ever happened, she was comforted.

"Tell me," he repeated, "what do the papers say about the book?"

"Say?" he echoed. "Why, simply that you've written the biggest book of the year, that's all!"

"Really! Oh, do tell me all they said!" She was fairly excited now, and in her enthusiasm she grasped Jefferson's broad, sunburnt hand which was lying outside the carriage rug. He tried to appear unconscious of the contact, which made his every nerve tingle, as he proceeded to tell her the gist of the reviews he had read that afternoon.

"Isn't that splendid!" she exclaimed, when he had finished. Then she added quickly:

"I wonder if your father has seen it?"

Jefferson grinned. He had something on his conscience, and this was a good opportunity to get rid of it. He replied laconically:

"He probably has read it by this time. I sent him a copy myself."

The instant the words were out of his mouth he was sorry, for Shirley's face had changed colour.

"You sent him a copy of 'The American Octopus?'" she cried. "Then he'll guess who wrote the book."

"Oh, no, he won't," rejoined Jefferson calmly. "He has no idea who sent it to him. I mailed it anonymously."

Shirley breathed a sigh of relief. It was so important that her identity should remain a secret. As daughter of a Supreme Court judge she had to be most careful. She would not embarrass her father for anything in the world. But it was smart of Jefferson to have sent Ryder, Sr., the book, so she smiled graciously on his son as she asked:

"How do you know he got it? So many letters and packages are sent to him that he never sees himself."

"Oh, he saw your book all right," laughed Jefferson. "I was around the house a good deal before sailing, and one day I caught him in the library reading it."

They both laughed, feeling like mischievous children who had played a successful trick on the hokeypokey man. Jefferson noted his companion's pretty dimples and fine teeth, and he thought how attractive she was, and stronger and stronger grew the idea within him that this was the woman who was intended by Nature to share his life. Her slender hand still covered his broad, sunburnt one, and he fancied he felt a slight pressure. But he was mistaken. Not the slightest sentiment entered into Shirley's thoughts of Jefferson. She regarded him only as a good comrade with whom she had secrets she confided in no one else. To that extent and to that extent alone he was privileged above other men. Suddenly he asked her:

"Have you heard from home recently?"

A soft light stole into the girl's face. Home! Ah, that was all she needed to make her cup of happiness full. Intoxicated with this new sensation of a first literary success, full of the keen pleasure this visit to the beautiful city was giving her, bubbling over with the joy of life, happy in the almost daily companionship of the man she liked most in the world after her father, there was only one thing lacking—home! She had left New York only a month before, and she was homesick already. Her father she missed most. She was fond of her mother, too, but the latter, being somewhat of a nervous invalid, had never been to her quite what her father had been. The playmate of her childhood, companion of her girlhood, her friend and adviser in womanhood, Judge Rossmore was to his daughter the ideal man and father. Answering Jefferson's question she said:

"I had a letter from father last week. Everything was going on at home as when I left. Father says he misses me sadly, and that mother is ailing as usual."

She smiled, and Jefferson smiled too. They both knew by experience that nothing really serious ailed Mrs. Rossmore, who was a good deal of a hypochondriac, and always so filled with aches and pains that, on the few occasions when she really felt well, she was genuinely alarmed.

The *fiacre* by this time had emerged from the Rue de Rivoli and was rolling smoothly along the fine wooden pavement in front of the historic Conciergerie prison where Marie Antoinette was confined before her execution. Presently they recrossed the Seine, and the cab, dodging the tram car rails, proceeded at a smart pace up the "Boul' Mich'," which is the familiar diminutive bestowed by the students upon that broad avenue which traverses the very heart of their beloved *Quartier Latin*. On the left frowned the scholastic walls of the learned Sorbonne, in the distance towered the majestic dome of the Panthéon where Rousseau, Voltaire and Hugo lay buried.

Like most of the principal arteries of the French capital, the boulevard was generously lined with trees, now in full bloom, and the sidewalks fairly seethed with a picturesque throng in which mingled promiscuously frivolous students, dapper shop clerks, sober citizens, and frisky, flirtatious little *ouvrières,* these last being all hatless, as is characteristic of the work-girl class, but singularly attractive in their neat black dresses and dainty low-cut shoes. There was also much in evidence another type of female whose extravagance of costume and boldness of manner loudly proclaimed her ancient profession.

On either side of the boulevard were shops and cafés, mostly cafés, with every now and then a *brasserie,* or beer hall. Seated in front of these establishments, taking their ease as if beer sampling constituted the only real interest in their lives, were hundreds of students, reckless and dare-devil, and suggesting almost anything except serious study. They all wore frock coats and tall silk hats, and some of the latter were wonderful specimens of the hatter's art. A few of the more eccentric students had long hair down to their shoulders, and wore baggy peg-top trousers of extravagant cut, which hung in loose folds over their sharp-pointed boots. On their heads were queer plug hats with flat brims.

Shirley laughed outright and regretted that she did not have her kodak to take back to America some idea of their grotesque appearance, and she listened with amused interest as Jefferson explained that these men

were notorious *poseurs,* aping the dress and manners
of the old-time student as he flourished in the days of
Randolph and Mimi and the other immortal charac-
ters of Murger's Bohemia. Nobody took them seriously except themselves, and for the most part they
were bad rhymesters of decadent verse. Shirley was
astonished to see so many of them busily engaged
smoking cigarettes and imbibing glasses of a pale-
green beverage, which Jefferson told her was absinthe.

" When do they read ? " she asked. " When do they
attend lectures ? "

" Oh," laughed Jefferson, " only the old-fashioned
students take their studies seriously. Most of the men
you see there are from the provinces, seeing Paris for
the first time, and having their fling. Incidentally
they are studying life. When they have sown their
wild oats and learned all about life—provided they are
still alive and have any money left—they will begin
to study books. You would be surprised to know how
many of these young men, who have been sent to the
University at a cost of goodness knows what sacrifices, return to their native towns in a few months
wrecked in body and mind, without having once set
foot in a lecture room, and, in fact, having done nothing except inscribe their names on the rolls."

Shirley was glad she knew no such men, and if she

ever married and had a son she would pray God to
spare her that grief and humiliation. She herself
knew something about the sacrifices parents make to
secure a college education for their children. Her
father had sent her to Vassar. She was a product of
the much-sneered-at higher education for women, and
all her life she would be grateful for the advantages
given her. Her liberal education had broadened her
outlook on life and enabled her to accomplish the little
she had. When she graduated her father had left
her free to follow her own inclinations. She had little
taste for social distractions, and still she could not
remain idle. For a time she thought of teaching to
occupy her mind, but she knew she lacked the necessary patience, and she could not endure the drudgery
of it, so, having won honors at college in English
composition, she determined to try her hand at literature. She wrote a number of essays and articles on
a hundred different subjects which she sent to the
magazines, but they all came back with politely worded
excuses for their rejection. But Shirley kept right
on. She knew she wrote well; it must be that her
subjects were not suitable. So she adopted new tactics, and persevered until one day came a letter of ac-
ceptance from the editor of one of the minor magazines. They would take the article offered—a sketch

of college life—and as many more in similar vein as Miss Rossmore could write. This success had been followed by other acceptances and other commissions, until at the present time she was a well-known writer for the leading publications. Her great ambition had been to write a book, and " The American Octopus," published under an assumed name, was the result.

The cab stopped suddenly in front of beautiful gilded gates. It was the Luxembourg, and through the tall railings they caught a glimpse of well-kept lawns, splashing fountains and richly dressed children playing. From the distance came the stirring strains of a brass band.

The coachman drove up to the curb and Jefferson jumped down, assisting Shirley to alight. In spite of Shirley's protest Jefferson insisted on paying.

" *Combien?* " he asked the *cocher*.

The jehu, a surly, thick-set man with a red face and small, cunning eyes like a ferret, had already sized up his fares for two *sacré* foreigners whom it would be flying in the face of Providence not to cheat, so with unblushing effrontery he answered:

" *Dix francs, Monsieur!* " And he held up ten fingers by way of illustration.

Jefferson was about to hand up a ten-franc piece when Shirley indignantly interfered. She would not submit to such an imposition. There was a regular tariff and she would pay that and nothing more. So, in better French than was at Jefferson's command, she exclaimed:

"Ten francs? *Pourquoi dix francs?* I took your cab by the hour. It is exactly two hours. That makes four francs." Then to Jefferson she added: "Give him a franc for a *pourboire*—that makes five francs altogether."

Jefferson, obedient to her superior wisdom, held out a five-franc piece, but the driver shrugged his shoulders disdainfully. He saw that the moment had come to bluster so he descended from his box fully prepared to carry out his bluff. He started in to abuse the two Americans whom in his ignorance he took for English.

"Ah, you *sale Anglais!* You come to France to cheat the poor Frenchman. You make me work all afternoon and then pay me nothing. Not with this coco! I know my rights and I'll get them, too."

All this was hurled at them in a patois French, almost unintelligible to Shirley, and wholly so to Jefferson. All he knew was that the fellow's attitude was becoming unbearably insolent and he stepped forward with a gleam in his eye that might have startled the man had he not been so busy shaking his fist at Shir-

ley. But she saw Jefferson's movement and laid her
hand on his arm.

" No, no, Mr. Ryder—no scandal, please. Look,
people are beginning to come up! Leave him to me.
I know how to manage him."

With this the daughter of a United States Supreme
Court judge proceeded to lay down the law to the
representative of the most lazy and irresponsible class
of men ever let loose in the streets of a civilised community. Speaking with an air of authority, she said:

" Now look here, my man, we have no time to bandy
words here with you. I took your cab at 3.30. It is
now 5.30. That makes two hours. The rate is two
francs an hour, or four francs in all. We offer you
five francs, and this includes a franc *pourboire*. If
this settlement does not suit you we will get into your
cab and you will drive us to the nearest police-station
where the argument can be continued."

The man's jaw dropped. He was obviously out-
classed. These foreigners knew the law as well as he
did. He had no desire to accept Shirley's suggestion
of a trip to the police-station, where he knew he would
get little sympathy, so, grumbling and giving vent
under his breath to a volley of strange oaths, he
grabbed viciously at the five-franc piece Jefferson held
out and, mounting his box, drove off.

# THE MOUSE

Proud of their victory, they entered the gardens, following the sweet-scented paths until they came to where the music was. The band of an infantry regiment was playing, and a large crowd had gathered. Many people were sitting on the chairs provided for visitors for the modest fee of two sous; others were promenading round and round a great circle having the musicians in its centre. The dense foliage of the trees overhead afforded a perfect shelter from the hot rays of the sun, and the place was so inviting and interesting, so cool and so full of sweet perfumes and sounds, appealing to and satisfying the senses, that Shirley wished they had more time to spend there. She was very fond of a good brass band, especially when heard in the open air. They were playing Strauss's *Blue Danube,* and the familiar strains of the delightful waltz were so infectious that both were seized by a desire to get up and dance.

There was constant amusement, too, watching the crowd, with its many original and curious types. There were serious college professors, with gold-rimmed spectacles, buxom *nounous* in their uniform cloaks and long ribbon streamers, nicely dressed children romping merrily but not noisily, more queer-looking students in shabby frock coats, tight at the waist, trousers too short, and comical hats, stylishly dressed women displaying the latest fashions, brilliantly uniformed army officers strutting proudly, dangling their swords—an attractive and interesting crowd, so different, thought the two Americans, from the cheap, evil-smelling, ill-mannered mob of aliens that invades their own Central Park the days when there is music, making it a nuisance instead of a pleasure. Here everyone belonged apparently to the better class; the women and children were richly and fashionably dressed, the officers looked smart in their multi-coloured uniforms, and, no matter how one might laugh at the students, there was an atmosphere of good-breeding and refinement everywhere which Shirley was not accustomed to see in public places at home. A sprinkling of workmen and people of the poorer class were to be seen here and there, but they were in the decided minority. Shirley, herself a daughter of the Revolution, was a staunch supporter of the immortal principles of Democracy and of the equality of man before the law. But all other talk of equality was the greatest sophistry and charlatanism. There could be no real equality so long as some people were cultured and refined and others were uneducated and vulgar. Shirley believed in an aristocracy of brains and soap. She insisted that no clean person, no matter how good a democrat, should be expected to sit close in public places to persons who were not on speaking terms with the bath-tub. In America this foolish theory of a democracy, which insists on throwing all classes, the clean and the unclean, promiscuously together, was positively revolting, making travelling in the public vehicles almost impossible, and it was not much better in the public parks. In France—also a Republic—where they likewise paraded conspicuously the clap-trap "Egalité, Fraternité," they managed these things far better. The French lower classes knew their place. They did not ape the dress, nor frequent the resorts of those above them in the social scale. The distinction between the classes was plainly and properly marked, yet this was not antagonistic to the ideal of true democracy; it had not prevented the son of a peasant from becoming President of the French Republic. Each district in Paris had its own amusement, its own theatres, its own parks. It was not a question of capital refusing to fraternize with labour, but the very natural desire of persons of refinement to mingle with clean people rather than to rub elbows with the Great Unwashed.

"Isn't it delightful here?" said Shirley. "I could stay here forever, couldn't you?"

"With you—yes," answered Jefferson, with a significant smile.

Shirley tried to look angry. She strictly discouraged these conventional, sentimental speeches which
constantly flung her sex in her face.

"Now, you know I don't like you to talk that way,
Mr. Ryder. It's most undignified. Please be sensible."

Quite subdued, Jefferson relapsed into a sulky silence. Presently he said:

"I wish you wouldn't call me Mr. Ryder. I meant
to ask you this before. You know very well that
you've no great love for the name, and if you persist
you'll end by including me in your hatred of the hero
of your book.'

Shirley looked at him with amused curiosity.

"What do you mean?" she asked. "What do you
want me to call you?"

"Oh, I don't know," he stammered, rather intimidated by this self-possessed young woman who looked
him calmly through and through. "Why not call me
Jefferson? Mr. Ryder is so formal."

Shirley laughed outright, a merry, unrestrained peal
of honest laughter, which made the passers-by turn
their heads and smile, too, commenting the while on
the stylish appearance of the two Americans whom
they took for sweethearts. After all, reasoned Shirley,
he was right. They had been together now nearly

every hour in the day for over a month. It was absurd to call him Mr. Ryder. So, addressing him with
mock gravity, she said:

"You're right, Mr. Ryder—I mean Jefferson.
You're quite right. You are Jefferson from this time
on, only remember "—here she shook her gloved finger
at him warningly—"mind you behave yourself! No
more such sentimental speeches as you made just now."

Jefferson beamed. He felt at least two inches taller,
and at that moment he would not have changed places
with any one in the world. To hide the embarrassment
his gratification caused him he pulled out his watch
and exclaimed:

"Why, it's a quarter past six. We shall have all
we can do to get back to the hotel and dress for dinner."

Shirley rose at once, although loath to leave.

"I had no idea it was so late," she said. "How the
time flies!" Then mockingly she added: "Come, Jefferson—be a good boy and find a cab."

They passed out of the Gardens by the gate facing
the Théâtre de l'Odéon, where there was a long string
of *fiacres* for hire. They got into one and in fifteen
minutes they were back at the Grand Hotel.

At the office they told Shirley that her aunt had
already come in and gone to her room, so she hurried

upstairs to dress for dinner while Jefferson proceeded to the Hotel de l'Athenée on the same mission. He had still twenty-five minutes before dinner time, and he needed only ten minutes for a wash and to jump into his dress suit, so, instead of going directly to his hotel, he sat down at the Café de la Paix. He was thirsty, and calling for a vermouth *frappé* he told the *garçon* to bring him also the American papers.

The crowd on the boulevard was denser than ever. The business offices and some of the shops were closing, and a vast army of employés, homeward bound, helped to swell the sea of humanity that pushed this way and that.

But Jefferson had no eyes for the crowd. He was thinking of Shirley. What singular, mysterious power had this girl acquired over him? He, who had scoffed at the very idea of marriage only a few months before, now desired it ardently, anxiously! Yes, that was what his life lacked—such a woman to be his companion and helpmate! He loved her—there was no doubt of that. His every thought, waking and sleeping, was of her, all his plans for the future included her. He would win her if any man could. But did she care for him? Ah, that was the cruel, torturing uncertainty! She appeared cold and indifferent, but per-

94

haps she was only trying him. Certainly she did not seem to dislike him.

The waiter returned with the vermouth and the newspapers. All he could find were the London *Times,* which he pronounced T-e-e-m-s, and some issues of the *New York Herald.* The papers were nearly a month old, but he did not care for that. Jefferson idly turned over the pages of the *Herald.* His thoughts were still running on Shirley, and he was paying little attention to what he was reading. Suddenly, however, his eyes rested on a headline which made him sit up with a start. It read as follows:

### JUDGE ROSSMORE IMPEACHED

#### JUSTICE OF THE SUPREME COURT TO BE TRIED ON BRIBERY CHARGES

The despatch, which was dated Washington two weeks back, went on to say that serious charges affecting the integrity of Judge Rossmore had been made the subject of Congressional inquiry, and that the result of the inquiry was so grave that a demand for impeachment would be at once sent to the Senate. It added that the charges grew out of the recent decision in the Great Northwestern Mining Company case, it being alleged that Judge Rossmore had accepted a large sum of money on condition of his handing down a decision favourable to the company.

Jefferson was thunderstruck. He read the despatch over again to make sure there was no mistake. No, it was very plain—Judge Rossmore of Madison Avenue. But how preposterous, what a calumny! The one judge on the bench at whom one could point and say with absolute conviction: "There goes an honest man!" And this judge was to be tried on a charge of bribery! What could be the meaning of it? Something terrible must have happened since Shirley's departure from home, that was certain. It meant her immediate return to the States and, of course, his own. He would see what could be done. He would make his father use his great influence. But how could he tell Shirley? Impossible, he could not! She would not believe him if he did. She would probably hear from home in some other way. They might cable. In any case he would say nothing yet. He paid for his vermouth and hurried away to his hotel to dress.

It was just striking seven when he re-entered the courtyard of the Grand Hotel. Shirley and Mrs. Blake were waiting for him. Jefferson suggested having dinner at the Café de Paris, but Shirley objected that as the weather was warm it would be more pleasant to dine in the open air, so they finally decided on the Pavillon d'Armonville where there was music and where they could have a little table to themselves in the garden.

They drove up the stately Champs Elysées, past the monumental Arc de Triomphe, and from there down to the Bois. All were singularly quiet. Mrs. Blake was worrying about her new gown. Shirley was tired, and Jefferson could not banish from his mind the terrible news he had just read. He avoided looking at Shirley until the latter noticed it and thought she must have offended him in some way. She was more sorry than she would have him know, for, with all her apparent coldness, Jefferson was rapidly becoming very indispensable to her happiness.

They dined sumptuously and delightfully with all the luxury of surroundings and all the delights of cooking that the French culinary art can perfect. A single glass of champagne had put Shirley in high spirits and she had tried hard to communicate some of her good humour to Jefferson who, despite all her efforts, remained quiet and preoccupied. Finally losing patience she asked him bluntly:

" Jefferson, what's the matter with you to-night? You've been sulky as a bear all evening."

Pleased to see she had not forgotten their compact

of the afternoon in regard to his name, Jefferson relaxed somewhat and said apologetically:

"Excuse me, I've been feeling a bit seedy lately. I think I need another sea voyage. That's the only time when I feel really first-class—when I'm on the water."

The mention of the sea started Shirley to talk about her future plans. She wasn't going back to America until September. She had arranged to make a stay of three weeks in London and then she would be free. Some friends of hers from home, a man and his wife who owned a steam yacht, were arranging a trip to the Mediterranean, including a run over to Cairo. They had asked her and Mrs. Blake to go and she was sure they would ask Jefferson, too. Would he go?

There was no way out of it. Jefferson tried to work up some enthusiasm for this yachting trip, which he knew very well could never come off, and it cut him to the heart to see this poor girl joyously making all these preparations and plans, little dreaming of the domestic calamity which at that very moment was hanging over her head.

It was nearly ten o'clock when they had finished. They sat a little longer listening to the gipsy music, weird and barbaric. Very pointedly, Shirley remarked:

"Father, I've changed my mind, I'm not going away." — Act II.

# THE MOUSE

" I for one preferred the music this afternoon."

" Why?" inquired Jefferson, ignoring the petulant note in her voice.

" Because you were more amiable!" she retorted rather crossly.

This was their first misunderstanding, but Jefferson said nothing. He could not tell her the thoughts and fears that had been haunting him all night. Soon afterward they re-entered their cab and returned to the boulevards which were ablaze with light and gaiety. Jefferson suggested going somewhere else, but Mrs. Blake was tired and Shirley, now quite irritated at what she considered Jefferson's unaccountable unsociability, declined somewhat abruptly. But she could never remain angry long, and when they said goodnight she whispered demurely:

" Are you cross with me, Jeff?"

He turned his head away and she saw that his face was singularly drawn and grave.

" Cross—no. Good-night. God bless you!" he said, hoarsely gulping down a lump that rose in his throat. Then grasping her hand he hurried away.

Completely mystified, Shirley and her companion turned to the office to get the key of their room. As the man handed it to Shirley he passed her also a cablegram which had just come. She changed colour.

She did not like telegrams. She always had a dread of them, for with her sudden news was usually bad news. Could this, she thought, explain Jefferson's strange behaviour? Trembling, she tore open the envelope and read:

*Come home at once.*

*Mother.*

# THE MOUSE

## CHAPTER V.

ROLLING, tumbling, splashing, foaming water as far as the eye could reach in every direction. A desolate waste, full of life, movement and colour, extending to the bleak horizon and like a vast ploughed field cut up into long and high liquid ridges, all scurrying in one direction in serried ranks and with incredible speed as if pursued by a fearful and unseen enemy. Serenely yet boisterously, gracefully yet resistlessly, the endless waves passed on—some small, others monstrous, with fleecy white combs rushing down their green sides like toy Niagaras and with a seething, boiling sound as when flame touches water. They went by in a stately, never ending procession, going nowhere, coming from nowhere, but full of dignity and importance, their breasts heaving with suppressed rage because there was nothing in their path that they might destroy. The dancing, leaping water reflected every shade and tint— now a rich green, then a deep blue and again a dirty gray as the sun hid for a moment behind a cloud, and as a gust of wind caught the top of the combers decapitating them at one mad rush, the spray was dashed high in the air, flashing out all the prismatic colours. Here and yonder, the white caps rose, disappeared and came again, and the waves grew and then diminished in size. Then others rose, towering, became larger, majestic, terrible; the milk-like comb rose proudly, soared a brief moment, then fell ignominiously, and the wave diminished passed on humiliated. Over head, a few scattered cirrus clouds flitted lazily across the blue dome of heaven, while a dozen Mother Carey chickens screamed hoarsely as they circled in the air. The strong and steady western breeze bore on its powerful pinions the sweet and eternal music of the wind and sea.

Shirley stood at the rail under the bridge of the ocean greyhound that was carrying her back to America with all the speed of which her mighty engines were capable. All day and all night, half naked stokers, so grimed with oil and coal dust as to lose the slightest semblance to human beings, feverishly shovelled coal, throwing it rapidly and evenly over roaring furnaces kept at a fierce white heat. The vast boilers, shaken by the titanic forces generating in their cavern-like depths, sent streams of scalding, hissing steam through a thousand valves, cylinders and pistons, turning wheels and cranks as it

distributed the tremendous power which was driving the
steel monster through the seas at the prodigious speed
of four hundred miles in the twenty-four hours. Like
a pulsating heart in some living thing, the mammoth
engines throbbed and panted, and the great vessel
groaned and creaked as she rose and fell to the heavy
swell, and again lurched forward in obedience to each
fresh propulsion from her fast spinning screws. Out
on deck, volumes of dense black smoke were pouring
from four gigantic smoke stacks and spread out in the
sky like some endless cinder path leading back over
the course the ship had taken.

They were four days out from port. Two days
more and they would sight Sandy Hook, and Shirley
would know the worst. She had caught the North
German Lloyd boat at Cherbourg two days after receiving the cablegram from New York. Mrs. Blake
had insisted on coming along in spite of her niece's
protests. Shirley argued that she had crossed alone
when coming; she could go back the same way. Besides, was not Mr. Ryder returning home on the
same ship? He would be company and protection
both. But Mrs. Blake was bent on making the voyage.
She had not seen her sister for many years and, moreover, this sudden return to America had upset her
own plans. She was a poor sailor, yet she loved the

ocean and this was a good excuse for a long trip.
Shirley was too exhausted with worry to offer further
resistance and by great good luck the two women had
been able to secure at the last moment a cabin to themselves amidships. Jefferson, less fortunate, was compelled, to his disgust, to share a stateroom with another
passenger, a fat German brewer who was returning to
Cincinnati, and who snored so loud at night that even
the thumping of the engines was completely drowned
by his eccentric nasal sounds.

The alarming summons home and the terrible shock
she had experienced the following morning when Jefferson showed her the newspaper article with its
astounding and heart rending news about her father
had almost prostrated Shirley. The blow was all the
greater for being so entirely unlooked for. That the
story was true she could not doubt. Her mother
would not have cabled except under the gravest circumstances. What alarmed Shirley still more was
that she had no direct news of her father. For a
moment her heart stood still—suppose the shock of
this shameful accusation had killed him? Her blood
froze in her veins, she clenched her fists and dug her
nails into her flesh as she thought of the dread possibility that she had looked upon him in life for the last
time. She remembered his last kind words when he

came to the steamer to see her off, and his kiss when he said good-bye and she had noticed a tear of which he appeared to be ashamed. The hot tears welled up in her own eyes and coursed unhindered down her cheeks.

What could these preposterous and abominable charges mean? What was this lie they had invented to ruin her father? That he had enemies she well knew. What strong man had not? Indeed, his proverbial honesty had made him feared by all evil-doers and on one occasion they had gone so far as to threaten his life. This new attack was more deadly than all— to sap and destroy his character, to deliberately fabricate lies and calumnies which had no foundation whatever. Of course, the accusation was absurd, the Senate would refuse to convict him, the entire press would espouse the cause of so worthy a public servant. Certainly, everything would be done to clear his character. But what was being done? She could do nothing but wait and wait. The suspense and anxiety were awful.

Suddenly she heard a familiar step behind her, and Jefferson joined her at the rail. The wind was due West and blowing half a gale, so where they were standing—one of the most exposed parts of the ship— it was difficult to keep one's feet, to say nothing of hearing anyone speak. There was a heavy sea run-

ning, and each approaching wave looked big enough
to engulf the vessel, but as the mass of moving water
reached the bow, the ship rose on it, light and graceful
as a bird, shook off the flying spray as a cat shakes
her fur after an unwelcome bath, and again drove forward as steady and with as little perceptible motion
as a railway train. Shirley was a fairly good sailor
and this kind of weather did not bother her in the
least, but when it got very rough she could not bear
the rolling and pitching and then all she was good for
was to lie still in her steamer chair with her eyes closed
until the water was calmer and the pitching ceased.

" It's pretty windy here, Shirley," shouted Jefferson,
steadying himself against a stanchion. " Don't you
want to walk a little? "

He had begun to call her by her first name quite
naturally, as if it were a matter of course. Indeed,
their relations had come to be more like those of
brother and sister than anything else. Shirley was too
much troubled over the news from home to have
a mind for other things, and in her distress she
had turned to Jefferson for advice and help as she
would have looked to an elder brother. He had felt
this impulse to confide in him and consult his opinion
and it had pleased him more than he dared betray. He
had shown her all the sympathy of which his warm,

generous nature was capable, yet secretly he did not regret that events had necessitated this sudden return home together on the same ship. He was sorry for Judge Rossmore, of course, and there was nothing he would not do on his return to secure a withdrawal of the charges. That his father would use his influence he had no doubt. But meantime he was selfish enough to be glad for the opportunity it gave him to be a whole week alone with Shirley. No matter how much one may be with people in city or country or even when stopping at the same hotel or house, there is no place in the world where two persons, especially when they are of the opposite sex, can become so intimate as on shipboard. The reason is obvious. The days are long and monotonous. There is nowhere to go, nothing to see but the ocean, nothing to do but read, talk or promenade. Seclusion in one's stuffy cabin is out of the question, the public sitting rooms are noisy and impossible, only a steamer chair on deck is comfortable and once there snugly wrapped up in a rug it is surprising how quickly another chair makes its appearance alongside and how welcome one is apt to make the intruder.

Thus events combined with the weather conspired to bring Shirley and Jefferson more closely together. The sea had been rough ever since they sailed, keeping Mrs. Blake confined to her stateroom almost continuously. They were, therefore, constantly in one another's company, and slowly, unconsciously, there was taking root in their hearts the germ of the only real and lasting love—the love born of something higher than mere physical attraction, the nobler, more enduring affection that is born of mutual sympathy, association and companionship.

"Isn't it beautiful?" exclaimed Shirley ecstatically. "Look at those great waves out there! See how majestically they soar and how gracefully they fall!"

"Glorious!" assented Jefferson sharing her enthusiasm. "There's nothing to compare with it. It's Nature's grandest spectacle. The ocean is the only place on earth that man has not defiled and spoiled. Those waves are the same now as they were on the day of creation."

"Not the day of creation. You mean during the aeons of time creation was evolving," corrected Shirley.

"I meant that of course," assented Jefferson. "When one says ' day ' that is only a form of speech."

"Why not be accurate?" persisted Shirley. "It was the use of that little word ' day ' which has given the theologians so many sleepless nights."

There was a roguish twinkle in her eye. She well

knew that he thought as she did on metaphysical questions, but she could not resist teasing him.

Like Jefferson, she was not a member of any church, although her nature was deeply religious. Hers was the religion the soul inculcates, not that which is learned by rote in the temple. She was a Christian because she thought Christ the greatest figure in world history, and also because her own conduct of life was modelled upon Christian principles and virtues. She was religious for religion's sake and not for public ostentation. The mystery of life awed her and while her intelligence could not accept all the doctrines of dogmatic religion she did not go so far as Jefferson, who was a frank agnostic. She would not admit that we do not know. The longings and aspirations of her own soul convinced her of the existence of a Supreme Being, First Cause, Divine Intelligence—call it what you will—which had brought out of chaos the wonderful order of the universe. The human mind was, indeed, helpless to conceive such a First Cause in any form and lay prostrate before the Unknown, yet she herself was an enthusiastic delver into scientific hypothesis and the teachings of Darwin, Spencer, Haeckel had satisfied her intellect if they had failed to content her soul. The theory of evolution as applied to life on her own little planet appealed strongly to her because it accounted plausibly for the presence of man on earth. The process through which we had passed could be understood by every intelligence. The blazing satellite, violently detached from the parent sun starting on its circumscribed orbit—that was the first stage, the gradual subsidence of the flames and the cooling of the crust—the second stage: the gases mingling and forming water which covered the earth—the third stage; the retreating of the waters and the appearance of the land—the fourth stage; the appearance of vegetation and animal life—the fifth stage; then, after a long interval and through constant evolution and change the appearance of man, which was the sixth stage. What stages still to come, who knows? This simple account given by science was, after all, practically identical with the biblical legend!

It was when Shirley was face to face with Nature in her wildest and most primitive aspects that this deep rooted religious feeling moved her most strongly. At these times she felt herself another being, exalted, sublimated, lifted from this little world with its petty affairs and vanities up to dizzy heights. She had felt the same sensation when for the first time she had viewed the glories of the snow clad Matterhorn, she had felt it when on a summer's night at sea she had sat on deck and watched with fascinated awe the resplendent radiance of the countless stars, she felt it now as she looked at the foaming, tumbling waves.

"It is so beautiful," she murmured as she turned to walk. The ship was rolling a little and she took Jefferson's arm to steady herself. Shirley was an athletic girl and had all the ease and grace of carriage that comes of much tennis and golf playing. Barely twenty-four years old, she was still in the first flush of youth and health, and there was nothing she loved so much as exercise and fresh air. After a few turns on deck, there was a ruddy glow in her cheeks that was good to see and many an admiring glance was cast at the young couple as they strode briskly up and down past the double rows of elongated steamer chairs.

They had the deck pretty much to themselves. It was only four o'clock, too early for the appetite-stimulating walk before dinner, and their fellow passengers were basking in the sunshine, stretched out on their chairs in two even rows like so many mummies on exhibition. Some were reading, some were dozing. Two or three were under the weather, completely prostrated, their bilious complexion of a deathly greenish hue. At each new roll of the ship, they closed their eyes as if resigned to the worst that might happen and their immediate neighbours furtively eyed each of their movements as if apprehensive of what any moment might bring forth. A few couples were flirting to their heart's content under the friendly cover of the lifeboats which, as on most of the transatlantic liners, were more useful in saving reputations than in saving life. The deck steward was passing round tea and biscuits, much to the disgust of the ill ones, but to the keen satisfaction of the stronger stomached passengers who on shipboard never seem to be able to get enough to eat and drink. On the bridge, the second officer, a tall, handsome man with the points of his moustache trained upwards à la Kaiser Wilhelm, was striding back and forth, every now and then sweeping the horizon with his glass and relieving the monotony of his duties by ogling the better looking women passengers.

" Hello, Shirley! " called out a voice from a heap of rugs as Shirley and Jefferson passed the rows of chairs.

They stopped short and discovered Mrs. Blake ensconced in a cozy corner, sheltered from the wind.

"Why, aunt Milly," exclaimed Shirley surprised. " I thought you were downstairs. I didn't think you could stand this sea."

" It is a little rougher than I care to have it," responded Mrs. Blake with a wry grimace and putting her hand to her breast as if to appease disturbing qualms. " It was so stuffy in the cabin I could not bear it. It's more pleasant here but it's getting a little cool and I think I'll go below. Where have you children been all afternoon?"

Jefferson volunteered to explain.

" The children have been rhapsodizing over the beauties of the ocean," he laughed. With a sly glance at Shirley, he added, " Your niece has been coaching me in metaphysics."

Shirley shook her finger at him.

" Now Jefferson, if you make fun of me I'll never talk seriously with you again."

*"Wie geht es, meine damen?"*

Shirley turned on hearing the guttural salutation. It was Captain Hegermann, the commander of the ship, a big florid Saxon with great bushy golden whiskers and a basso voice like Edouard de Reszké. He was imposing in his smart uniform and gold braid and his manner had the self-reliant, authoritative air usual in men who have great responsibilities and are accustomed to command. He was taking his afternoon stroll and had stopped to chat with his lady passengers. He had already passed Mrs. Blake a dozen times and not noticed her, but now her pretty niece was with her, which altered the situation. He talked

to the aunt and looked at Shirley, much to the annoyance of Jefferson, who muttered things under his
breath.

"When shall we be in, captain?" asked Mrs. Blake
anxiously, forgetting that this was one of the questions
which according to ship etiquette must never be asked
of the officers.

But as long as he could ignore Mrs. Blake and gaze
at Shirley Capt. Hegermann did not mind. He
answered amiably:

"At the rate we are going, we ought to sight Fire
Island sometime to-morrow evening. If we do, that
will get us to our dock about 11 o'clock Friday morning, I fancy." Then addressing Shirley direct he said:

"And you, fraulein, I hope you won't be glad the
voyage is over?"

Shirley sighed and a worried, anxious look came into
her face.

"Yes, Captain, I shall be very glad. It is not
pleasure that is bringing me back to America so soon."

The captain elevated his eyebrows. He was sorry
the young lady had anxieties to keep her so serious,
and he hoped she would find everything all right on
her arrival. Then, politely saluting, he passed on, only
to halt again a few paces on where his bewhiskered
gallantry met with more encouragement.

# THE MOUSE

Mrs. Blake rose from her chair. The air was decidedly cooler, she would go downstairs and prepare for dinner. Shirley said she would remain on deck a little longer. She was tired of walking, so when her aunt left them she took her chair and told Jefferson to get another. He wanted nothing better, but before seating himself he took the rugs and wrapped Shirley up with all the solicitude of a mother caring for her first born. Arranging the pillow under her head, he asked:

" Is that comfortable?"

She nodded, smiling at him.

" You're a good boy, Jeff. But you'll spoil me."

" Nonsense," he stammered as he took another chair and put himself by her side. " As if any fellow wouldn't give his boots to do a little job like that for you!"

She seemed to take no notice of the covert compliment. In fact, she already took it as a matter of course that Jefferson was very fond of her.

Did she love him? She hardly knew. Certainly she thought more of him than of any other man she knew and she readily believed that she could be with him for the rest of her life and like him better every day. Then, too, they had become more intimate during the last few days. This trouble, this unknown peril had drawn them together. Yes, she would be sorry if she were to see Jefferson paying attention to another woman. Was this love? Perhaps.

These thoughts were running through her mind as they sat there side by side isolated from the main herd of passengers, each silent, watching through the open rail the foaming water as it rushed past. Jefferson had been casting furtive glances at his companion and as he noted her serious, pensive face he thought how pretty she was. He wondered what she was thinking of and suddenly inspired no doubt by the mysterious power that enables some people to read the thoughts of others, he said abruptly:

"Shirley, I can read your thoughts. You were thinking of me."

She was startled for a moment but immediately recovered her self possession. It never occurred to her to deny it. She pondered for a moment and then replied:

"You are right, Jeff, I was thinking of you. How did you guess?"

He leaned over her chair and took her hand. She made no resistance. Her delicate, slender hand lay passively in his big brown one and met his grasp frankly, cordially. He whispered:

"What were you thinking of me—good or bad?"

116

# THE MOUSE

" Good, of course.  How could I think anything bad of you ? "

She turned her eyes on him in wonderment.  Then she went on:

" I was wondering how a girl could distinguish between the feeling she has for a man she merely likes, and the feeling she has for a man she loves."

Jefferson bent eagerly forward so as to lose no word that might fall from those coveted lips.

" In what category would I be placed? " he asked.

" I don't quite know," she answered, laughingly. Then seriously, she added: " Jeff, why should we act like children?  Your actions, more than your words, have told me that you love me.  I have known it all along.  If I have appeared cold and indifferent it is because "—she hesitated.

" Because? " echoed Jefferson anxiously, as if his whole future depended on that reason.

" Because I was not sure of myself.  Would it be womanly or honourable on my part to encourage you, unless I felt I reciprocated your feelings?  You are young, one day you will be very rich, the whole world lies before you.  There are plenty of women who would willingly give you their love."

" No—no! " he burst out in vigorous protest, " it is you I want. Shirley, you alone."

Grasping her hand more closely, he went on, passion vibrating in every note of his voice. "I love you, Shirley. I've loved you from the very first evening I met you. I want you to be my wife."

Shirley looked straight up into the blue eyes so eagerly bent down on hers, so entreating in their expression, and in a gentle voice full of emotion she answered:

"Jefferson, you have done me the greatest honour a man can do a woman. Don't ask me to answer you now. I like you very much—I more than like you. Whether it is love I feel for you—that I have not yet determined. Give me time. My present trouble and then my literary work——"

"I know," agreed Jefferson, "that this is hardly the time to speak of such matters. Your father has first call on your attention. But as to your literary work. I do not understand."

"Simply this. I am ambitious. I have had a little success—just enough to crave for more. I realize that marriage would put an extinguisher on all aspirations in that direction."

"Is marriage so very commonplace?" grumbled Jefferson.

"Not commonplace, but there is no room in marriage for a woman having personal ambitions of her

118

own. · Once married her duty is to her husband and her children—not to herself."

"That is right," he replied; "but which is likely to give you greater joy—a literary success or a happy wifehood? When you have spent your best years and given the public your best work they will throw you over for some new favorite. You'll find yourself an old woman with nothing more substantial to show as your life work than that questionable asset, a literary reputation. How many literary reputations to-day conceal an aching heart and find it difficult to make both ends meet? How different with the woman who married young and obeys Nature's behest by contributing her share to the process of evolution. Her life is spent basking in the affection of her husband and the chubby smiles of her dimpled babes, and when in the course of time she finds herself in the twilight of her life, she has at her feet a new generation of her own flesh and blood. Isn't that better than a literary reputation?"

He spoke so earnestly that Shirley looked at him in surprise. She knew he was serious but she had not suspected that he thought so deeply on these matters. Her heart told her that he was uttering the true philosophy of the ages. She said:

"Why, Jefferson, you talk like a book. Perhaps you

are right, I have no wish to be a blue stocking and deserted in my old age, far from it. But give me time to think. Let us first ascertain the extent of this disaster which has overtaken my father. Then if you still care for me and if I have not changed my mind," here she glanced slyly at him, " we will resume our discussion."

Again she held out her hand which he had released.

" Is it a bargain? " she asked.

" It's a bargain," he murmured, raising the white hand to his lips. A fierce longing rose within him to take her in his arms and kiss passionately the mouth that lay temptingly near his own, but his courage failed him. After all, he reasoned, he had not yet the right.

A few minutes later they left the deck and went downstairs to dress for dinner. That same evening they stood again at the rail watching the mysterious phosphorescence as it sparkled in the moonlight. Her thoughts travelling faster than the ship, Shirley suddenly asked:

" Do you really think Mr. Ryder will use his influence to help my father? "

Jefferson set his jaw fast and the familiar Ryder gleam came into his eyes as he responded:

" Why not? My father is all powerful. He has made and unmade judges and legislators and even presidents. Why should he not be able to put a stop to these preposterous proceedings? I will go to him directly we land and we'll see what can be done."

So the time on shipboard had passed, Shirley alternately buoyed up with hope and again depressed by the gloomiest forebodings. The following night they passed Fire Island and the next day the huge steamer dropped anchor at Quarantine.

## CHAPTER VI.

A MONTH had passed since the memorable meeting of the directors of the Southern and Transcontinental Railroad in New York and during that time neither John Burkett Ryder nor Judge Rossmore had been idle. The former had immediately set in motion the machinery he controlled in the Legislature at Washington, while the judge neglected no step to vindicate himself before the public.

Ryder, for reasons of his own—probably because he wished to make the blow the more crushing when it did fall—had insisted on the proceedings at the board meeting being kept a profound secret and some time elapsed before the newspapers got wind of the coming Congressional inquiry. No one had believed the stories about Judge Rossmore but now that a quasi-official seal had been set on the current gossip, there was a howl of virtuous indignation from the journalistic muck rakers. What was the country coming to? they cried in double leaded type. After the embezzling by life insurance officers, the rascality of the railroads, the looting of city treasuries, the greed of the Trusts,

the grafting of the legislators, had arisen a new and
more serious scandal—the corruption of the Judiciary.
The last bulwark of the nation had fallen, the country
lay helpless at the mercy of legalized sandbaggers.
Even the judges were no longer to be trusted, the most
respected one among them all had been unable to resist
the tempter. The Supreme Court, the living voice of
the Constitution, was honeycombed with graft. Public life was rotten to the core!

Neither the newspapers nor the public stopped to
ascertain the truth or the falsity of the charges against
Judge Rossmore. It was sufficient that the bribery
story furnished the daily sensation which newspaper
editors and newspaper readers must have. The world
is ever more prompt to believe ill rather than good of
a man, and no one, except in Rossmore's immediate
circle of friends, entertained the slightest doubt of
his guilt. It was common knowledge that the " big
interests " were behind the proceedings, and that Judge
Rossmore was a scapegoat, sacrificed by the System
because he had been blocking their game. If Rossmore had really accepted the bribe, and few now believed him spotless, he deserved all that was coming
to him. Senator Roberts was very active in Washington preparing the case against Judge Rossmore. The
latter being a democrat and " the interests " controlling

a Republican majority in the House, it was a foregone conclusion that the inquiry would be against him, and that a demand would at once be made upon the Senate for his impeachment.

Almost prostrated by the misfortune which had so suddenly and unexpectedly come upon him, Judge Rossmore was like a man demented. His reason seemed to be tottering, he spoke and acted like a man in a dream. Naturally he was entirely incapacitated for work and he had applied to Washington to be temporarily relieved from his judicial duties. He was instantly granted a leave of absence and went at once to his home in Madison Avenue, where he shut himself up in his library, sitting for hours at his desk wrestling with documents and legal tomes in a pathetic endeavour to find some way out, trying to elude this net in which unseen hands had entangled him.

What an end to his career! To have struggled and achieved for half a century, to have built up a reputation year by year, as a man builds a house brick by brick, only to see the whole crumble to his feet like dust! To have gained the respect of the country, to have made a name as the most incorruptible of public servants and now to be branded as a common bribe taker! Could he be dreaming? It was too incredible! What would his daughter say—his Shirley? Ah, the

thought of the expression of incredulity and wonder
on her face when she heard the news cut him to the
heart like a knife thrust. Yet, he mused, her very un-
willingness to believe it should really be his consolation.
Ah, his wife and his child—they knew he had been innocent of wrong doing. The very idea was ridiculous.
At most he had been careless. Yes, he was certainly to
blame. He ought to have seen the trap so carefully
prepared and into which he had walked as if blind-
folded. That extra $50,000 worth of stock, on which
he had never received a cent interest, had been the
decoy in a carefully thought out plot. They, the
plotters, well knew how ignorant he was of financial
matters and he had been an easy victim. Who would
believe his story that the stock had been sent to him
with a plausibly-worded letter to the effect that it
represented a bonus on his own investment? Now he
came to think of it, calmly and reasonably, he would
not believe it himself. As usual, he had mislaid or
destroyed the secretary's letter and there was only his
word against the company's books to substantiate what
would appear a most improbable if not impossible
occurrence.

It was his conviction of his own good faith that
made his present dilemma all the more cruel. Had
he really been a grafter, had he really taken the stock

as a bribe he would not care so much, for then he would have foreseen and discounted the chances of exposure. Yes, there was no doubt possible. He was the victim of a conspiracy, there was an organized plot to ruin him, to get him out of the way. The " interests " feared him, resented his judicial decisions and they had halted at nothing to accomplish their purpose. How could he fight them back, what could he do to protect himself? He had no proofs of a conspiracy, his enemies worked in the dark, there was no way in which he could reach them or know who they were.

He thought of John Burkett Ryder. Ah, he remembered now. Ryder was the man who had recommended the investment in Alaskan stock. Of course, why did he not think of it before? He recollected that at the time he had been puzzled at receiving so much stock and he had mentioned it to Ryder, adding that the secretary had told him it was customary. Oh, why had he not kept the secretary's letter? But Ryder would certainly remember it. He probably still had his two letters in which he spoke of making the investment. If those letters could be produced at the Congressional inquiry they would clear him at once. So losing no time, and filled with renewed hope he wrote to the Colossus a strong, manly letter which would

have melted an iceberg, urging Mr. Ryder to come
forward now at this critical time and clear him of this
abominable charge, or in any case to kindly return
the two letters he must have in his possession, as they
would go far to help him at the trial. Three days
passed and no reply from Ryder. On the fourth came
a polite but frigid note from Mr. Ryder's private secretary. Mr. Ryder had received Judge Rossmore's letter and in reply begged to state that he had a vague
recollection of some conversation with the judge in
regard to investments, but he did not think he had
advised the purchase of any particular stock, as that
was something he never did on principle, even with
his most intimate friends. He had no wish to be held
accountable in case of loss, etc. As to the letter which
Judge Rossmore mentioned as having written to Mr.
Ryder in regard to having received more stock than
he had bought, of that Mr. Ryder had no recollection
whatsoever. Judge Rossmore was probably mistaken
as to the identity of his correspondent. He regretted
he could not be of more service to Judge Rossmore,
and remained his very obedient servant.

It was very evident that no help was to be looked
for in that quarter. There was even decided hostility
in Ryder's reply. Could it be true that the financier
was really behind these attacks upon his character, was

127

it possible that one man merely to make more money would deliberately ruin his fellow man whose hand he had grasped in friendship? He had been unwilling to believe it when his friend ex-judge Stott had pointed to Ryder as the author of all his misfortunes, but this unsympathetic letter with its falsehoods, its lies plainly written all over its face, was proof enough. Yes, there was now no doubt possible. John Burkett Ryder was his enemy and what an enemy! Many a man had committed suicide when he had incurred the enmity of the Colossus. Judge Rossmore, completely discouraged, bowed his head to the inevitable.

His wife, a nervous, sickly woman, was helpless to comfort or aid him. She had taken their misfortune as a visitation of an inscrutable Deity. She knew, of course, that her husband was wholly innocent of the accusations brought against him and if his character could be cleared and himself rehabilitated before the world, she would be the first to rejoice. But if it pleased the Almighty in His wisdom to sorely try her husband and herself and inflict this punishment upon them it was not for the finite mind to criticise the ways of Providence. There was probably some good reason for the apparent cruelty and injustice of it which their earthly understanding failed to grasp. Mrs. Rossmore found much comfort in this philosophy, which gave a satisfactory ending to both ends of the problem, and she was upheld in her view by the rector of the church which she had attended regularly each Sunday for the past five and twenty years. Christian resignation in the hour of trial, submission to the will of Heaven were, declared her spiritual adviser, the fundamental principles of religion. He could only hope that Mrs. Rossmore would succeed in imbuing her husband with her Christian spirit. But when the judge's wife returned home and saw the keen mental distress of the man who had been her companion for twenty-five long years, the comforter in her sorrows, the joy and pride of her young wifehood, she forgot all about her smug churchly consoler, and her heart went out to her husband in a spontaneous burst of genuine human sympathy. Yes, they must do something at once. Where men had failed perhaps a woman could do something. She wanted to cable at once for Shirley, who was everything in their household—organizer, manager, adviser—but the judge would not hear of it. No, his daughter was enjoying her holiday in blissful ignorance of what had occurred. He would not spoil it for her. They would see; perhaps things would improve. But he sent for his old friend ex-Judge Stott.

They were life-long friends, having become acquainted nearly thirty years ago at the law school, at the time when both were young men about to enter on a public career. Stott, who was Rossmore's junior, had begun as a lawyer in New York and soon acquired a reputation in criminal practice. He afterwards became assistant district attorney and later, when a vacancy occurred in the city magistrature, he was successful in securing the appointment. On the bench he again met his old friend Rossmore and the two men once more became closely intimate. The regular court hours, however, soon palled on a man of Judge Stott's nervous temperament and it was not long before he retired to take up once more his criminal practice. He was still a young man, not yet fifty, and full of vigor and fight. He had a blunt manner but his heart was in the right place, and he had a record as clean as his close shaven face. He was a hard worker, a brilliant speaker and one of the cleverest cross-examiners at the bar. This was the man to whom Judge Rossmore naturally turned for legal assistance.

Stott was out West when he first heard of the proceedings against his old friend, and this indignity put upon the only really honest man in public life whom he knew, so incensed him that he was already hurrying back to his aid when the summons reached him.

Meantime, a fresh and more serious calamity had

overwhelmed Judge Rossmore. Everything seemed to combine to break the spirit of this man who had dared defy the power of organized capital. Hardly had the news of the Congressional inquiry been made public, than the financial world was startled by an extraordinary slump in Wall Street. There was nothing in the news of the day to justify a decline, but prices fell and fell. The bears had it all their own way, the big interests hammered stocks all along the line, "coppers" especially being the object of attack. The market closed feverishly and the next day the same tactics were pursued. From the opening, on selling orders coming from no one knew where, prices fell to nothing, a stampede followed and before long it became a panic. Pandemonium reigned on the floor of the Stock Exchange. White faced, dishevelled brokers shouted and struggled like men possessed to execute the orders of their clients. Big financial houses, which stood to lose millions on a falling market, rallied and by rush orders to buy, attempted to stem the tide, but all to no purpose. One firm after another went by the board unable to weather the tempest, until just before closing time, the stock ticker announced the failure of the Great Northwestern Mining Co. The drive in the market had been principally directed against its securities, and after vainly endeavoring to check the bear raid, it had been compelled to declare itself bankrupt. It was heavily involved, assets nil, stock almost worthless. It was probable that the creditors would not see ten cents on the dollar. Thousands were ruined and Judge Rossmore among them. All the savings of a lifetime—nearly $55,000 were gone. He was practically penniless, at a time when he needed money most. He still owned his house in Madison Avenue, but that would have to go to settle with his creditors. By the time everything was paid there would only remain enough for a modest competence. As to his salary, of course he could not touch that so long as this accusation was hanging over his head. And if he were impeached it would stop altogether. The salary, therefore, was not to be counted on. They must manage as best they could and live more cheaply, taking a small house somewhere in the outskirts of the city where he could prepare his case quietly without attracting attention.

Stott thought this was the best thing they could do and he volunteered to relieve his friend by taking on his own hands all the arrangements of the sale of the house and furniture, which offer the judge accepted only too gladly. Meantime, Mrs. Rossmore went to Long Island to see what could be had, and she found at the little village of Massapequa just what they were looking for—a commodious, neatly-furnished two-story cottage at a modest rental. Of course, it was nothing like what they had been accustomed to, but it was clean and comfortable, and as Mrs. Rossmore said, rather tactlessly, beggars cannot be choosers. Perhaps it would not be for long. Instant possession was to be had, so deposit was paid on the spot and a few days later the Rossmores left their mansion on Madison Avenue and took up their residence in Massapequa, where their advent created quite a fluster in local social circles.

Massapequa is one of the thousand and one flourishing communities scattered over Long Island, all of which are apparently modelled after the same pattern. Each is an exact duplicate of its neighbour in everything except the name—the same untidy railroad station, the same sleepy stores, the same attractive little frame residences, built for the most part on the " Why pay Rent? Own your own Home " plan. A healthy boom in real estate imparts plenty of life to them all and Massapequa is particularly famed as being the place where the cat jumped to when Manhattan had to seek an outlet for its congested population and ever-increasing army of home seekers. Formerly large tracts of flat farm lands, only sparsely shaded by trees, Massapequa, in common with other villages of its kind, was utterly destitute of any natural attractions. There was the one principal street leading to the station, with a few scattered stores on either side, a church and a bank. Happily, too, for those who were unable to survive the monotony of the place, it boasted of a pretty cemetery. There were also a number of attractive cottages with spacious porches hung with honeysuckle and of these the Rossmores occupied one of the less pretentious kind.

But although Massapequa, theoretically speaking, was situated only a stone's throw from the metropolis, it might have been situated in the Great Sahara so far as its inhabitants took any active interest in the doings of gay Gotham. Local happenings naturally had first claim upon Massapequa's attention—the prowess of the local baseball team, Mrs. Robinson's tea party and the highly exciting sessions of the local Pinochle Club furnishing food for unlimited gossip and scandal. The newspapers reached the village, of course, but only the local news items aroused any real interest, while the women folk usually restricted their readings to those pages devoted to Daily Hints for the Home, Mrs. Sayre's learned articles on Health and Beauty and Fay Stanton's Daily Fashions. It was not surprising, therefore, that the fame of Judge Rossmore and the scandal in which he was at present involved had not penetrated as far as Massapequa and that the natives were considerably mystified as to who the new arrivals in their midst might be.

Stott had been given a room in the cottage so that he might be near at hand to work with the judge in the preparation of the defence, and he came out from the city every evening. It was now June. The Senate would not take action until it convened in December, but there was a lot of work to be done and no time to be lost.

The evening following the day of their arrival they were sitting on the porch enjoying the cool evening air after dinner. The judge was smoking. He was not a slave to the weed, but he enjoyed a quiet pipe after meals, claiming that it quieted his nerves and enabled him to think more clearly. Besides, it was necessary to keep at bay the ubiquitous Long Island mosquito. Mrs. Rossmore had remained for a moment in the dining-room to admonish Eudoxia, their new and only maid-of-all-work, not to wreck too much of the crockery when she removed the dinner dishes. Suddenly Stott, who was perusing an evening paper, asked:

" By the way, where's your daughter? Does she know of this radical change in your affairs? "

Judge Rossmore started. By what mysterious

agency had this man penetrated his own most intimate thoughts? He was himself thinking of Shirley that very moment, and by some inexplicable means—telepathy modern psychologists called it—the thought current had crossed to Stott, whose mind, being in full sympathy, was exactly attuned to receive it. Removing the pipe from his mouth the judge replied:

"Shirley's in Paris. Poor girl, I hadn't the heart to tell her. She has no idea of what's happened. I didn't want to spoil her holiday."

He was silent for a moment. Then, after a few more puffs he added confidentially in a low tone, as if he did not care for his wife to hear:

"The truth is, Stott, I couldn't bear to have her return now. I couldn't look my own daughter in the face."

A sound as of a great sob which he had been unable to control cut short his speech. His eyes filled with tears and he began to smoke furiously as if ashamed of this display of emotion. Stott, blowing his nose with suspicious vigor, replied soothingly:

"You mustn't talk like that. Everything will come out all right, of course. But I think you are wrong not to have told your daughter. Her place is here at your side. She ought to be told even if only in justice

136

to her. If you don't tell her someone else will, or, what's worse, she'll hear of it through the newspapers."

"Ah, I never thought of that!" exclaimed the judge, visibly perturbed at the suggestion about the newspapers.

"Don't you agree with me?" demanded Stott, appealing to Mrs. Rossmore, who emerged from the house at that instant. "Don't you think your daughter should be informed of what has happened?"

"Most assuredly I do," answered Mrs. Rossmore determinedly. "The judge wouldn't hear of it, but I took the law into my own hands. I've cabled for her."

"You cabled for Shirley?" cried the judge incredulously. He was so unaccustomed to seeing his ailing, vacillating wife do anything on her own initiative and responsibility that it seemed impossible. "You cabled for Shirley?" he repeated.

"Yes," replied Mrs. Rossmore triumphantly and secretly pleased that for once in her life she had asserted herself. "I cabled yesterday. I simply couldn't bear it alone any longer."

"What did you say?" inquired the judge apprehensively.

"I just told her to come home at once. To-morrow we ought to get an answer."

Stott meantime had been figuring on the time of

Shirley's probable arrival. If the cablegram had been received in Paris the previous evening it would be too late to catch the French boat. The North German Lloyd steamer was the next to leave and it touched at Cherbourg. She would undoubtedly come on that. In a week at most she would be here. Then it became a question as to who should go to meet her at the dock. The judge could not go, that was certain. It would be too much of an ordeal. Mrs. Rossmore did not know the lower part of the city well, and had no experience in meeting ocean steamships. There was only one way out—would Stott go? Of course he would and he would bring Shirley back with him to Massapequa. So during the next few days while Stott and the judge toiled preparing their case, which often necessitated brief trips to the city, Mrs. Rossmore, seconded with sulky indifference by Eudoxia, was kept busy getting a room ready for her daughter's arrival.

Eudoxia, who came originally from County Cork, was an Irish lady with a thick brogue and a husky temper. She was amiable enough so long as things went to her satisfaction, but when they did not suit her she was a termagant. She was neither beautiful nor graceful, she was not young nor was she very clean. Her usual condition was dishevelled, her face was all askew, and when she dressed up she looked like

a valentine. Her greatest weakness was a propensity
for smashing dishes, and when reprimanded she would
threaten to take her traps and skidoo. This news of
the arrival of a daughter failed to fill her with enthusiasm. Firstly, it meant more work; secondly she had
not bargained for it. When she took the place it was
on the understanding that the family consisted only of
an elderly gentleman and his wife, that there was practically no work, good wages, plenty to eat, with the
privilege of an evening out when she pleased. Instead
of this millennium she soon found Stott installed as a
permanent guest and now a daughter was to be foisted
on her. No wonder hard working girls were getting
sick and tired of housework!

As already hinted there was no unhealthy curiosity
among Massapequans regarding their new neighbors
from the city but some of the more prominent people
of the place considered it their duty to seek at least a
bowing acquaintance with the Rossmores by paying
them a formal visit. So the day following the conversation on the porch when the judge and Stott had gone
to the city on one of their periodical excursions, Mrs.
Rossmore was startled to see a gentleman of clerical
appearance accompanied by a tall, angular woman
enter their gate and ring the bell.

The Rev. Percival Pontifex Deetle and his sister

Miss Jane Deetle prided themselves on being leaders in the best social circle in Massapequa. The incumbent of the local Presbyterian church, the Rev. Deetle, was a thin, sallow man of about thirty-five. He had a diminutive face with a rather long and very pointed nose which gave a comical effect to his physiognomy. Theology was written all over his person and he wore the conventional clerical hat which, owing to his absurdly small face, had the unfortunate appearance of being several sizes too large for him. Miss Deetle was a gaunt and angular spinster who had an unhappy trick of talking with a jerk. She looked as if she were constantly under self-restraint and was liable at any moment to explode into a fit of rage and only repressed herself with considerable effort. As they came up the stoop, Eudoxia, already instructed by Mrs. Rossmore, was ready for them. With her instinctive respect for the priestly garb she was rather taken back on seeing a clergyman, but she brazened it out:

"Mr. Rossmore's not home." Then shaking her head, she added: "They don't see no visitors."

Unabashed, the Rev. Deetle drew a card from a case and handing it to the girl said pompously:

"Then we will see Mrs. Rossmore. I saw her at the window as we came along. Here, my girl, take her this card. Tell her that the Reverend Pontifex

Deetle and Miss Deetle have called to present their compliments."

Brushing past Eudoxia, who vainly tried to close the door, the Rev. Deetle coolly entered the house, followed by his sister, and took a seat in the parlour.

" She'll blame me for this," wailed the girl, who had not budged and who stood there fingering the Rev. Deetle's card.

" Blame you?  For what? " demanded the clerical visitor in surprise.

" She told me to say she was out—but I can't lie to a minister of the Gospel—leastways not to his face. I'll give her your card, sir."

The reverend caller waited until Eudoxia had disappeared, then he rose and looked around curiously at the books and pictures.

" Hum—not a Bible or a prayer book or a hymn book, not a picture or anything that would indicate the slightest reverence for holy things."

He picked up a few papers that were lying on the table and after glancing at them threw them down in disgust.

" Law reports—Wall Street reports—the god of this world.  Evidently very ordinary people, Jane."

He looked at his sister, but she sat stiffly and primly in her chair and made no reply.  He repeated:

" Didn't you hear me? I said they are ordinary people."

" I've no doubt," retorted Miss Deetle, " and as such they will not thank us for prying into their affairs."

" Prying, did you say? " said the parson, resenting this implied criticism of his actions.

" Just plain prying," persisted his sister angrily. " I don't see what else it is."

The Rev. Pontifex straightened up and threw out his chest as he replied:

" It is protecting my flock. As Leader of the Unified All Souls Baptismal Presbytery, it is my duty to visit the widows and orphans of this community."

" These people are neither widows or orphans," objected Miss Deetle.

" They are strangers," insisted the Rev. Pontifex, " and it is my duty to minister to them—if they need it. Furthermore it is my duty to my congregation to find out who is in their midst. No less than three of the Lady Trustees of my church have asked me who and what these people are and whence they came."

" The Lady Trustees are a pack of old busybodies," growled his sister.

Her brother raised his finger warningly.

" Jane, do you know you are uttering a blasphemy? These Rossmore people have been here two weeks,

# THE MOUSE

They have visited no one, no one **visits them**. They have avoided a temple of worship, they have acted most mysteriously. Who are they? What are they hiding? Is it fair to my church, is it fair to my flock? It is not a bereavement, for they don't wear mourning. I'm afraid it may be some hidden scandal——"

Further speculations on his part were interrupted by the entrance of Mrs. Rossmore, who thought rightly that the quickest way to get rid of her unwelcome visitors was to hurry downstairs as quickly as possible.

" Miss Deetle—Mr. Deetle. I am much honoured," was her not too effusive greeting.

The Reverend Pontifex, anxious to make a favourable impression, was all smiles and bows. The idea of a possible scandal had for the moment ceased to worry him.

" The honour is ours," he stammered. " I—er—we —er—my sister Jane and I called to——"

" Won't you sit down? " said Mrs. Rossmore, waving him to a chair. He danced around her in a manner that made her nervous.

" Thank you so much," he said with a smile that was meant to be amiable. He took a seat at the further end of the room and an awkward pause followed. Finally his sister prompted him:

" You wanted to see Mrs. Rossmore about the festival," she said.

" Oh, of course, I had quite forgotten. How stupid of me. The fact is, Mrs. Rossmore," he went on, " we are thinking of giving a festival next week—a festival with strawberries—and our trustees thought, in fact it occurred to me also that if you and Mr. Rossmore would grace the occasion with your presence it would give us an opportunity—so to speak—get better acquainted, and er——"

Another awkward pause followed during which he sought inspiration by gazing fixedly in the fireplace. Then turning on Mrs. Rossmore so suddenly that the poor woman nearly jumped out of her chair he asked:

" Do you like strawberries? "

" It's very kind of you," interrupted Mrs. Rossmore, glad of the opportunity to get a word in edgeways. " Indeed, I appreciate your kindness most keenly but my husband and I go nowhere, nowhere at all. You see we have met with reverses and——"

" Reverses," echoed the clerical visitor, with difficulty keeping his seat. This was the very thing he had come to find out and here it was actually thrown at him. He congratulated himself on his cleverness in having inspired so much confidence and thought with glee of his triumph when he returned with the full story to the Lady Trustees. Simulating, therefore, the deepest sympathy he tried to draw his hostess out:

"Dear me, how sad! You met with reverses."

Turning to his sister, who was sitting in her corner like a petrified mummy, he added:

"Jane, do you hear? How inexpressibly sad! They have met with reverses!"

He paused, hoping that Mrs. Rossmore would go on to explain just what their reverses had been, but she was silent. As a gentle hint he said softly:

"Did I interrupt you, Madam?"

"Not at all, I did not speak," she answered.

Thus baffled, he turned the whites of his eyes up to the ceiling and said:

"When reverses come we naturally look for spiritual consolation. My dear Mrs. Rossmore, in the name of the Unified All Souls Baptismal Presbytery I offer you that consolation."

Mrs. Rossmore looked helplessly from one to the other embarrassed as to what to say. Who were these strangers that intruded on her privacy offering a consolation she did not want? Miss Deetle, as if glad of the opportunity to joke at her brother's expense, said explosively:

"My dear Pontifex, you have already offered a

strawberry festival which Mrs. Rossmore has been unable to accept."

"Well, what of it?" demanded Mr. Deetle, glaring at his sister for the irrelevant interruption.

"You are both most kind," murmured Mrs. Rossmore; "but we could not accept in any case. My daughter is returning home from Paris next week."

"Ah, your daughter—you have a daughter?" exclaimed Mr. Deetle, grasping at the slightest straw to add to his stock of information. "Coming from Paris, too! Such a wicked city!"

He had never been to Paris, he went on to explain, but he had read enough about it and he was grateful that the Lord had chosen Massapequa as the field of his labours. Here at least, life was sweet and wholesome and one's hopes of future salvation fairly reasonable. He was not a brilliant talker when the conversation extended beyond Massapequa but he rambled on airing his views on the viciousness of the foreigner in general, until Mrs. Rossmore, utterly wearied, began to wonder when they would go. Finally he fell back upon the weather.

"We are very fortunate in having such pleasant weather, don't you think so, Madam? Oh, Massapequa is a lovely spot, isn't it? We think it's the one place to live in. We are all one happy family. That's why my sister and I called to make your acquaintance."

"You are very good, I'm sure. I shall tell my husband you came and he'll be very pleased."

Having exhausted his conversational powers and seeing that further efforts to pump Mrs. Rossmore were useless, the clerical visitor rose to depart:

"It looks like rain. Come, Jane, we had better go. Good-bye, Madam, I am delighted to have made this little visit and I trust you will assure Mr. Rossmore that All Souls Unified Baptismal Presbytery always has a warm welcome for him."

They bowed and Mrs. Rossmore bowed. The agony was over and as the door closed on them Mrs. Rossmore gave a sigh of relief.

That evening Stott and the judge came home earlier than usual and from their dejected appearance Mrs. Rossmore divined bad news. The judge was painfully silent throughout the meal and Stott was unusually grave. Finally the latter took her aside and broke it to her gently. In spite of their efforts and the efforts of their friends the Congressional inquiry had resulted in a finding against the judge and a demand had already been made upon the Senate for his impeachment. They could do nothing now but fight it in the Senate with all the influence they could muster. It was going

147

to be hard but Stott was confident that right would prevail. After dinner as they were sitting in silence on the porch, each measuring the force of this blow which they had expected yet had always hoped to ward off, the crunching sound of a bicycle was heard on the quiet country road. The rider stopped at their gate and came up the porch holding out an envelope to the judge, who, guessing the contents, had started forward. He tore it open. It was a cablegram from Paris and read as follows:

*Am sailing on the Kaiser Wilhelm to-day.*

*Shirley.*

## CHAPTER VII.

THE pier of the North German Lloyd Steamship
Company, at Hoboken, fairly sizzled with
bustle and excitement. The Kaiser Wilhelm
had arrived at Sandy Hook the previous evening and
was now lying out in midstream. She would tie up
at her dock within half an hour. Employés of the line,
baggage masters, newspaper reporters, Custom House
officers, policemen, detectives, truck drivers, express-
men, longshoremen, telegraph messengers and anxious
friends of incoming passengers surged back and forth
in seemingly hopeless confusion. The shouting of
orders, the rattling of cab wheels, the shrieking of
whistles was deafening. From out in the river came
the deep toned blasts of the steamer's siren, in grotesque contrast with the strident tooting of a dozen
diminutive tugs which, puffing and snorting, were
slowly but surely coaxing the leviathan into her berth
alongside the dock. The great vessel, spick and span
after a coat of fresh paint hurriedly put on during the
last day of the voyage, bore no traces of gale, fog and
stormy seas through which she had passed on her

3,000 mile run across the ocean. Conspicuous on the bridge, directing the docking operations, stood Capt. Hegermann, self satisfied and smiling, relieved that the responsibilities of another trip were over, and at his side, sharing the honours, was the grizzled pilot who had brought the ship safely through the dangers of Gedney's Channel, his shabby pea jacket, old slouch hat, top boots and unkempt beard standing out in sharp contrast with the immaculate white duck trousers, the white and gold caps and smart full dress uniforms of the ship's officers. The rails on the upper decks were seen to be lined with passengers, all dressed in their shore going clothes, some waving handkerchiefs at friends they already recognized, all impatiently awaiting the shipping of the gangplank.

Stott had come early. They had received word at Massapequa the day before that the steamer had been sighted off Fire Island and that she would be at her pier the next morning at 10 o'clock. Stott arrived at 9.30 and so found no difficulty in securing a front position among the small army of people, who, like himself, had come down to meet friends.

As the huge vessel swung round and drew closer, Stott easily picked out Shirley. She was scanning eagerly through a binocular the rows of upturned faces on the dock, and he noted that a look of disap-

pointment crossed her face at not finding the object of
her search. She turned and said something to a lady
in black and to a man who stood at her side. Who
they might be Stott had no idea. Fellow passengers,
no doubt. One becomes so intimate on shipboard; it
seems a friendship that must surely last a lifetime,
whereas—the custom officers have not finished rummaging through your trunks when these easily-made
steamer friends are already forgotten. Presently Shirley took another look and her glass soon lighted on
him. Instantly she recognized her father's old friend.
She waved a handkerchief and Stott raised his hat.
Then she turned quickly and spoke again to her
friends, whereupon they all moved in the direction of
the gangplank, which was already being lowered.

Shirley was one of the first to come ashore. Stott
was waiting for her at the foot of the gangplank and
she threw her arms round his neck and kissed him.
He had known her ever since she was a little tot in
arms, and bystanders who noticed them meet had no
doubt that they were father and daughter. Shirley
was deeply moved; a great lump in her throat seemed
to choke her utterance. So far she had been able
to bear up, but now that home was so near her heart
failed her. She had hoped to find her father on the
dock. Why had he not come? Were things so bad

then? She questioned Judge Stott anxiously, fearfully.

He reassured her. Both her mother and father were well. It was too long a trip for them to make, so he had volunteered.

"Too long a trip," echoed Shirley puzzled. "This is not far from our house. Madison Avenue is no distance. That could not have kept father away."

"You don't live on Madison Avenue any longer. The house and its contents have been sold," replied Stott gravely, and in a few words he outlined the situation as it was.

Shirley listened quietly to the end and only the increasing pallor of her face and an occasional nervous twitching at the corner of her mouth betrayed the shock that this recital of her father's misfortunes was to her. Ah, this she had little dreamed of! Yet why not? It was but logic. When wrecked in reputation, one might as well be wrecked in fortune, too. What would their future be, how could that proud, sensitive man her father bear this humiliation, this disgrace? To be condemned to a life of obscurity, social ostracism, and genteel poverty! Oh, the thought was unendurable! She herself could earn money, of course. If her literary work did not bring in enough, she could teach and what she earned would help out. Certainly her parents should never want for anything so long as she could supply it. She thought bitterly how futile now were plans of marriage, even if she had ever entertained such an idea seriously. Henceforward, she did not belong to herself. Her life must be devoted to clearing her father's name. These reflections were suddenly interrupted by the voice of Mrs. Blake calling out:

" Shirley, where have you been? We lost sight of you as we left the ship, and we have been hunting for you ever since."

Her aunt, escorted by Jefferson Ryder, had gone direct to the Customs desk and in the crush they had lost trace of her. Shirley introduced Stott.

" Aunt Milly, this is Judge Stott, a very old friend of father's. Mrs. Blake, my mother's sister. Mother will be surprised to see her. They haven't met for ten years."

" This visit is going to be only a brief one," said Mrs. Blake. " I really came over to chaperone Shirley more than anything else."

" As if I needed chaperoning with Mr. Ryder for an escort ! " retorted Shirley. Then presenting Jefferson to Stott she said:

" This is Mr. Jefferson Ryder—Judge Stott. Mr. Ryder has been very kind to me abroad."

The two men bowed and shook hands.

" Any relation to J. B.? " asked Stott good humouredly.

" His son—that's all," answered Jefferson laconically.

Stott now looked at the young man with more interest. Yes, there was a resemblance, the same blue eyes,
the fighting jaw. But how on earth did Judge Rossmore's daughter come to be travelling in the company
of John Burkett Ryder's son? The more he thought of
it the more it puzzled him, and while he cogitated
Shirley and her companions wrestled with the United
States Customs, and were undergoing all the tortures
invented by Uncle Sam to punish Americans for going
abroad.

Shirley and Mrs. Blake were fortunate in securing
an inspector who was fairly reasonable. Of course,
he did not for a moment believe their solemn statement, already made on the ship, that they had nothing
dutiable, and he rummaged among the most intimate
garments of their wardrobe in a wholly indecent and
unjustifiable manner, but he was polite and they fared
no worse than all the other women victims of this, the
most brutal custom house inspection system in the
world.

Jefferson had the misfortune to be allotted an inspector who was half seas over with liquor and the man

was so insolent and threatening in manner that it was only by great self-restraint that Jefferson controlled himself. He had no wish to create a scandal on the dock, nor to furnish good "copy" for the keen-eyed, long-eared newspaper reporters who would be only too glad of such an opportunity for a "scare head." But when the fellow compelled him to open every trunk and valise and then put his grimy hands to the bottom and by a quick upward movement jerked the entire contents out on the dock he interfered:

"You are exceeding your authority," he exclaimed hotly. "How dare you treat my things in this manner?"

The drunken uniformed brute raised his bloodshot, bleary eyes and took Jefferson in from tip to toe. He clenched his fist as if about to resort to violence, but he was not so intoxicated as to be quite blind to the fact that this passenger had massive square shoulders, a determined jaw and probably a heavy arm. So contenting himself with a sneer, he said:

"This ain't no country for blooming English dooks. You're not in England now you know. This is a free country. See?"

"I see this," replied Jefferson, furious. "that you

are a drunken ruffian and a disgrace to the uniform you wear. I shall report your conduct immediately," with which he proceeded to the Customs desk to lodge a complaint.

He might have spared himself the trouble. The silver haired, distinguished looking old officer in charge knew that Jefferson's complaint was well founded, he knew that this particular inspector was a drunkard and a discredit to the government which employed him, but at the same time he also knew that political influence had been behind his appointment and that it was unsafe to do more than mildly reprimand him. When, therefore, he accompanied Jefferson to the spot where the contents of the trunks lay scattered in confusion all over the dock, he merely expostulated with the officer, who made some insolent reply. Seeing that it was useless to lose further time, Jefferson repacked his trunks as best he could and got them on a cab. Then he hurried over to Shirley's party and found them already about to leave the pier.

"Come and see us, Jeff," whispered Shirley as their cab drove through the gates.

"Where," he asked, "Madison Avenue?"

She hesitated for a moment and then replied quickly:

"No, we are stopping down on Long Island for the

Summer—at a cute little place called Massapequa.
Run down and see us."

He raised his hat and the cab drove on.

There was greater activity in the Rossmore cottage
at Massapequa than there had been any day since the
judge and his wife went to live there. Since daybreak
Eudoxia had been scouring and polishing in honour of
the expected arrival and a hundred times Mrs. Rossmore had climbed the stairs to see that everything was
as it should be in the room which had been prepared for
Shirley. It was not, however, without a passage at
arms that Eudoxia consented to consider the idea of
an addition to the family. Mrs. Rossmore had said to
her the day before:

" My daughter will be here to-morrow, Eudoxia."

A look expressive of both displeasure and astonishment marred the classic features of the hireling. Putting her broom aside and placing her arms akimbo she
exclaimed in an injured tone:

" And it's a dayther you've got now? So it's three
in family you are! When I took the place it's two you
tould me there was!

"Well, with your kind permission," replied Mrs.

Rossmore, "there will be three in future. There is nothing in the Constitution of the United States that says we can't have a daughter without consulting our help, is there?"

The sarcasm of this reply did not escape even the dull-edged wits of the Irish drudge. She relapsed into a dignified silence and a few minutes later was discovered working with some show of enthusiasm.

The judge was nervous and fidgety. He made a pretence to read, but it was plain to see that his mind was not on his book. He kept leaving his chair to go and look at the clock; then he would lay the volume aside and wander from room to room like a lost soul. His thoughts were on the dock at Hoboken.

By noon every little detail had been attended to and there was nothing further to do but sit and wait for the arrival of Stott and Shirley. They were to be expected any moment now. The passengers had probably got off the steamer by eleven o'clock. It would take at least two hours to get through the Customs and out to Massapequa. The judge and his wife sat on the porch counting the minutes and straining their ears to catch the first sound of the train from New York.

"I hope Stott broke the news to her gently," said the judge.

# THE MOUSE

"I wish we had gone to meet her ourselves," sighed his wife.

The judge was silent and for a moment or two he puffed vigorously at his pipe, as was his habit when disturbed mentally. Then he said:

"I ought to have gone, Martha, but I was afraid. I'm afraid to look my own daughter in the face and tell her that I am a disgraced man, that I am to be tried by the Senate for corruption, perhaps impeached and turned off the bench as if I were a criminal. Shirley won't believe it, sometimes I can't believe it myself. I often wake up in the night and think of it as part of a dream, but when the morning comes it's still true —it's still true!"

He smoked on in silence. Then happening to look up he noticed that his wife was weeping. He laid his hand gently on hers.

"Don't cry, dear, don't make it harder for me to bear. Shirley must see no trace of tears."

"I was thinking of the injustice of it all," replied Mrs. Rossmore, wiping her eyes.

"Fancy Shirley in this place, living from hand to mouth," went on the judge.

"That's the least," answered his wife. "She's a fine, handsome girl, well educated and all the rest of it. She ought to make a good marriage." No matter what state of mind Mrs. Rossmore might be in, she never lost sight of the practical side of things.

"Hardly with her father's disgrace hanging over her head," replied the judge wearily. "Who," he added, "would have the courage to marry a girl whose father was publicly disgraced?"

Both relapsed into another long silence, each mentally reviewing the past and speculating on the future. Suddenly Mrs. Rossmore started. Surely she could not be mistaken! No, the clanging of a locomotive bell was plainly audible. The train was in. From the direction of the station came people with parcels and hand bags and presently there was heard the welcome sound of carriage wheels crunching over the stones. A moment later they saw coming round the bend in the road a cab piled up with small baggage.

"Here they are! Here they are!" cried Mrs. Rossmore. "Come, Eudoxia!" she called to the servant, while she herself hurried down to the gate. The judge, fully as agitated as herself, only showing his emotion in a different way, remained on the porch pale and anxious.

The cab stopped at the curb and Stott alighted, first helping out Mrs. Blake. Mrs. Rossmore's astonishment on seeing her sister was almost comical.

"Milly!" she exclaimed.

"Father! Father! What have they
done to you?"—*Page 161.*

# THE MOUSE

They embraced first and explained afterwards. Then Shirley got out and was in her mother's arms.

"Where's father?" was Shirley's first question.

"There—he's coming!"

The judge, unable to restrain his impatience longer, ran down from the porch towards the gate. Shirley, with a cry of mingled grief and joy, precipitated herself on his breast.

"Father! Father!" she cried between her sobs. "What have they done to you?"

"There—there, my child. Everything will be well—everything will be well."

Her head lay on his shoulder and he stroked her hair with his hand, unable to speak from pent up emotion.

Mrs. Rossmore could not recover from her stupefaction on seeing her sister. Mrs. Blake explained that she had come chiefly for the benefit of the voyage and announced her intention of returning on the same steamer.

"So you see I shall bother you only a few days," she said.

"You'll stay just as long as you wish," rejoined Mrs. Rossmore. "Happily we have just one bedroom left." Then turning to Eudoxia, who was wrestling with the baggage, which formed a miniature Matterhorn on the sidewalk, she gave instructions:

"Eudoxia, you'll take this lady's baggage to the small bedroom adjoining Miss Shirley's. She is going to stop with us for a few days."

Taken completely aback at the news of this new addition, Eudoxia looked at first defiance. She seemed on the point of handing in her resignation there and then. But evidently she thought better of it, for, taking a cue from Mrs. Rossmore, she asked in the sarcastic manner of her mistress:

"Four is it now, M'm? I suppose the Constitootion of the United States allows a family to be as big as one likes to make it. It's hard on us girls, but if it's the law, it's all right, M'm. The more the merrier!" With which broadside, she hung the bags all over herself and staggered off to the house.

Stott explained that the larger pieces and the trunks would come later by express. Mrs. Rossmore took him aside while Mrs. Blake joined Shirley and the judge.

"Did you tell Shirley?" asked Mrs. Rossmore. "How did she take it?"

"She knows everything," answered Stott, "and takes it very sensibly. We shall find her of great

162

moral assistance in our coming fight in the Senate,"
he added confidently.

Realizing that the judge would like to be left alone
with Shirley, Mrs. Rossmore invited Mrs. Blake to go
upstairs and see the room she would have, while Stott
said he would be glad of a washup. When they had
gone Shirley sidled up to her father in her old familiar
way.

" I've just been longing to see you, father," she said.
She turned to get a good look at him and noticing the
lines of care which had deepened during her absence
she cried : " Why, how you've changed! I can scarcely
believe it's you. Say something. Let me hear the
sound of your voice, father."

The judge tried to smile.

" Why, my dear girl, I——"

Shirley threw her arms round his neck.

" Ah, yes, now I know it's you," she cried.

" Of course it is, Shirley, my dear girl. Of course
it is. Who else should it be?"

"Yes, but it isn't the same," insisted Shirley. "There
is no ring to your voice. It sounds hollow and empty,
like an echo. And this place," she added dolefully,
" this awful place——"

She glanced around at the cracked ceilings, the
cheaply papered walls, the shabby furniture, and her

heart sank as she realized the extent of their misfortune. She had come back prepared for the worst, to help win the fight for her father's honour, but to have to struggle against sordid poverty as well, to endure that humiliation in addition to disgrace—ah, that was something she had not anticipated! She changed colour and her voice faltered. Her father had been closely watching for just such signs and he read her thoughts.

"It's the best we can afford, Shirley," he said quietly. "The blow has been complete. I will tell you everything. You shall judge for yourself. My enemies have done for me at last."

"Your enemies?" cried Shirley eagerly. "Tell me who they are so I may go to them."

"Yes, dear, you shall know everything. But not now. You are tired after your journey. To-morrow sometime Stott and I will explain everything."

"Very well, father, as you wish," said Shirley gently. "After all," she added in an effort to appear cheerful, "what matter where we live so long as we have each other?"

She drew away to hide her tears and left the room on pretence of inspecting the house. She looked into the dining-room and kitchen and opened the cupboards, and when she returned there were no visible signs of trouble in her face.

# THE MOUSE

"It's a cute little house, isn't it?" she said. "I've always wanted a little place like this—all to ourselves. Oh, if you only knew how tired I am of New York and its great ugly houses, its retinue of servants and its domestic and social responsibilities! We shall be able to live for ourselves now, eh, father?"

She spoke with a forced gaiety that might have deceived anyone but the judge. He understood the motive of her sudden change in manner and silently he blessed her for making his burden lighter.

"Yes, dear, it's not bad," he said. "There's not much room, though."

"There's quite enough," she insisted. "Let me see." She began to count on her fingers. "Upstairs—three rooms, eh? and above that three more——"

"No," smiled the judge, "then comes the roof?"

"Of course," she laughed, "how stupid of me—a nice gable roof, a sloping roof that the rain runs off beautifully. Oh, I can see that this is going to be awfully jolly—just like camping out. You know how I love camping out. And you have a piano, too."

She went over to the corner where stood one of those homely instruments which hardly deserve to be dignified by the name piano, with a cheap, gaudily painted case outside and a tin pan effect inside, and which are usually to be found in the poorer class of country boarding houses. Shirley sat down and ran her fingers over the keys, determined to like everything.

"It's a little old," was her comment, "but I like these zither effects. It's just like the sixteenth century spinet. I can see you and mother dancing a stately minuet," she smiled.

"What's that about mother dancing?" demanded Mrs. Rossmore, who at that instant entered the room. Shirley arose and appealed to her:

"Isn't it absurd, mother, when you come to think of it, that anybody should accuse father of being corrupt and of having forfeited the right to be judge? Isn't it still more absurd that we should be helpless and dejected and unhappy because we are on Long Island instead of Madison Avenue? Why should Manhattan Island be a happier spot than Long Island? Why shouldn't we be happy anywhere; we have each other. And we do need each other. We never knew how much till to-day, did we? We must stand by each other now. Father is going to clear his name of this preposterous charge and we're going to help him, aren't we, mother? We're not helpless just because we are women. We're going to work, mother and I."

"Work?" echoed Mrs. Rossmore, somewhat scandalized.

"Work," repeated Shirley very decisively.

The judge interfered. He would not hear of it.

"You work, Shirley? Impossible!

"Why not? My book has been selling well while I was abroad. I shall probably write others. Then I shall write, too, for the newspapers and magazines. It will add to our income."

"Your book—'The American Octopus,' is selling well?" inquired the judge, interested.

"So well," replied Shirley, "that the publishers wrote me in Paris that the fourth edition was now on the press. That means good royalties. I shall soon be a fashionable author. The publishers will be after me for more books and we'll have all the money we want. Oh, it is so delightful, this novel sensation of a literary success!" she exclaimed with glee. "Aren't you proud of me, dad?"

The judge smiled indulgently. Of course he was glad and proud. He always knew his Shirley was a clever girl. But by what strange fatality, he thought to himself, had his daughter in this book of hers assailed the very man who had encompassed his own ruin? It seemed like the retribution of heaven. Neither his daughter nor the financier was conscious of the fact that each was indirectly connected with the impeachment proceedings. Ryder could not dream that

" Shirley Green," the author of the book which flayed him so mercilessly, was the daughter of the man he was trying to crush. Shirley, on the other hand, was still unaware of the fact that it was Ryder who had lured her father to his ruin.

Mrs. Rossmore now insisted on Shirley going to her room to rest. She must be tired and dusty. After changing her travelling dress she would feel refreshed and more comfortable. When she was ready to come down again luncheon would be served. So leaving the judge to his papers, mother and daughter went upstairs together, and with due maternal pride Mrs. Rossmore pointed out to Shirley all the little arrangements she had made for her comfort. Then she left her daughter to herself while she hurried downstairs to look after Eudoxia and luncheon.

When, at last, she could lock herself in her room where no eye could see her, Shirley threw herself down on the bed and burst into a torrent of tears. She had kept up appearances as long as it was possible, but now the reaction had set in. She gave way freely to her pent up feelings, she felt that unless she could relieve herself in this way her heart would break. She had been brave until now, she had been strong to hear everything and see everything, but she could not keep it up forever. Stott's words to her on the dock had in part prepared her for the worst, he had told her what to expect at home, but the realization was so much more vivid. While hundreds of miles of ocean still lay between, it had all seemed less real, almost attractive as a romance in modern life, but now she was face to face with the grim reality—this shabby cottage, cheap neighbourhood and commonplace surroundings, her mother's air of resignation to the inevitable, her father's pale, drawn face telling so eloquently of the keen mental anguish through which he had passed. She compared this pitiful spectacle with what they had been when she left for Europe, the fine mansion on Madison Avenue with its rich furnishings and well-trained servants, and her father's proud aristocratic face illumined with the consciousness of his high rank in the community, and the attention he attracted every time he appeared on the street or in public places as one of the most brilliant and most respected judges on the bench. Then to have come to this all in the brief space of a few months! It was incredible, terrible, heart rending! And what of the future? What was to be done to save her father from this impeachment which she knew well would hurry him to his grave? He could not survive that humiliation, that degradation. He must be saved in the Senate, but how—how?

She dried her eyes and began to think. Surely her

woman's wit would find some way. She thought of Jefferson. Would he come to Massapequa? It was hardly probable. He would certainly learn of the change in their circumstances and his sense of delicacy would naturally keep him away for some time even if other considerations, less unselfish, did not. Perhaps he would be attracted to some other girl he would like as well and who was not burdened with a tragedy in her family. Her tears began to flow afresh until she hated herself for being so weak while there was work to be done to save her father. She loved Jefferson. Yes, she had never felt so sure of it as now. She felt that if she had him there at that moment she would throw herself in his arms crying: " Take me, Jefferson, take me away, where you will, for I love you! I love you! " But Jefferson was not there and the rickety chairs in the tiny bedroom and the cheap prints on the walls seemed to jibe at her in her misery. If he were there, she thought as she looked into a cracked mirror, he would think her very ugly with her eyes all red from crying. He would not marry her now in any case. No self-respecting man would. She was glad that she had spoken to him as she had in regard to marriage, for while a stain remained upon her father's name marriage was out of the question. She might have yielded on the question of the literary career, but she would never allow a man to taunt her afterwards with the disgrace of her own flesh and blood. No, henceforth her place was at her father's side until his character was cleared. If the trial in the Senate were to go against him, then she could never see Jefferson again. She would give up all idea of him and everything else. Her literary career would be ended, her life would be a blank. They would have to go abroad, where they were not known, and try and live down their shame, for no matter how innocent her father might be the world would believe him guilty. Once condemned by the Senate, nothing could remove the stigma. She would have to teach in order to contribute towards the support, they would manage somehow. But what a future, how unnecessary, how unjust!

Suddenly she thought of Jefferson's promise to interest his father in their case and she clutched at the hope this promise held out as a drowning man clutches at a drifting straw. Jefferson would not forget his promise and he would come to Massapequa to tell her of what he had done. She was sure of that. Perhaps, after all, there was where their hope lay. Why had she not told her father at once? It might have relieved his mind. John Burkett Ryder, the Colossus, the man of unlimited power! He could save her father and he would. And the more she thought about it, the more cheerful and more hopeful she became, and she started to dress quickly so that she might hurry down to tell her father the good news. She was actually sorry now that she had said so many hard things of Mr. Ryder in her book and she was worrying over the thought that her father's case might be seriously prejudiced if the identity of the author were ever revealed, when there came a knock at her door. It was Eudoxia.

" Please, miss, will you come down to lunch?"

# THE MOUSE

## CHAPTER VIII

A WHIRLING maelstrom of human activity and dynamic energy—the city which above all others is characteristic of the genius and virility of the American people—New York, with its congested polyglot population and teeming millions, is assuredly one of the busiest, as it is one of the most strenuous and most noisy places on earth. Yet, despite its swarming streets and crowded shops, ceaselessly thronged with men and women eagerly hurrying here and there in the pursuit of business or elusive pleasure, all chattering, laughing, shouting amid the deafening, multisonous roar of traffic incidental to Gotham's daily life, there is one part of the great metropolis where there is no bustle, no noise, no crowd, where the streets are empty even in daytime, where a passer-by is a curiosity and a child a phenomenon. This deserted village in the very heart of the big town is the millionaires' district, the boundaries of which are marked by Carnegie hill on the north, Fiftieth Street on the south, and by Fifth and Madison Avenues respectively on the west and east. There is nothing more mournful than the outward aspect of these princely residences which, abandoned and empty for three-quarters of the year, stand in stately loneliness, as if ashamed of their isolation and utter uselessness. Their blinds drawn, affording no hint of life within, enveloped the greater part of the time in the stillness and silence of the tomb, they appear to be under the spell of some baneful curse. No merry-voiced children romp in their carefully railed off gardens, no sounds of conversation or laughter come from their hermetically closed windows, not a soul goes in or out, at most, at rare intervals, does one catch a glimpse of a gorgeously arrayed servant gliding about in ghostly fashion, supercilious and suspicious, and addressing the chance visitor in awed whispers as though he were the guardian of a house of affliction. It is, indeed, like a city of the dead.

So it appeared to Jefferson as he walked up Fifth Avenue, bound for the Ryder residence, the day following his arrival from Europe. Although he still lived at his father's house, for at no time had there been an open rupture, he often slept in his studio, finding it more convenient for his work, and there he had gone straight from the ship. He felt, however, that it was his duty to see his mother as soon as possible; besides he was anxious to fulfil his promise to Shirley and find what his father could do to help Judge

Rossmore. He had talked about the case with several men the previous evening at the club and the general impression seemed to be that, guilty or innocent, the judge would be driven off the bench. The " interests " had forced the matter as a party issue, and the Republicans being in control in the Senate the outcome could hardly be in doubt. He had learned also of the other misfortunes which had befallen Judge Rossmore and he understood now the reason for Shirley's grave face on the dock and her little fib about summering on Long Island. The news had been a shock to him, for, apart from the fact that the judge was Shirley's father, he admired him immensely as a man. Of his perfect innocence there could, of course, be no question: these charges of bribery had simply been trumped up by his enemies to get him off the bench. That was very evident. The " interests " feared him and so had sacrificed him without pity, and as Jefferson walked along Central Park, past the rows of superb palaces which face its eastern wall, he wondered in which particular mansion had been hatched this wicked, iniquitous plot against a wholly blameless American citizen. Here, he thought, were the citadels of the plutocrats, America's aristocracy of money, the strongholds of her Coal, Railroad, Oil, Gas and Ice barons, the castles of her monarchs of Steel, Copper, and Finance. Each of

these million-dollar residences, he pondered, was filled
from cellar to roof with costly furnishings, master-
pieces of painting and sculpture, priceless art treasures
of all kinds purchased in every corner of the globe
with the gold filched from a Trust-ridden people. For
every stone in those marble halls a human being, other
than the owner, had been sold into bondage, for each
of these magnificent edifices, which the plutocrat put
up in his pride only to occupy it two months in the
year, ten thousand American men, women and children
had starved and sorrowed.

Europe, thought Jefferson as he strode quickly along,
pointed with envy to America's unparalleled prosperity,
spoke with bated breath of her great fortunes. Rather
should they say her gigantic robberies, her colossal
frauds! As a nation we were not proud of our multi-
millionaires. How many of them would bear the search-
light of investigation? Would his own father? How
many millions could one man make by honest methods?
America was enjoying unprecedented prosperity, not
because of her millionaires, but in spite of them. The
United States owed its high rank in the family of
nations to the country's vast natural resources, its in-
exhaustible vitality, its great wheat fields, the industrial and mechanical genius of its people. It was the
plain American citizen who had made the greatness

of America, not the millionaires who, forming a class by themselves of unscrupulous capitalists, had created an arrogant oligarchy which sought to rule the country by corrupting the legislature and the judiciary. The plutocrats—these were the leeches, the sores in the body politic. An organized band of robbers, they had succeeded in dominating legislation and in securing control of every branch of the nation's industry, crushing mercilessly and illegally all competition. They were the Money Power, and such a menace were they to the welfare of the people that, it had been estimated, twenty men in America had it in their power, by reason of the vast wealth which they controlled, to come together, and within twenty-four hours arrive at an understanding by which every wheel of trade and commerce would be stopped from revolving, every avenue of trade blocked and every electric key struck dumb. Those twenty men could paralyze the whole country, for they controlled the circulation of the currency and could create a panic whenever they might choose. It was the rapaciousness and insatiable greed of these plutocrats that had forced the toilers to combine for self-protection, resulting in the organization of the Labor Unions which, in time, became almost as tyrannical and unreasonable as the bosses. And the breach between capital on the one hand and labour on the other was widening daily, masters and servants snarling over wages and hours, the quarrel ever increasing in bitterness and acrimony until one day the extreme limit of patience would be reached and industrial strikes would give place to bloody violence.

Meantime the plutocrats, wholly careless of the significant signs of the times and the growing irritation and resentment of the people, continued their illegal practices, scoffing at public opinion, snapping their fingers at the law, even going so far in their insolence as to mock and jibe at the President of the United States. Feeling secure in long immunity and actually protected in their wrong doing by the courts—the legal machinery by its very elaborateness defeating the ends of justice—the Trust kings impudently defied the country and tried to impose their own will upon the people. History had thus repeated itself. The armed feudalism of the middle ages had been succeeded in twentieth century America by the tyranny of capital.

Yet, ruminated the young artist as he neared the Ryder residence, the American people had but themselves to blame for their present thralldom. Forty years before Abraham Lincoln had warned the country when at the close of the war he saw that the race for wealth was already making men and women money-mad. In 1864 he wrote these words:

178

# THE MOUSE

"Yes, we may congratulate ourselves that this cruel war is nearing its close. It has cost a vast amount of treasure and blood. The best blood of the flower of American youth has been freely offered upon our country's altar that the nation might live. It has been indeed a trying hour for the Republic, but I see in the near future a crisis approaching that unnerves me and causes me to tremble for the safety of my country. As a result of the war, corporations have been enthroned and an era of corruption in high places will follow and the money power of the country will endeavor to prolong its reign by working upon the prejudices of the people until all the wealth is aggregated in a few hands and the Republic is destroyed."

Truly prophetic these solemn words were to-day. Forgetting the austere simplicity of their forebears, a love of show and ostentation had become the ruling passion of the American people. Money, MONEY, MONEY! was to-day the only standard, the only god! The whole nation, frenzied with a wild lust for wealth no matter how acquired, had tacitly acquiesced in all sorts of turpitude, every description of moral depravity, and so had fallen an easy victim to the band of capitalistic adventurers who now virtually ruled the land. With the thieves in power, the courts were powerless, the demoralization was general and the world was afforded the edifying spectacle of an entire country given up to an orgy of graft—treason in the Senate—corruption in the Legislature, fraudulent elections, leaks in government reports, trickery in Wall Street, illegal corners in coal, meat, ice and other prime necessaries of life, the deadly horrors of the Beef and Drug Trusts, railroad conspiracies, insurance scandals, the wrecking of savings banks, police dividing spoils with pickpockets and sharing the wages of prostitutes, magistrates charged with blackmailing—a foul stench of social rottenness and decay! What, thought Jefferson, would be the outcome—Socialism or Anarchy?

Still, he mused, one ray of hope pierced the general gloom—the common sense, the vigour and the intelligence of the true American man and woman, the love for a " square deal " which was characteristic of the plain people, the resistless force of enlightened public opinion. The country was merely passing through a dark phase in its history, it was the era of the grafters. There would come a reaction, the rascals would be exposed and driven off, and the nation would go on upward toward its high destiny. The country was fortunate, too, in having a strong president, a man of high principles and undaunted courage who had already shown his capacity to deal with the critical situa-

tion. America was lucky with her presidents. Picked
out by the great political parties as mere figureheads,
sometimes they deceived their sponsors, and showed
themselves men and patriots. Such a president was
Theodore Roosevelt. After beginning vigorous war-
fare on the Trusts, attacking fearlessly the most ras-
cally of the band, the chief of the nation had sounded
the slogan of alarm in regard to the multi-million-
aires. The amassing of colossal fortunes, he had declared, must be stopped—a man might accumulate more
than sufficient for his own needs and for the needs of
his children, but the evil practice of perpetuating great
and ever-increasing fortunes for generations yet unborn was recognized as a peril to the State. To have
had the courage to propose such a sweeping and radical
restrictive measure as this should alone, thought Jefferson, ensure for Theodore Roosevelt a place among
America's greatest and wisest statesmen. He and
Americans of his calibre would eventually perform the
titanic task of cleansing these Augean stables, the
muck and accumulated filth of which was sapping the
health and vitality of the nation.

Jefferson turned abruptly and went up the wide
steps of an imposing white marble edifice, which took
up the space of half a city block. A fine example of
French Renaissance architecture, with spire roofs,

round turrets and mullioned windows dominating the
neighbouring houses, this magnificent home of the
plutocrat, with its furnishings and art treasures, had
cost John Burkett Ryder nearly ten millions of dollars.
It was one of the show places of the town, and when
the "rubber neck" wagons approached the Ryder
mansion and the guides, through their megaphones,
expatiated in awe-stricken tones on its external and
hidden beauties, there was a general craning of verte-
bræ among the "seeing New York"-ers to catch a
glimpse of the abode of the richest man in the world.

Only a few privileged ones were ever permitted to
penetrate to the interior of this ten-million-dollar home.
Ryder was not fond of company, he avoided strangers
and lived in continual apprehension of the subpœna
server. Not that he feared the law, only he usually
found it inconvenient to answer questions in court
under oath. The explicit instructions to the servants,
therefore, were to admit no one under any pretext
whatever unless the visitor had been approved by the
Hon. Fitzroy Bagley, Mr. Ryder's aristocratic private
secretary, and to facilitate this preliminary inspection
there had been installed between the library upstairs
and the front door one of those ingenious electric
writing devices, such as are used in banks, on which
a name is hastily scribbled, instantly transmitted else-

where, immediately answered and the visitor promptly admitted or as quickly shown the door.

Indeed the house, from the street, presented many of the characteristics of a prison. It had massive doors behind a row of highly polished steel gates, which would prove as useful in case of attempted invasion as they were now ornamental, and heavily barred windows, while on either side of the portico were great marble columns hung with chains and surmounted with bronze lions rampant. It was unusual to keep the town house open so late in the summer, but Mr. Ryder was obliged for business reasons to be in New York at this time, and Mrs. Ryder, who was one of the few American wives who do not always get their own way, had good-naturedly acquiesced in the wishes of her lord.

Jefferson did not have to ring at the paternal portal. The sentinel within was at his post; no one could approach that door without being seen and his arrival and appearance signalled upstairs. But the great man's son headed the list of the privileged ones, so without ado the smartly dressed flunkey opened wide the doors and Jefferson was under his father's roof.

"Is my father in?" he demanded of the man.

"No, sir," was the respectful answer. "Mr. Ryder has gone out driving, but Mr. Bagley is upstairs."

Then after a brief pause he added: " Mrs. Ryder is in, too."

In this household where the personality of the mistress was so completely overshadowed by the stronger personality of the master the latter's secretary was a more important personage to the servants than the unobtrusive wife.

Jefferson went up the grand staircase hung on either side with fine old portraits and rare tapestries, his feet sinking deep in the rich velvet carpet. On the first landing was a piece of sculptured marble of inestimable worth, seen in the soft warm light that sifted through a great pictorial stained-glass window overhead, the subject representing Ajax and Ulysses contending for the armour of Achilles. To the left of this, at the top of another flight leading to the library, was hung a fine full-length portrait of John Burkett Ryder. The ceilings here as in the lower hall were richly gilt and adorned with paintings by famous modern artists. When he reached this floor Jefferson was about to turn to the right and proceed direct to his mother's suite when he heard a voice near the library door. It was Mr. Bagley giving instructions to the butler.

The Honourable Fitzroy Bagley, a younger son of a British peer, had left his country for his country's good, and in order to turn an honest penny, which he had never succeeded in doing at home, he had entered the service of America's foremost financier, hoping to gather a few of the crumbs that fell from the rich man's table and disguising the menial nature of his position under the high-sounding title of private secretary. His job called for a spy and a toady and he filled these requirements admirably. Excepting with his employer, of whom he stood in craven fear, his manner was condescendingly patronizing to all with whom he came in contact, as if he were anxious to impress on these American plebeians the signal honour which a Fitzroy, son of a British peer, did them in deigning to remain in their "blarsted" country. In Mr. Ryder's absence, therefore, he ran the house to suit himself, bullying the servants and not infrequently issuing orders that were contradictory to those already given by Mrs. Ryder. The latter offered no resistance, she knew he was useful to her husband and, what to her mind was a still better reason for letting him have his own way, she had always had the greatest reverence for the British aristocracy. It would have seemed to her little short of vulgarity to question the actions of anyone who spoke with such a delightful English accent. Moreover, he dressed with irreproachable taste, was an acknowledged authority on dinner menus and social functions and knew his Burke backwards—altogether an accomplished and invaluable person.

Jefferson could not bear the sight of him; in fact, it was this man's continual presence in the house that had driven him to seek refuge elsewhere. He believed him to be a scoundrel as he certainly was a cad. Nor was his estimate of the English secretary far wrong. The man, like his master, was a grafter, and the particular graft he was after now was either to make a marriage with a rich American girl or to so compromise her that the same end would be attained. He was shrewd enough to realize that he had little chance to get what he wanted in the open matrimonial market, so he determined to attempt a raid and carry off an heiress under her father's nose, and the particular proboscis he had selected was that of his employer's friend, Senator Roberts. The senator and Miss Roberts were frequently at the Ryder House and in course of time the aristocratic secretary and the daughter had become quite intimate. A flighty girl, with no other purpose in life beyond dress and amusement and having what she termed " a good time," Kate thought it excellent pastime to flirt with Mr. Bagley, and when she discovered that he was serious in his attentions she felt flattered rather than indignant. After all, she argued, he was of noble birth. If his two brothers died he would be peer of England, and she had enough money for both. He might not make a bad husband. But she was careful to keep her own counsel and not let her father have any suspicion of what was going on. She knew that his heart was set on her marrying Jefferson Ryder and she knew better than anyone how impossible that dream was. She herself liked Jefferson quite enough to marry him, but if his eyes were turned in another direction—and she knew all about his attentions to Miss Rossmore—she was not going to break her heart about it. So she continued to flirt secretly with the Honourable Fitzroy while she still led the Ryders and her own father to think that she was interested in Jefferson.

"Jorkins," Mr. Bagley was saying to the butler, "Mr. Ryder will occupy the library on his return. See that he is not disturbed."

"Yes, sir," replied the butler respectfully. The man turned to go when the secretary called him back.

"And, Jorkins, you will station another man at the front entrance. Yesterday it was left unguarded, and a man had the audacity to address Mr. Ryder as he was getting out of his carriage. Last week a reporter tried to snapshot him. Mr. Ryder was furious. These things must not happen again, Jorkins. I shall hold you responsible."

"Very good, sir." The butler bowed and went downstairs. The secretary looked up and saw Jefferson. His face reddened and his manner grew nervous.

"Hello! Back from Europe, Jefferson? How jolly! Your mother will be delighted. She's in her room upstairs."

Declining to take the hint, and gathering from Bagley's embarrassed manner that he wanted to get rid of him, Jefferson lingered purposely. When the butler had disappeared, he said:

"This house is getting more and more like a barracks every day. You've got men all over the place. One can't move a step without falling over one."

Mr. Bagley drew himself up stiffly, as he always did when assuming an air of authority.

"Your father's personality demands the utmost precaution," he replied. "We cannot leave the life of the richest and most powerful financier in the world at the mercy of the rabble."

"What rabble?" inquired Jefferson, amused.

"The common rabble—the lower class—the riffraff," explained Mr. Bagley.

"Pshaw!" laughed Jefferson. "If our financiers were only half as respectable as the common rabble,

188

as you call them, they would need no bars to their houses."

Mr. Bagley sneered and shrugged his shoulders.

"Your father has warned me against your socialistic views." Then, with a lofty air, he added: "For four years I was third groom of the bedchamber to the second son of England's queen. I know my responsibilities."

"But you are not groom of the bedchamber here," retorted Jefferson.

"Whatever I am," said Mr. Bagley haughtily, "I am answerable to your father alone."

"By the way, Bagley," asked Jefferson, "when do you expect father to return? I want to see him."

"I'm afraid it's quite impossible," answered the secretary with studied insolence. "He has three important people to see before dinner. There's the National Republican Committee and Sergeant Ellison of the Secret Service from Washington—all here by appointment. It's quite impossible."

"I didn't ask you if it were possible. I said I wanted to see him and I will see him," answered Jefferson quietly but firmly, and in a tone and manner which did not admit of further opposition. "I'll go and leave word for him on his desk," he added.

He started to enter the library when the secretary,

who was visibly perturbed, attempted to bar his way.

"There's some one in there," he said in an undertone. "Someone waiting for your father."

"Is there?" replied Jefferson coolly. "I'll see who it is," with which he brushed past Mr. Bagley and entered the library.

He had guessed aright. A woman was there. It was Kate Roberts.

"Hello, Kate! how are you?" They called each other by their first names, having been acquainted for years, and while theirs was an indifferent kind of friendship they had always been on good terms. At one time Jefferson had even begun to think he might do what his father wished and marry the girl, but it was only after he had met and known Shirley Rossmore that he realized how different one woman can be from another. Yet Kate had her good qualities. She was frivolous and silly as are most girls with no brains and nothing else to do in life but dress and spend money, but she might yet be happy with some other fellow, and that was why it made him angry to see this girl with $100,000 in her own right playing into the hands of an unscrupulous adventurer. He had evidently disturbed an interesting *tête-à-tête*. He decided to say nothing, but mentally he resolved to spoil

Mr. Bagley's game and save Kate from her own folly. On hearing his voice Kate turned and gave a little cry of genuine surprise.

"Why, is it you, Jeff? I thought you were in Europe."

"I returned yesterday," he replied somewhat curtly. He crossed over to his father's desk where he sat down to scribble a few words, while Mr. Bagley, who had followed him in scowling, was making frantic dumb signs to Kate.

"I fear I intrude here," said Jefferson pointedly.

"Oh, dear no, not at all," replied Kate in some confusion. "I was waiting for my father. How is Paris?" she asked.

"Lovely as ever," he answered.

"Did you have a good time?" she inquired.

"I enjoyed it immensely. I never had a better one."

"You probably were in good company," she said significantly. Then she added: "I believe Miss Rossmore was in Paris."

"Yes, I think she was there," was his non-committal answer.

To change the conversation, which was becoming decidedly personal, he picked up a book that was lying on his father's desk and glanced at the title. It was "The American Octopus."

" Is father still reading this? " he asked. " He was at it when I left."

" Everybody is reading it," said Kate. " The book has made a big sensation. Do you know who the hero is? "

" Who? " he asked with an air of the greatest innocence.

" Why, no less a personage than your father—John Burkett Ryder himself! Everybody says it's he—the press and everybody that's read it. He says so himself."

" Really? " he exclaimed with well-simulated surprise. " I must read it."

" It has made a strong impression on Mr. Ryder," chimed in Mr. Bagley. " I never knew him to be so interested in a book before. He's trying his best to find out who the author is. It's a jolly well written book and raps you American millionaires jolly well— what? "

" Whoever wrote the book," interrupted Kate, " is somebody who knows Mr. Ryder exceedingly well. There are things in it that an outsider could not possibly know."

" Phew! " Jefferson whistled softly to himself. He was treading dangerous ground. To conceal his embarrassment, he rose.

# THE MOUSE

"If you'll excuse me, I'll go and pay my filial respects upstairs. I'll see you again." He gave Kate a friendly nod, and without even glancing at Mr. Bagley left the room.

The couple stood in silence for a few moments after he disappeared. Then Kate went to the door and listened to his retreating footsteps. When she was sure that he was out of earshot she turned on Mr. Bagley indignantly.

"You see what you expose me to. Jefferson thinks this was a rendezvous."

"Well, it was to a certain extent," replied the secretary unabashed. "Didn't you ask me to see you here?"

"Yes," said Kate, taking a letter from her bosom, "I wanted to ask you what this means?"

"My dear Miss Roberts—Kate—I"—stammered the secretary.

"How dare you address me in this manner when you know I and Mr. Ryder are engaged?"

No one knew better than Kate that this was not true, but she said it partly out of vanity, partly out of a desire to draw out this Englishman who made such bold love to her.

"Miss Roberts," replied Mr. Bagley loftily, "in that note I expressed my admiration—my love for you.

Your engagement to Mr. Jefferson Ryder is, to say the least, a most uncertain fact." There was a tinge of sarcasm in his voice that did not escape Kate.

"You must not judge from appearances," she answered, trying to keep up the outward show of indignation which inwardly she did not feel. "Jeff and I may hide a passion that burns like a volcano. All lovers are not demonstrative, you know."

The absurdity of this description as applied to her relations with Jefferson appealed to her as so comical that she burst into laughter in which the secretary joined.

"Then why did you remain here with me when the Senator went out with Mr. Ryder, senior?" he demanded.

"To tell you that I cannot listen to your nonsense any longer," retorted the girl.

"What?" he cried, incredulously. "You remain here to tell me that you cannot listen to me when you could easily have avoided listening to me without telling me so. Kate, your coldness is not convincing."

"You mean you think I want to listen to you?" she demanded.

"I do," he answered, stepping forward as if to take her in his arms.

"Mr. Bagley!" she exclaimed, recoiling.

" A week ago," he persisted, " you called me Fitz-roy. Once, in an outburst of confidence, you called me Fitz."

" You hadn't asked me to marry you then," she laughed mockingly. Then edging away towards the door she waved her hand at him playfully and said teasingly: " Good-bye, Mr. Bagley, I am going up-stairs to Mrs. Ryder. I will await my father's return in her room. I think I shall be safer."

He ran forward to intercept her, but she was too quick for him. The door slammed in his face and she was gone.

Meantime Jefferson had proceeded upstairs, passing through long and luxuriously carpeted corridors with panelled frescoed walls, and hung with grand old tapes tries and splendid paintings, until he came to his mother's room. He knocked.

" Come in! " called out the familiar voice.

He entered. Mrs. Ryder was busy at her escritoire looking over a mass of household accounts.

" Hello, mother! " he cried, running up and hugging her in his boyish, impulsive way. Jefferson had always been devoted to his mother, and while he de-plored her weakness in permitting herself to be so completely under the domination of his father, she had always found him an affectionate and loving son.

"Jefferson!" she exclaimed when he released her. "My dear boy, when did you arrive?"

"Only yesterday. I slept at the studio last night. You're looking bully, mother. How's father?"

Mrs. Ryder sighed while she looked her son over proudly. In her heart she was glad Jefferson had turned out as he had. Her boy certainly would never be a financier to be attacked in magazines and books. Answering his question she said:

"Your father is as well as those busybodies in the newspapers will let him be. He's considerably worried just now over that new book 'The American Octopus.' How dare they make him out such a monster? He's no worse than other successful business men. He's richer, that's all, and it makes them jealous. He's out driving now with Senator Roberts. Kate is somewhere in the house—in the library, I think."

"Yes, I found her there," replied Jefferson dryly. "She was with that cad, Bagley. When is father going to find that fellow out?"

"Oh, Jefferson," protested his mother, "how can you talk like that of Mr. Bagley. He is such a perfect gentleman. His family connections alone should entitle him to respect. He is certainly the best secretary your father ever had. I'm sure I don't know what we

196

should do without him. He knows everything that a gentleman should."

"And a good deal more, I wager," growled Jefferson. "He wasn't groom of the backstairs to England's queen for nothing." Then changing the topic, he said suddenly: "Talking about Kate, mother, we have got to reach some definite understanding. This talk about my marrying her must stop. I intend to take the matter up with father to-day."

"Oh, of course, more trouble!" replied his mother in a resigned tone. She was so accustomed to having her wishes thwarted that she was never surprised at anything. "We heard of your goings on in Paris. That Miss Rossmore was there, was she not?"

"That has got nothing to do with it," replied Jefferson warmly. He resented Shirley's name being dragged into the discussion. Then more calmly he went on: "Now, mother, be reasonable, listen. I purpose to live my own life. I have already shown my father that I will not be dictated to, and that I can earn my own living. He has no right to force this marriage on me. There has never been any misunderstanding on Kate's part. She and I understand each other thoroughly."

"Well, Jefferson, you may be right from your point of view," replied his mother weakly. She invariably

ended by agreeing with the last one who argued with
her. "You are of age, of course. Your parents have
only a moral right over you. Only remember this: it
would be foolish of you to do anything now to anger
your father. His interests are your interests. Don't
do anything to jeopardize them. Of course, you can't
be forced to marry a girl you don't care for, but your
father will be bitterly disappointed. He had set his
heart on this match. He knows all about your infatuation for Miss Rossmore and it has made him furious.
I suppose you've heard about her father?"

"Yes, and it's a dastardly outrage," blurted out
Jefferson. "It's a damnable conspiracy against one of
the most honourable men that ever lived, and I mean
to ferret out and expose the authors. I came here to-
day to ask father to help me."

"You came to ask your father to help you?" echoed
his mother incredulously.

"Why not?" demanded Jefferson. "Is it true then
that he is selfishness incarnate? Wouldn't he do that
much to help a friend?"

"You've come to the wrong house, Jeff. You ought
to know that. Your father is far from being Judge
Rossmore's friend. Surely you have sense enough to
realize that there are two reasons why he would not
raise a finger to help him. One is that he has always

been his opponent in public life, the other is that you want to marry his daughter."

Jefferson sat as if struck dumb. He had not thought of that. Yes, it was true. His father and the father of the girl he loved were mortal enemies. How was help to be expected from the head of those " interests " which the judge had always attacked, and now he came to think of it, perhaps his own father was really at the bottom of these abominable charges! He broke into a cold perspiration and his voice was altered as he said:

" Yes, I see now, mother. You are right." Then he added bitterly: " That has always been the trouble at home. No matter where I turn, I am up against a stone wall—the money interests. One never hears a glimmer of fellow-feeling, never a word of human sympathy, only cold calculation, heartless reasoning, money, money, money! Oh, I am sick of it. I don't want any of it. I am going away where I'll hear no more of it."

His mother laid her hand gently on his shoulder.

" Don't talk that way, Jefferson. Your father is not a bad man at heart, you know that. His life has been devoted to money making and he has made a greater fortune than any man living or dead. He is only what his life has made him. He has a good heart. And he loves you—his only son. But his business enemies —ah! those he never forgives."

Jefferson was about to reply when suddenly a dozen electric bells sounded all over the house.

"What's that?" exclaimed Jefferson, alarmed, and starting towards the door.

"Oh, that's nothing," smiled his mother. "We have had that put in since you went away. Your father must have just come in. Those bells announce the fact. It was done so that if there happened to be any strangers in the house they could be kept out of the way until he reached the library safely."

"Oh," laughed Jefferson, "he's afraid some one will kidnap him? Certainly he would be a rich prize. I wouldn't care for the job myself, though. They'd be catching a tartar."

His speech was interrupted by a timid knock at the door.

"May I come in to say good-bye?" asked a voice which they recognized as Kate's. She had successfully escaped from Mr. Bagley's importunities and was now going home with the Senator. She smiled amiably at Jefferson and they chatted pleasantly of his trip abroad. He was sincerely sorry for this girl whom they were trying to foist on him. Not that he thought she really cared for him, he was well aware that hers was a nature that made it impossible to feel very deeply on any subject, but the idea of this ready-made marriage was so foreign, so revolting to the American mind! He thought it would be a kindness to warn her against Bagley.

"Don't be foolish, Kate," he said. "I was not blind just now in the library. That man is no good."

As is usual when one's motives are suspected, the girl resented his interference. She knew he hated Mr. Bagley and she thought it mean of him to try and get even in this way. She stiffened up and replied coldly:

"I think I am able to look after myself, Jefferson. Thanks, all the same."

He shrugged his shoulders and made no reply. She said good-bye to Mrs. Ryder, who was again immersed in her tradespeople bills, and left the room, escorted by Jefferson, who accompanied her downstairs and on to the street where Senator Roberts was waiting for her in the open victoria. The senator greeted with unusual cordiality the young man whom he still hoped to make his son-in-law.

"Come and see us, Jefferson," he said. "Come to dinner any evening. We are always alone and Kate and I will be glad to see you."

"Jefferson has so little time now, father. His work and—his friends keep him pretty busy."

Jefferson had noted both the pause and the sarcasm, but he said nothing. He smiled and the senator raised his hat. As the carriage drove off the young man noticed that Kate glanced at one of the upper windows where Mr. Bagley stood behind a curtain watching. Jefferson returned to the house. The psychological moment had arrived. He must go now and confront his father in the library.

## CHAPTER IX

THE library was the most important room in the Ryder mansion, for it was there that the Colossus carried through his most important business deals, and its busiest hours were those which most men devote to rest. But John Burkett Ryder never rested. There could be no rest for any man who had a thousand millions of dollars to take care of. Like Macbeth, he could sleep no more. When the hum of business life had ceased down town and he returned home from the tall building in lower Broadway, then his real work began. The day had been given to mere business routine; in his own library at night, free from inquisitive ears and prying eyes, he could devise new schemes for strengthening his grip upon the country, he could evolve more gigantic plans for adding to his already countless millions.

Here the money Moloch held court like any king, with as much ceremony and more secrecy, and having for his courtiers some of the most prominent men in the political and industrial life of the nation. Corrupt senators, grafting Congressmen, ambitious railroad presidents, insolent coal barons who impudently claimed they administered the coal lands in trust for the Almighty, unscrupulous princes of finance and commerce, all visited this room to receive orders or pay from the head of the " System." Here were made and unmade governors of States, mayors of cities, judges, heads of police, cabinet ministers, even presidents. Here were turned over to confidential agents millions of dollars to overturn the people's vote in the National elections; here were distributed yearly hundreds of thousands of dollars to grafters, large and small, who had earned it in the service of the "interests."

Here, secretly and unlawfully, the heads of railroads met to agree on rates which by discriminating against one locality in favour of another crushed out competition, raised the cost to the consumer, and put millions in the pockets of the Trust. Here were planned tricky financial operations, with deliberate intent to mislead and deceive the investing public, operations which would send stocks soaring one day, only a week later to put Wall Street on the verge of panic. Half a dozen suicides might result from the coup, but twice as many millions of profits had gone into the coffers of the " System." Here, too, was perpetrated the most heinous crime that can be committed against a free people—the conspiring of the Trusts abetted by the railroads, to arbitrarily raise the prices of the necessaries of life—meat, coal, oil, ice, gas—wholly without other justification than that of greed, which, with these men, was the unconquerable, all-absorbing passion. In short, everything that unscrupulous leaders of organized capital could devise to squeeze the life blood out of the patient, defenceless toiler was done within these four walls.

It was a handsome room, noble in proportions and abundantly lighted by three large and deeply recessed, mullioned windows, one in the middle of the room and one at either end. The lofty ceiling was a marvellously fine example of panelled oak of Gothic design, decorated with gold, and the shelves for books which lined the walls were likewise of oak, richly carved. In the centre of the wall facing the windows was a massive and elaborately designed oak chimney-piece, reaching up to the ceiling, and having in the middle panel over the mantel a fine three-quarter length portrait of George Washington. The room was furnished sumptuously yet quietly, and fully in keeping with the rich collection of classic and modern authors that filled the bookcases, and in corners here and there stood pedestals with marble busts of Shakespeare, Goethe and

Voltaire. It was the retreat of a scholar rather than of a man of affairs.

When Jefferson entered, his father was seated at his desk, a long black cigar between his lips, giving instructions to Mr. Bagley. Mr. Ryder looked up quickly as the door opened and the secretary made a movement forward as if to eject the intruder, no matter who he might be. They were not accustomed to having people enter the sanctum of the Colossus so unceremoniously. But when he saw who it was, Mr. Ryder's stern, set face relaxed and he greeted his son amiably.

" Why, Jeff, my boy, is that you? Just a moment, until I get rid of Bagley, and I'll be with you."

Jefferson turned to the book shelves and ran over the titles while the financier continued his business with the secretary.

" Now, Bagley. Come, quick. What is it? "

He spoke in a rapid, explosive manner, like a man who has only a few moments to spare before he must rush to catch a train. John Ryder had been catching trains all his life, and he had seldom missed one.

" Governor Rice called. He wants an appointment," said Mr. Bagley, holding out a card.

" I can't see him. Tell him so," came the answer,

quick as a flash. "Who else?" he demanded. "Where's your list?"

Mr. Bagley took from the desk a list of names and read them over.

"General Abbey telephoned. He says you promised——"

"Yes, yes," interrupted Ryder impatiently, "but not here. Down town, to-morrow, any time. Next?"

The secretary jotted down a note against each name and then said:

"There are some people downstairs in the reception room. They are here by appointment."

"Who are they?"

"The National Republican Committee and Sergeant Ellison of the Secret Service from Washington," replied Mr. Bagley.

"Who was here first?" demanded the financier.

"Sergeant Ellison, sir."

"Then I'll see him first, and the Committee afterwards. But let them all wait until I ring. I wish to speak with my son."

He waved his hand and the secretary, knowing well from experience that this was a sign that there must be no further discussion, bowed respectfully and left the room. Jefferson turned and advanced towards his father, who held out his hand.

"Well, Jefferson," he said kindly, "did you have a good time abroad?"

"Yes, sir, thank you. Such a trip is a liberal education in itself."

"Ready for work again, eh? I'm glad you're back, Jefferson. I'm busy now, but one of these days I want to have a serious talk with you in regard to your future. This artist business is all very well—for a pastime. But it's not a career—surely you can appreciate that—for a young man with such prospects as yours. Have you ever stopped to think of that?"

Jefferson was silent. He did not want to displease his father; on the other hand, it was impossible to let things drift as they had been doing. There must be an understanding sooner or later. Why not now?

"The truth is, sir," he began timidly, "I'd like a little talk with you now, if you can spare the time."

Ryder, Sr., looked first at his watch and then at his son, who, ill at ease, sat nervously on the extreme edge of a chair. Then he said with a smile:

"Well, my boy, to be perfectly frank, I can't—but —I will. Come, what is it?" Then, as if to apologize for his previous abruptness, he added, "I've had a very busy day, Jeff. What with Trans-Continental and Trans-Atlantic and Southern Pacific, and Wall

208

Street, and Rate Bills, and Washington I feel like Atlas shouldering the world."

"The world wasn't intended for one pair of shoulders to carry, sir," rejoined Jefferson calmly.

His father looked at him in amazement. It was something new to hear anyone venturing to question or comment upon anything he said.

"Why not?" he demanded, when he had recovered from his surprise. "Julius Cæsar carried it. Napoleon carried it—to a certain extent. However, that's neither here nor there. What is it, boy?"

Unable to remain a moment inactive, he commenced to pick among the mass of papers on his desk, while Jefferson was thinking what to say. The last word his father uttered gave him a cue, and he blurted out protestingly:

"That's just it, sir. You forget that I'm no longer a boy. It's time to treat me as if I were a man."

Ryder, Sr., leaned back in his chair and laughed heartily.

"A man at twenty-eight? That's an excellent joke Do you know that a man doesn't get his horse sense till he's forty?"

"I want you to take me seriously," persisted Jefferson.

Ryder, Sr., was not a patient man. His moments

of good humour were of brief duration. Anything that savoured of questioning his authority always angered him. The smile went out of his face and he retorted explosively:

"Go on—damn it all! Be serious if you want, only don't take so long about it. But understand one thing. I want no preaching, no philosophical or socialistic twaddle. No Tolstoi—he's a great thinker, and you're not. No Bernard Shaw—he's funny, and you're not. Now go ahead."

This beginning was not very encouraging, and Jefferson felt somewhat intimidated. But he realized that he might not have another such opportunity, so he plunged right in.

"I should have spoken to you before if you had let me," he said. "I often——"

"If I let you?" interrupted his father. "Do you expect me to sit and listen patiently to your wild theories of social reform? You asked me one day why the wages of the idle rich was wealth and the wages of hard work was poverty, and I told you that I worked harder in one day than a tunnel digger works in a life-time. Thinking is a harder game than any. You must think or you won't know. Napoleon knew more about war than all his generals put together. I know more about money than any man living to-day. The man who knows is the man who wins. The man who takes advice isn't fit to give it. That's why I never take yours. Come, don't be a fool, Jeff—give up this art nonsense. Come back to the Trading Company. I'll make you vice-president, and I'll teach you the business of making millions."

Jefferson shook his head. It was hard to have to tell his own father that he did not think the million-making business quite a respectable one, so he only murmured:

"It's impossible, father. I am devoted to my work. I even intend to go away and travel a few years and see the world. It will help me considerably."

Ryder, Sr., eyed his son in silence for a few moments; then he said gently:

"Don't be obstinate, Jeff. Listen to me. I know the world better than you do. You mustn't go away. You are the only flesh and blood I have."

He stopped speaking for a moment, as if overcome by a sudden emotion over which he had no control. Jefferson remained silent, nervously toying with a paper cutter. Seeing that his words had made no effect, Ryder thumped his desk with his fist and cried:

"You see my weakness. You see that I want you with me, and now you take advantage—you take advantage——"

"No, father, I don't," protested Jefferson; "but I want to go away. Although I have my studio and am practically independent, I want to go where I shall be perfectly free—where my every move will not be watched—where I can meet my fellow-man heart to heart on an equal basis, where I shall not be pointed out as the son of Ready Money Ryder. I want to make a reputation of my own as an artist."

"Why not study theology and become a preacher?" sneered Ryder. Then, more amiably, he said: "No, my lad, you stay here. Study my interests—study the interests that will be yours some day."

"No," said Jefferson doggedly, "I'd rather go— my work and my self-respect demand it."

"Then go, damn it, go!" cried his father in a burst of anger. "I'm a fool for wasting my time with an ungrateful son." He rose from his seat and began to pace the room.

"Father," exclaimed Jefferson starting forward, "you do me an injustice."

"An injustice?" echoed Mr. Ryder turning round. "Ye gods! I've given you the biggest name in the commercial world; the most colossal fortune ever accumulated by one man is waiting for you, and you say I've done you an injustice!"

"Yes—we are rich," said Jefferson bitterly. "But

at what a cost! You do not go into the world and hear the sneers that I get everywhere. You may succeed in muzzling the newspapers and magazines, but you cannot silence public opinion. People laugh when they hear the name Ryder—when they do not weep. All your millions cannot purchase the world's respect. You try to throw millions to the public as a bone to a dog, and they decline the money on the ground that it is tainted. Doesn't that tell you what the world thinks of your methods?"

Ryder laughed cynically. He went back to his desk, and, sitting facing his son, he replied:

"Jefferson, you are young. It is one of the symptoms of youth to worry about public opinion. When you are as old as I am you will understand that there is only one thing which counts in this world—money. The man who has it possesses power over the man who has it not, and power is what the ambitious man loves most."

He stopped to pick up a book. It was "The American Octopus." Turning again to his son, he went on:

"Do you see this book? It is the literary sensation of the year. Why? Because it attacks me—the richest man in the world. It holds me up as a monster, a tyrant, a man without soul, honour or conscience, caring only for one thing—money; having but one passion—the love of power, and halting at nothing, not even at crime, to secure it. That is the portrait they draw of your father."

Jefferson said nothing. He was wondering if his sire had a suspicion who wrote it and was leading up to that. But Ryder, Sr., continued:

"Do I care? The more they attack me the more I like it. Their puny pen pricks have about the same effect as mosquito bites on the pachyderm. What I am, the conditions of my time made me. When I started in business a humble clerk, forty years ago, I had but one goal—success; I had but one aim—to get rich. I was lucky. I made a little money, and I soon discovered that I could make more money by outwitting my competitors in the oil fields. Railroad conditions helped me. The whole country was money mad. A wave of commercial prosperity swept over the land and I was carried along on its crest. I grew enormously rich, my millions increasing by leaps and bounds. I branched out into other interests, successful always, until my holdings grew to what they are to-day—the wonder of the twentieth century. What do I care for the world's respect when my money makes the world my slave? What respect can I have for a people that cringe before money and let it rule them? Are you aware that not a factory wheel

214

turns, not a vote is counted, not a judge is appointed, not a legislator seated, not a president elected without my consent? I am the real ruler of the United States —not the so-called government at Washington. They are my puppets and this is my executive chamber. This power will be yours one day, boy, but you must know how to use it when it comes."

"I never want it, father," said Jefferson firmly. "To me your words savour of treason. I couldn't imagine that American talking that way." He pointed to the mantel, at the picture of George Washington.

Ryder, Sr., laughed. He could not help it if his son was an idealist. There was no use getting angry, so he merely shrugged his shoulders and said:

"All right, Jeff. We'll discuss the matter later, when you've cut your wisdom teeth. Just at present you're in the clouds. But you spoke of my doing you an injustice. How can my love of power do you an injustice?"

"Because," replied Jefferson, "you exert that power over your family as well as over your business associates. You think and will for everybody in the house, for everyone who comes in contact with you. Yours is an influence no one seems able to resist. You robbed me of my right to think. Ever since I was old enough to think, you have thought for me; ever since I was old enough to choose, you have chosen for me. You have chosen that I should marry Kate Roberts. That is the one thing I wished to speak to you about. The marriage is impossible."

Ryder, Sr., half sprang from his seat. He had listened patiently, he thought, to all that his headstrong son had said, but that he should repudiate in this unceremonious fashion what was a tacit understanding between the two families, and, what was more, run the risk of injuring the Ryder interests—that was inconceivable. Leaving his desk, he advanced into the centre of the room, and folding his arms confronted Jefferson.

"So," he said sternly, "this is your latest act of rebellion, is it? You are going to welsh on your word? You are going to jilt the girl?"

"I never gave my word," answered Jefferson hotly. "Nor did Kate understand that an engagement existed. You can't expect me to marry a girl I don't care a straw about. It would not be fair to her."

"Have you stopped to think whether it would be fair to me?" thundered his father.

His face was pale with anger, his jet-black eyes flashed, and his white hair seemed to bristle with rage. He paced the floor for a few moments, and then turning to Jefferson, who had not moved, he said more calmly:

"Don't be a fool, Jeff. I don't want to think for you, or to choose for you, or to marry for you. I did not interfere when you threw up the position I made for you in the Trading Company and took that studio. I realized that you were restless under the harness, so I gave you plenty of rein. But I know so much better than you what is best for you. Believe me I do. Don't—don't be obstinate. This marriage means a great deal to my interests—to your interests. Kate's father is all powerful in the Senate. He'll never forgive this disappointment. Hang it all, you liked the girl once, and I made sure that——"

He stopped suddenly, and the expression on his face changed as a new light dawned upon him.

"It isn't that Rossmore girl, is it?" he demanded. His face grew dark and his jaw clicked as he said between his teeth: "I told you some time ago how I felt about her. If I thought that it was Rossmore's daughter! You know what's going to happen to him, don't you?"

Thus appealed to, Jefferson thought this was the most favourable opportunity he would have to redeem his promise to Shirley. So, little anticipating the tempest he was about to unchain, he answered:

" I am familiar with the charges that they have trumped up against him. Needless to say, I consider him entirely innocent. What's more, I firmly believe he is the victim of a contemptible conspiracy. And I'm going to make it my business to find out who the plotters are. I came to ask you to help me. Will you?"

For a moment Ryder was speechless from utter astonishment. Then, as he realized the significance of his son's words and their application to himself he completely lost control of himself. His face became livid, and he brought his fist down on his desk with a force that shook the room.

" I will see him in hell first!" he cried. "Damn him! He has always opposed me. He has always defied my power, and now his daughter has entrapped my son. So it's her you want to go to, eh? Well, I can't make you marry a girl you don't want, but I can prevent you throwing yourself away on the daughter of a man who is about to be publicly disgraced, and, by God, I will."

" Poor old Rossmore," said Jefferson bitterly. " If the history of every financial transaction were made known, how many of us would escape public disgrace? Would you?" he cried.

Ryder, Sr., rose, his hands working dangerously.

He made a movement as if about to advance on his son, but by a supreme effort he controlled himself.

"No, upon my word, it's no use disinheriting you, you wouldn't care. I think you'd be glad; on my soul, I do!" Then calming down once more, he added: "Jefferson, give me your word of honour that your object in going away is not to find out this girl and marry her unknown to me. I don't mind your losing your heart, but, damn it, don't lose your head. Give me your hand on it."

Jefferson reluctantly held out his hand.

"If I thought you would marry that girl unknown to me, I'd have Rossmore sent out of the country and the woman too. Listen, boy. This man is my enemy, and I show no mercy to my enemies. There are more reasons than one why you cannot marry Miss Rossmore. If she knew one of them she would not marry you."

"What reasons?" demanded Jefferson.

"The principal one," said Ryder, slowly and deliberately, and eyeing his son keenly as if to judge of the effect of his words, "the principal one is that it was through my agents that the demand was made for her father's impeachment."

"Ah," cried Jefferson, "then I guessed aright!

Oh, father, how could you have done that? If you only knew him!"

Ryder, Sr., had regained command of his temper, and now spoke calmly enough.

" Jefferson, I don't have to make any apologies to you for the way I conduct my business. The facts contained in the charge were brought to my attention. I did not see why I should spare him. He never spared me. I shall not interfere, and the probabilities are that he will be impeached. Senator Roberts said this afternoon that it was a certainty. You see yourself how impossible a marriage with Miss Rossmore would be, don't you?"

" Yes, father, I see now. I have nothing more to say."

" Do you still intend going away?"

" Yes," replied Jefferson bitterly. " Why not? You have taken away the only reason why I should stay."

" Think it well over, lad. Marry Kate or not, as you please, but I want you to stay here."

" It's no use. My mind is made up," answered Jefferson decisively.

The telephone rang, and Jefferson got up to go. Mr. Ryder took up the receiver.

" Hallo! What's that? Sergeant Ellison? Yes, send him up."

# THE MOUSE

Putting the telephone down, Ryder, Sr., rose, and crossing the room accompanied his son to the door.

"Think it well over, Jeff. Don't be hasty."

"I have thought it over, sir, and I have decided to go."

A few moments later Jefferson left the house.

Ryder, Sr., went back to his desk and sat for a moment in deep thought. For the first time in his life he was face to face with defeat; for the first time he had encountered a will as strong as his own. He who could rule parliaments and dictate to governments now found himself powerless to rule his own son. At all costs, he mused, the boy's infatuation for Judge Rossmore's daughter must be checked, even if he had to blacken the girl's character as well as the father's, or, as a last resort, send the entire family out of the country. He had not lost sight of his victim since the carefully prepared crash in Wall Street, and the sale of the Rossmore home following the bankruptcy of the Great Northwestern Mining Company. His agents had reported their settlement in the quiet little village on Long Island, and he had also learned of Miss Rossmore's arrival from Europe, which coincided strangely with the home-coming of his own son. He decided, therefore, to keep a closer watch on Massapequa now than ever, and that is why to-day's call of

Sergeant Ellison, a noted sleuth in the government service, found so ready a welcome.

The door opened, and Mr. Bagley entered, followed by a tall, powerfully built man whose robust physique and cheap looking clothes contrasted strangely with the delicate, ultra-fashionably attired English secretary.

"Take a seat, Sergeant," said Mr. Ryder, cordially motioning his visitor to a chair. The man sat down gingerly on one of the rich leather-upholstered chairs. His manner was nervous and awkward, as if intimidated in the presence of the financier.

"Are the Republican Committee still waiting?" demanded Mr. Ryder.

"Yes, sir," replied the secretary.

"I'll see them in a few minutes. Leave me with Sergeant Ellison."

Mr. Bagley bowed and retired.

"Well, Sergeant, what have you got to report?"

He opened a box of cigars that stood on the desk and held it out to the detective.

"Take a cigar," he said amiably.

The man took a cigar, and also the match which Mr. Ryder held out. The financier knew how to be cordial with those who could serve him.

"Thanks. This is a good one," smiled the sleuth,

sniffing at the weed. "We don't often get a chance at such as these."

"It ought to be good," laughed Ryder. "They cost two dollars apiece."

The detective was so surprised at this unheard of extravagance that he inhaled a puff of smoke which almost choked him. It was like burning money.

Ryder, with his customary bluntness, came right down to business.

"Well, what have you been doing about the book?" he demanded. "Have you found the author of 'The American Octopus'?"

"No, sir, I have not. I confess I'm baffled. The secret has been well k pt. The publishers have shut up like a clam. There's only one thing that I'm pretty well sure of."

"What's that?" demanded Ryder, interested.

"That no such person as Shirley Green exists."

"Oh," exclaimed e financier, "then you think it is a mere *nom de plume?*"

"Yes, sir."

"And what do you think was the reason for preserving the anonymity?"

"Well, you see, sir, the book deals with a big subject. It gives some hard knocks, and the author, no

doubt, felt a little timid about launching it under his
or her real name.  At least that's my theory, sir."

"And a good one, no doubt," said Mr. Ryder.  Then
he added: "That makes me all the more anxious to
find out who it is.  I would willingly give this moment a check for $5,000 to know who wrote it.  Who-
ever it is, knows me as well as I know myself.  We
must find the author."

The sleuth was silent for a moment.  Then he said:
"There might be one way to reach the author, but
it will be successful only in the event of her being
willing to be known and come out into the open.  Suppose you write to her in care of the publishers.  They
would certainly forward the letter to wherever she
may be.  If she does not want you to know who she
is she will ignore your letter and remain in the back-
ground.  If, on the contrary, she has no fear of you,
and is willing to meet you, she will answer the letter."

"Ah, I never thought of that!" exclaimed Ryder.
"It's a good idea.  I'll write such a letter at once.  It
shall go to-night."

He unhooked the telephone and asked Mr. Bagley
to come up.  A few seconds later the secretary entered
the room.

"Bagley," said Mr. Ryder, "I want you to write a
letter for me to Miss Shirley Green, author of that

book 'The American Octopus.' We will address it care of her publishers, Littleton & Co. Just say that if convenient I should like a personal interview with her at my office, No. 36 Broadway, in relation to her book, 'The American Octopus.' See that it is mailed to-night. That's all."

Mr. Bagley bowed and retired. Mr. Ryder turned to the secret service agent.

"There, that's settled. We'll see how it works. And now, Sergeant, I have another job for you, and if you are faithful to my interests you will not find me un-appreciative. Do you know a little place on Long Island called Massapequa?"

"Yes," grinned the detective, "I know it. They've got some fine specimens of 'skeeters' there."

Paying no attention to this jocularity, Mr. Ryder continued:

"Judge Rossmore is living there—pending the out-come of his case in the Senate. His daughter has just arrived from Europe. My son Jefferson came home on the same ship. They are a little more friendly than I care to have them. You understand. I want to know if my son visits the Rossmores, and if he does I wish to be kept informed of all that's going on. You understand?"

"Perfectly, sir. You shall know everything."

Mr. Ryder took a blank check from his desk and proceeded to fill it up. Then handing it to the detective, he said:

"Here is $500 for you. Spare neither trouble or expense."

"Thank you, sir," said the man as he pocketed the money. "Leave it to me."

"That's about all, I think. Regarding the other matter, we'll see how the letter works."

He touched a bell and rose, which was a signal to the visitor that the interview was at an end. Mr. Bagley entered.

"Sergeant Ellison is going," said Mr. Ryder. "Have him shown out, and send the Republican Committee up."

# THE MOUSE

## CHAPTER X

"WHAT!" exclaimed Shirley, changing colour, "you believe that John Burkett Ryder is at the bottom of this infamous accusation against father?"

It was the day following her arrival at Massapequa, and Shirley, the judge and Stott were all three sitting on the porch. Until now, by common consent, any mention of the impeachment proceedings had been avoided by everyone. The previous afternoon and evening had been spent listening to an account of Shirley's experiences in Europe and a smile had flitted across even the judge's careworn face as his daughter gave a humorous description of the picturesque Paris student with their long hair and peg-top trousers, while Stott simply roared with laughter. Ah, it was good to laugh again after so much trouble and anxiety! But while Shirley avoided the topic that lay nearest her heart, she was consumed with a desire to tell her father of the hope she had of enlisting the aid of John Burkett Ryder. The great financier was certainly able to do anything he chose, and had not his son Jefferson promised to win him over to their cause? So, to-day, after Mrs. Rossmore and her sister had gone down to the village to make some purchases Shirley timidly broached the matter. She asked Stott and her father to tell her everything, to hold back nothing. She wanted to hear the worst.

Stott, therefore, started to review the whole affair from the beginning, explaining how her father in his capacity as Judge of the Supreme Court had to render decisions, several of which were adverse to the corporate interests of a number of rich men, and how since that time these powerful interests had used all their influence to get him put off the Bench. He told her about the Transcontinental case and how the judge had got mysteriously tangled up in the Great Northern Mining Company, and of the scandalous newspaper rumours, followed by the news of the Congressional inquiry. Then he told her about the panic in Wall Street, the sale of the house on Madison Avenue and the removal to Long Island.

" That is the situation," said Stott when he had finished. " We are waiting now to see what the Senate will do. We hope for the best. It seems impossible that the Senate will condemn a man whose whole life is like an open book, but unfortunately the Senate is strongly Republican and the big interests are in com-

228

plete control. Unless support comes from some unexpected quarter we must be prepared for anything."

Support from some unexpected quarter! Stott's
closing words rang in Shirley's head. Was that not
just what she had to offer? Unable to restrain herself
longer and her heart beating tumultuously from suppressed emotion, she cried:

"We'll have that support! We'll have it! I've got
it already! I wanted to surprise you! Father, the
most powerful man in the United States will save you
from being dishonoured!"

The two men leaned forward in eager interest.
What could the girl mean? Was she serious or merely
jesting?

But Shirley was never more serious in her life. She
was jubilant at the thought that she had arrived home
in time to invoke the aid of this powerful ally. She
repeated enthusiastically:

"We need not worry any more. He has but to say
a word and these proceedings will be instantly dropped.
They would not dare act against his veto. Did you
hear, father, your case is as good as won!"

"What do you mean, child? Who is this unknown
friend?"

"Surely you can guess when I say the most power-

ful man in the United States? None other than John
Burkett Ryder!"

She stopped short to watch the effect which this
name would have on her hearers. But to her surprise
neither her father nor Stott displayed the slightest emotion or even interest. Puzzled at this cold reception,
she repeated:

"Did you hear, father—John Burkett Ryder will
come to your assistance. I came home on the same
ship as his son and he promised to secure his father's
aid."

The judge puffed heavily at his pipe and merely
shook his head, making no reply. Stott explained:

"We can't look for help from that quarter, Shirley.
You don't expect a man to cut loose his own kite,
do you?"

"What do you mean?" demanded Shirley, mystified.

"Simply this—that John Burkett Ryder is the very
man who is responsible for all your father's misfortunes."

The girl sank back in her seat pale and motionless,
as if she had received a blow. Was it possible? Could
Jefferson's father have done them such a wrong as
this? She well knew that Ryder, Sr., was a man who
would stop at nothing to accomplish his purpose—this

she had demonstrated conclusively in her book—but
she had never dreamed that his hand would ever be
directed against her own flesh and blood. Decidedly
some fatality was causing Jefferson and herself to
drift further and further apart. First, her father's
trouble. That alone would naturally have separated
them. And now this discovery that Jefferson's father
had done hers this wrong. All idea of marriage was
henceforth out of the question. That was irre-
vocable. Of course, she could not hold Jefferson to
blame for methods which he himself abhorred. She
would always think as much of him as ever, but
whether her father emerged safely from the trial in
the Senate or not—no matter what the outcome of the
impeachment proceedings might be, Jefferson could
never be anything else than a Ryder and from now on
there would be an impassable gulf between the Rossmores and the Ryders. The dove does not mate with
the hawk.

"Do you really believe this, that John Ryder deliberately concocted the bribery charge with the sole
purpose of ruining my father?" demanded Shirley
when she had somewhat recovered.

"There is no other solution of the mystery possible," answered Stott. "The Trusts found they could
not fight him in the open, in a fair, honest way, so

they plotted in the dark. Ryder was the man who had most to lose by your father's honesty on the bench. Ryder was the man he hit the hardest when he enjoined his Transcontinental Railroad. Ryder, I am convinced, is the chief conspirator."

"But can such things be in a civilized community?" cried Shirley indignantly. "Cannot he be exposed, won't the press take the matter up, cannot we show conspiracy?"

"It sounds easy, but it isn't," replied Stott. "I have had a heap of experience with the law, my child, and I know what I'm talking about. They're too clever to be caught tripping. They've covered their tracks well, be sure of that. As to the newspapers—when did you ever hear of them championing a man when he's down?"

"And you, father—do you believe Ryder did this?"

"I have no longer any doubt of it," answered the judge. "I think John Ryder would see me dead before he would raise a finger to help me. His answer to my demand for my letters convinced me that he was the arch plotter."

"What letters do you refer to?" demanded Shirley.

"The letters I wrote to him in regard to my making an investment. He advised the purchase of certain stock. I wrote him two letters at the time, which let-

ters if I had them now would go a long way to clearing me of this charge of bribery, for they plainly
showed that I regarded the transaction as a *bona fide*
investment. Since this trouble began I wrote to Ryder
asking him to return me these letters so I might use
them in my defence. The only reply I got was an
insolent note from his secretary saying that Mr. Ryder
had forgotten all about the transaction, and in any case
had not the letters I referred to."

"Couldn't you compel him to return them?" asked
Shirley.

"We could never get at him," interrupted Stott.
"The man is guarded as carefully as the Czar."

"Still," objected Shirley, "it is possible that he may
have lost the letters or even never received them."

"Oh, he has them safe enough," replied Stott. "A
man like Ryder keeps every scrap of paper, with the
idea that it may prove useful some day. The letters
are lying somewhere in his desk. Besides, after the
Transcontinental decision he was heard to say that
he'd have Judge Rossmore off the Bench inside of a
year."

"And it wasn't a vain boast—he's done it," muttered the judge.

Shirley relapsed into silence. Her brain was in a
whirl. It was true then. This merciless man of

money, this ogre of monopolistic corporations, this
human juggernaut had crushed her father merely because by his honesty he interfered with his shady business deals! Ah, why had she spared him in her book?
She felt now that she had been too lenient, not bitter
enough, not sufficiently pitiless. Such a man was entitled to no mercy. Yes, it was all clear enough now.
John Burkett Ryder, the head of " the System," the
plutocrat whose fabulous fortune gave him absolute
control over the entire country, which invested him
with a personal power greater than that of any king,
this was the man who now dared attack the Judiciary,
the corner stone of the Constitution, the one safe-
guard of the people's liberty. Where would it end?
How long would the nation tolerate being thus ruthlessly trodden under the unclean heels of an insolent
oligarchy? The capitalists, banded together for the
sole purpose of pillage and loot, had already succeeded
in enslaving the toiler. The appalling degradation of
the working classes, the sordidness and demoralizing
squalor in which they passed their lives, the curse of
drink, the provocation to crime, the shame of the
sweat shops—all which evils in our social system she
had seen as a Settlement worker, were directly trace-
able to Centralized Wealth. The labor unions regu-
lated wages and hours, but they were powerless to

control the prices of the necessaries of life. The Trusts could at pleasure create famine or plenty. They usually willed to make it famine so they themselves might acquire more millions with which to pay for marble palaces, fast motor cars, ocean-going yachts and expensive establishments at Newport. Food was ever dearer and of poorer quality, clothes cost more, rents and taxes were higher. She thought of the horrors in the packing houses at Chicago recently made the subject of a sensational government report—putrid, pestiferous meats put up for human food amid conditions of unspeakable foulness, freely exposed to deadly germs from the expectorations of work people suffering from tuberculosis, in unsanitary rotten buildings soaked through with blood and every conceivable form of filth and decay, the beef barons careless and indifferent to the dictates of common decency so long as they could make more money. And while our public gasped in disgust at the sickening revelations of the Beef scandal and foreign countries quickly cancelled their contracts for American prepared meats, the millionaire packer, insolent in the possession of wealth stolen from a poisoned public, impudently appeared in public in his fashionable touring car, with head erect and self-satisfied, wholly indifferent to his shame.

These and other evidences of the plutocracy's cruel grip upon the nation had ended by exasperating the people. There must be a limit somewhere to the turpitudes of a degenerate class of *nouveaux riches*. The day of reckoning was fast approaching for the grafters and among the first to taste the vengeance of the people would be the Colossus. But while waiting for the people to rise in their righteous wrath, Ryder was all powerful, and if it were true that he had instituted these impeachment proceedings her father had little chance. What could be done? They could not sit and wait, as Stott had said, for the action of the Senate. If it were true that Ryder controlled the Senate as he controlled everything else her father was doomed. No, they must find some other way.

And long after the judge and Stott had left for the city Shirley sat alone on the porch engrossed in thought, taxing her brain to find some way out of the darkness. And when presently her mother and aunt returned they found her still sitting there, silent and preoccupied. If they only had those two letters, she thought. They alone might save her father. But how could they be got at? Mr. Ryder had put them safely away, no doubt. He would not give them up. She wondered how it would be to go boldly to him and appeal to whatever sense of honour and fairness that might be lying latent within him. No, such a man would not know what the terms " honour," " fairness " meant. She pondered upon it all day and at night when she went tired to bed it was her last thought as she dropped off to sleep.

The following morning broke clear and fine. It was one of those glorious, ideal days of which we get perhaps half a dozen during the whole summer, days when the air is cool and bracing, champagne-like in its exhilarating effect, and when Nature dons her brightest dress, when the atmosphere is purer, the grass greener, the sky bluer, the flowers sweeter and the birds sing in more joyous chorus, when all creation seems in tune. Days that make living worth while, when one can forget the ugliness, the selfishness, the empty glitter of the man-made city and walk erect and buoyant in the open country as in the garden of God.

Shirley went out for a long walk. She preferred to go alone so she would not have to talk. Hers was one of those lonely, introspective natures that resent the intrusion of aimless chatter when preoccupied with serious thoughts. Long Island was unknown territory to her and it all looked very flat and uninteresting, but she loved the country and found keen delight in the fresh, pure air and the sweet scent of new mown hay wafted from the surrounding fields. In her soft, loose-fitting linen dress, her white canvas shoes, garden hat trimmed with red roses, and lace parasol, she made an attractive picture and every passer-by—with the exception of one old farmer and he was half blind—turned to look at this good-looking girl, a stranger in those parts and whose stylish appearance suggested Fifth Avenue rather than the commonplace purlieus of Massapequa.

Every now and then Shirley espied in the distance the figure of a man which she thought she recognized as that of Jefferson. Had he come, after all? The blood went coursing tumultuously through her veins only a moment later to leave her face a shade paler as the man came nearer and she saw he was a stranger. She wondered what he was doing, if he gave her a thought, if he had spoken to his father and what the latter had said. She could realize now what Mr. Ryder's reply had been. Then she wondered what her future life would be. She could do nothing, of course, until the Senate had passed upon her father's case, but it was imperative that she get to work. In a day or two, she would call on her publishers and learn how her book was selling. She might get other commissions. If she could not make enough money in literary work she would have to teach. It was a dreary outlook at best, and she sighed as she thought of the ambitions that had once stirred her breast. All the brightness seemed to have gone out of her life, her father disgraced, Jefferson now practically lost to her —only her work remained

As she neared the cottage on her return home she caught sight of the letter carrier approaching the gate. Instantly she thought of Jefferson, and she hurried to intercept the man. Perhaps he had written instead of coming.

" Miss Shirley Rossmore? " said the man eyeing her interrogatively.

" That's I," said Shirley.

The postman handed her a letter and passed on. Shirley glanced quickly at the superscription. No, it was not from Jefferson; she knew his handwriting too well. The envelope, moreover, bore the firm name of her publishers. She tore it open and found that it merely contained another letter which the publishers had forwarded. This was addressed to Miss Shirley Green and ran as follows:

*Dear Madam.*—If convenient, I should like to see you at my office, No. 36 Broadway, in relation to your book " The American Octopus." Kindly inform me as to the day and hour at which I may expect you.

Yours truly,

JOHN BURKETT RYDER,

per B.

Shirley almost shouted from sheer excitement. At

first she was alarmed—the name John Burkett Ryder was such a bogey to frighten bad children with, she thought he might want to punish her for writing about him as she had. She hurried to the porch and sat there reading the letter over and over and her brain began to evolve ideas. She had been wondering how she could get at Mr. Ryder and here he was actually asking her to call on him. Evidently he had not the slightest idea of her identity, for he had been able to reach her only through her publishers and no doubt he had exhausted every other means of discovering her address. The more she pondered over it the more she began to see in this invitation a way of helping her father. Yes, she would go and beard the lion in his den, but she would not go to his office. She would accept the invitation only on condition that the interview took place in the Ryder mansion where undoubtedly the letters would be found. She decided to act immediately. No time was to be lost, so she procured a sheet of paper and an envelope and wrote as follows:

MR. JOHN BURKETT RYDER,

    *Dear Sir.*—I do not call upon gentlemen at their business office.

                             Yours, etc.,

                                SHIRLEY GREEN.

Her letter was abrupt and at first glance seemed hardly calculated to bring about what she wanted—an invitation to call at the Ryder home, but she was shrewd enough to see that if Ryder wrote to her at all it was because he was most anxious to see her and her abruptness would not deter him from trying again. On the contrary, the very unusualness of anyone thus dictating to him would make him more than ever desirous of making her acquaintance. So Shirley mailed the letter and awaited with confidence for Ryder's reply. So certain was she that one would come that she at once began to form her plan of action. She would leave Massapequa at once, and her whereabouts must remain a secret even from her own family. As she intended to go to the Ryder house in the assumed character of Shirley Green, it would never do to run the risk of being followed home by a Ryder detective to the Rossmore cottage. She would confide in one person only—Judge Stott. He would know where she was and would be in constant communication with her. But, otherwise, she must be alone to conduct the campaign as she judged fit. She would go at once to New York and take rooms in a boarding house where she would be known as Shirley Green. As for funds to meet her expenses, she had her diamonds, and would they not be filling a more useful purpose if sold to defray the cost of saving her father than in mere personal adornment? So that evening, while her mother was talking with the judge, she beckoned Stott over to the corner where she was sitting:

" Judge Stott," she began, " I have a plan."

He smiled indulgently at her

" Another friend like that of yesterday? " he asked.

" No," replied the girl, " listen. I am in earnest now and I want you to help me. You said that no one on earth could resist John Burkett Ryder, that no one could fight against the Money Power. Well, do you know what I am going to do? "

There was a quiver in her voice and her nostrils were dilated like those of a thoroughbred eager to run the race. She had risen from her seat and stood facing him, her fists clenched, her face set and determined. Stott had never seen her in this mood and he gazed at her half admiringly, half curiously.

" What will you do? " he asked with a slightly ironical inflection in his voice.

" I am going to fight John Burkett Ryder! " she cried.

Stott looked at her open-mouthed.

" You? " he said.

" Yes, I," said Shirley. " I'm going to him and I intend to get those letters if he has them."

Stott shook his head.

" My dear child," he said, " what are you talking

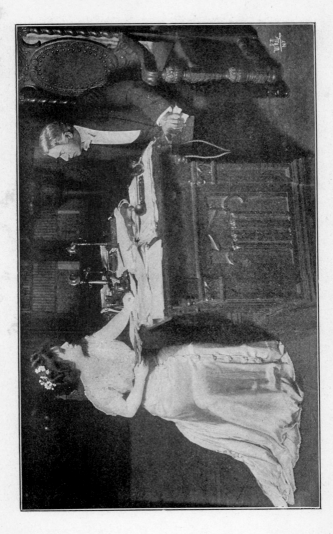

"How do you classify him?"

"As the greatest criminal the world has ever produced."—Act III.

about? How can you expect to reach Ryder? We couldn't."

" I don't know just how yet," replied Shirley, " but I'm going to try. I love my father and I'm going to leave nothing untried to save him."

" But what can you do? " persisted Stott. " The matter has been sifted over and over by some of the greatest minds in the country."

" Has any woman sifted it over? " demanded Shirley.

" No, but—" stammered Stott.

" Then it's about time one did," said the girl decisively. " Those letters my father speaks of—they would be useful, would they not? "

" They would be invaluable."

" Then I'll get them. If not——"

" But I don't understand how you're going to get at Ryder," interrupted Stott.

" This is how," replied Shirley, passing over to him the letter she had received that afternoon.

As Stott recognized the well-known signature and read the contents the expression of his face changed. He gasped for breath and sank into a chair from sheer astonishment.

" Ah, that's different! " he cried, " that's different! "

Briefly Shirley outlined her plan, explaining that

she would go to live in the city immediately and conduct her campaign from there. If she was successful it might save her father and if not no harm could come of it.

Stott demurred at first. He did not wish to bear alone the responsibility of such an adventure. There was no knowing what might happen to her, visiting a strange house under an assumed name. But when he saw how thoroughly in earnest she was and that she was ready to proceed without him he capitulated. He agreed that she might be able to find the missing letters or if not that she might make some impression on Ryder himself. She could show interest in the judge's case as a disinterested outsider and so might win his sympathies. From being a sceptic, Stott now became enthusiastic. He promised to co-operate in every way and to keep Shirley's whereabouts an absolute secret. The girl, therefore, began to make her preparations for departure from home by telling her parents that she had accepted an invitation to spend a week or two with an old college chum in New York.

That same evening her mother, the judge, and Stott went for a stroll after dinner and left her to take care of the house. They had wanted Shirley to go, too, but she pleaded fatigue. The truth was that she wanted to be alone so she could ponder undisturbed

over her plans. It was a clear, starlit night, with
no moon, and Shirley sat on the porch listening to the
chirping of the crickets and idly watching the flashes
of the mysterious fireflies. She was in no mood for
reading and sat for a long time rocking herself engrossed in her thoughts. Suddenly she heard someone
unfasten the garden gate. It was too soon for the return of the promenaders; it must be a visitor. Through
the uncertain penumbra of the garden she discerned
approaching a form which looked familiar. Yes, now
there was no doubt possible. It was, indeed, Jefferson
Ryder.

She hurried down the porch to greet him. No matter what the father had done she could never think
any the less of the son. He took her hand and for
several moments neither one spoke. There are times
when silence is more eloquent than speech and this
was one of them. The gentle grip of his big strong
hand expressed more tenderly than any words the
sympathy that lay in his heart for the woman he loved.
Shirley said quietly:

"You have come at last, Jefferson."

"I came as soon as I could," he replied gently. "I
saw father only yesterday."

"You need not tell me what he said," Shirley hastened to say.

Jefferson made no reply. He understood what she meant. He hung his head and hit viciously with his walking stick at the pebbles that lay at his feet. She went on:

"I know everything now. It was foolish of me to think that Mr. Ryder would ever help us."

"I can't help it in any way," blurted out Jefferson. "I have not the slightest influence over him. His business methods I consider disgraceful—you understand that, don't you, Shirley?"

The girl laid her hand on his arm and replied kindly:

"Of course, Jeff, we know that. Come up and sit down."

He followed her on the porch and drew up a rocker beside her.

"They are all out for a walk," she explained.

"I'm glad," he said frankly. "I wanted a quiet talk with you. I did not care to meet anyone. My name must be odious to your people."

Both were silent, feeling a certain awkwardness. They seemed to have drifted apart in some way since those delightful days in Paris and on the ship. Then he said:

"I'm going away, but I couldn't go until I saw you."

" You are going away?" exclaimed Shirley, surprised.

"Yes," he said, " I cannot stand it any more at home. I had a hot talk with my father yesterday about one thing and another. He and I don't chin well together. Besides this matter of your father's impeachment has completely discouraged me. All the wealth in the world could never reconcile me to such methods! I'm ashamed of the rôle my own flesh and blood has played in that miserable affair. I can't express what I feel about it."

"Yes," sighed Shirley, " it is hard to believe that you are the son of that man!"

"How is your father?" inquired Jefferson. " How does he take it?"

" Oh, his heart beats and he can see and hear and speak," replied Shirley sadly, " but he is only a shadow of what he once was. If the trial goes against him, I don't think he'll survive it."

" It is monstrous," cried Jefferson. " To think that my father should be responsible for this thing!"

" We are still hoping for the best," added Shirley, " but the outlook is dark."

" But what are you going to do?" he asked. "These surroundings are not for you—" He looked around at the cheap furnishings which he could see through the open window and his face showed real concern.

"I shall teach or write, or go out as governess," replied Shirley with a tinge of bitterness. Then smiling sadly she added: "Poverty is easy; it is unmerited disgrace which is hard."

The young man drew his chair closer and took hold of the hand that lay in her lap. She made no resistance.

"Shirley," he said, "do you remember that talk we had on the ship? I asked you to be my wife. You led me to believe that you were not indifferent to me. I ask you again to marry me. Give me the right to take care of you and yours. I am the son of the world's richest man, but I don't want his money. I have earned a competence of my own—enough to live on comfortably. We will go away where you and your father and mother will make their home with us. Do not let the sins of the fathers embitter the lives of the children."

"Mine has not sinned," said Shirley bitterly.

"I wish I could say the same of mine," replied Jefferson. "It is because the clouds are dark about you that I want to come into your life to comfort you."

The girl shook her head.

"No, Jefferson, the circumstances make such a marriage impossible. Your family and everybody else would say that I had inveigled you into it. It is even more impossible now than I thought it was when I spoke to you on the ship. Then I was worried about my father's trouble and could give no thought to anything else. Now it is different. Your father's action has made our union impossible for ever. I thank you for the honour you have done me. I do like you. I like you well enough to be your wife, but I will not accept this sacrifice on your part. Your offer, coming at such a critical time, is dictated only by your noble, generous nature, by your sympathy for our misfortune. Afterwards, you might regret it. If my father were convicted and driven from the bench and you found you had married the daughter of a disgraced man you would be ashamed of us all, and if I saw that it would break my heart."

Emotion stopped her utterance and she buried her face in her hands weeping silently.

" Shirley," said Jefferson gently, " you are wrong. I love you for yourself, not because of your trouble. You know that. I shall never love any other woman but you. If you will not say ' yes ' now, I shall go away as I told my father I would and one day I shall come back and then if you are still single I shall ask you again to be my wife."

" Where are you going? " she asked.

" I shall travel for a year and then, may be, I shall stay a couple of years in Paris, studying at the Beaux Arts.  Then I may go to Rome.  If I am to do anything worth while in the career I have chosen I must have that European training."

" Paris!  Rome! " echoed Shirley.  " How I envy you!  Yes, you are right.  Get away from this country where the only topic, the only thought is money, where the only incentive to work is dollars.  Go where there are still some ideals, where you can breathe the atmosphere of culture and art."

Forgetting momentarily her own troubles, Shirley chatted on about life in the art centres of Europe, advised Jefferson where to go, with whom to study.  She knew people in Paris, Rome and Munich and she would give him letters to them.  Only, if he wanted to perfect himself in the languages, he ought to avoid Americans and cultivate the natives.  Then, who could tell? if he worked hard and was lucky, he might have something exhibited at the Salon and return to America a famous painter.

" If I do," smiled Jefferson, " you shall be the first to congratulate me.  I shall come and ask you to be my wife.  May I? " he added.

Shirley smiled gravely.

" Get famous first. You may not want me then."

" I shall always want you," he whispered hoarsely, bending over her. In the dim light of the porch he saw that her tear-stained face was drawn and pale. He rose and held out his hand.

" Good-bye," he said simply.

" Good-bye, Jefferson." She rose and put her hand in his. " We shall always be friends. I, too, am going away."

" You going away—where to? " he asked surprised.

" I have work to do in connection with my father's case," she said.

" You? " said Jefferson puzzled. " You have work to do—what work? "

" I can't say what it is, Jefferson. There are good reasons why I can't. You must take my word for it that it is urgent and important work." Then she added: " You go your way, Jefferson; I will go mine. It was not our destiny to belong to each other. You will become famous as an artist. And I——"

" And you—" echoed Jefferson.

" I—I shall devote my life to my father. I'ts no use, Jefferson—really—I've thought it all out. You must not come back to me—you understand. We must be alone with our grief—father and I. Good-bye."

He raised her hand to his lips.

"Good-bye, Shirley. Don't forget me. I shall come back for you."

He went down the porch and she watched him go out of the gate and down the road until she could see his figure no longer. Then she turned back and sank into her chair and burying her face in her handkerchief she gave way to a torrent of tears which afforded some relief to the weight on her heart. Presently the others returned from their walk and she told them about the visitor.

"Mr. Ryder's son, Jefferson, was here. We crossed on the same ship. I introduced him to Judge Stott on the dock."

The judge looked surprised, but he merely said:

"I hope for his sake that he is a different man from his father."

"He is," replied Shirley simply, and nothing more was said.

Two days went by, during which Shirley went on completing the preparations for her visit to New York. It was arranged that Stott should escort her to the city. Shortly before they started for the train a letter arrived for Shirley. Like the first one it had been forwarded by her publishers. It read as follows:

252

# THE MOUSE

Miss Shirley Green,

    *Dear Madam.*—I shall be happy to see you at my residence—Fifth Avenue—any afternoon that you w ll mention.

Yours very truly,

John Burkett Ryder,

per B.

Shirley smiled in triumph as, unseen by her father and mother, she passed it over to Stott. She at once sat down and wrote this reply:

Mr. John Burkett Ryder,

    *Dear Sir.*—I am sorry that I am unable to comply with your request. I prefer the invitation to call at your private residence should come from Mrs. Ryder.

Yours, etc.,

Shirley Green.

She laughed as she showed this to Stott:

"He'll write me again," she said, "and next time his wife will sign the letter."

An hour later she left Massapequa for the city.

## CHAPTER XI

THE HON. FITZROY BAGLEY had every
reason to feel satisfied with himself. His
*affaire de cœur* with the Senator's daughter
was progressing more smoothly than ever, and nothing
now seemed likely to interfere with his carefully prepared plans to capture an American heiress. The
interview with Kate Roberts in the library, so awkwardly disturbed by Jefferson's unexpected intrusion,
had been followed by other interviews more secret and
more successful, and the plausible secretary had contrived so well to persuade the girl that he really
thought the world of her, and that a brilliant future
awaited her as his wife, that it was not long before
he found her in a mood to refuse him nothing.

Bagley urged immediate marriage; he insinuated
that Jefferson had treated her shamefully and that she
owed it to herself to show the world that there were
other men as good as the one who had jilted her.
He argued that in view of the Senator being bent on
the match with Ryder's son it would be worse than
useless for him, Bagley, to make formal application

for her hand, so, as he explained, the only thing which remained was a runaway marriage. Confronted with the *fait accompli*, papa Roberts would bow to the inevitable. They could get married quietly in town, go away for a short trip, and when the Senator had gotten over his first disappointment they would be welcomed back with open arms.

Kate listened willingly enough to this specious reasoning. In her heart she was piqued at Jefferson's indifference and she was foolish enough to really believe that this marriage with a British nobleman, twice removed, would be in the nature of a triumph over him. Besides, this project of an elopement appealed strangely to her frivolous imagination; it put her in the same class as all her favourite novel heroines. And it would be capital fun!

Meantime, Senator Roberts, in blissful ignorance of this little plot against his domestic peace, was growing impatient and he approached his friend Ryder once more on the subject of his son Jefferson. The young man, he said, had been back from Europe some time. He insisted on knowing what his attitude was towards his daughter. If they were engaged to be married he said there should be a public announcement of the fact. It was unfair to him and a slight to his daughter to let matters hang fire in this unsatisfactory way and he hinted that both himself and his daughter might demand their passports from the Ryder mansion unless some explanation were forthcoming.

Ryder was in a quandary. He had no wish to quarrel with his useful Washington ally; he recognized the reasonableness of his complaint. Yet what could he do? Much as he himself desired the marriage, his son was obstinate and showed little inclination to settle down. He even hinted at attractions in another quarter. He did not tell the Senator of his recent interview with his son when the latter made it very plain that the marriage could never take place. Ryder, Sr., had his own reasons for wishing to temporize. It was quite possible that Jefferson might change his mind and abandon his idea of going abroad and he suggested to the Senator that perhaps if he, the Senator, made the engagement public through the newspapers it might have the salutary effect of forcing his son's hand.

So a few mornings later there appeared among the society notes in several of the New York papers this paragraph:

"The engagement is announced of Miss Katherine Roberts, only daughter of senator Roberts of Wisconsin, to Jefferson Ryder, son of Mr. John Burkett Ryder."

Two persons in New York happened to see the item about the same time and both were equally interested, although it affected them in a different manner. One was Shirley Rossmore, who had chanced to pick up the newspaper at the breakfast table in her boarding house.

"So soon?" she murmured to herself. Well, why not? She could not blame Jefferson. He had often spoken to her of this match arranged by his father and they had laughed over it as a typical marriage of convenience modelled after the Continental pattern. Jefferson, she knew, had never cared for the girl nor taken the affair seriously. Some powerful influences must have been at work to make him surrender so easily. Here again she recognized the masterly hand of Ryder, Sr., and more than ever she was eager to meet this extraordinary man and measure her strength with his. Her mind, indeed, was too full of her father's troubles to grieve over her own however much she might have been inclined to do so under other circumstances, and all that day she did her best to banish the paragraph from her thoughts. More than a week had passed since she left Massapequa and what with corresponding with financiers, calling on editors and publishers, every moment of her time had been kept busy. She had found a quiet and reasonable priced boarding house off Washington Square and here Stott had called several times to see her. Her correspondence with

Mr. Ryder had now reached a phase when it was impossible to invent any further excuses for delaying the interview asked for. As she had foreseen, a day or two after her arrival in town she had received a note from Mrs. Ryder asking her to do her the honour to call and see her, and Shirley, after waiting another two days, had replied making an appointment for the following day at three o'clock. This was the same day on which the paragraph concerning the Ryder-Roberts engagement appeared in the society chronicles of the metropolis.

Directly after the meagre meal which in New York boarding houses is dignified by the name of luncheon, Shirley proceeded to get ready for this portentous visit to the Ryder mansion. She was anxious to make a favourable impression on the financier, so she took some pains with her personal appearance. She always looked stylish, no matter what she wore, and her poverty was of too recent date to make much difference to her wardrobe, which was still well supplied with Paris-made gowns. She selected a simple close-fitting gown of gray chiffon cloth and a picture hat of Leghorn straw heaped with red roses, Shirley's favourite flower. Thus arrayed, she sallied forth at two o'clock —a little gray mouse to do battle with the formidable lion.

# THE MOUSE

The sky was threatening, so instead of walking a short way up Fifth Avenue for exercise, as she had intended doing, she cut across town through Ninth Street, and took the surface car on Fourth Avenue. This would put her down at Madison Avenue and Seventy-fourth Street, which was only a block from the Ryder residence. She looked so pretty and was so well dressed that the passers-by who looked after her wondered why she did not take a cab instead of standing on a street corner for a car. But one's outward appearance is not always a faithful index to the condition of one's pocketbook, and Shirley was rapidly acquiring the art of economy.

It was not without a certain trepidation that she began this journey. So far, all her plans had been based largely on theory, but now that she was actually on her way to Mr. Ryder all sorts of misgivings beset her. Suppose he knew her by sight and roughly accused her of obtaining access to his house under false pretences and then had her ejected by the servants? How terrible and humiliating that would be! And even if he did not how could she possibly find those letters with him watching her, and all in the brief time of a conventional afternoon call? It had been an absurd idea from the first. Stott was right; she saw that now. But she had entered upon it and she was not going to confess herself beaten until she had tried. And as the car sped along Madison Avenue, gradually drawing nearer to the house which she was going to enter disguised as it were, like a burglar, she felt cold chills run up and down her spine—the same sensation that one experiences when one rings the bell of a dentist's where one has gone to have a tooth extracted. In fact, she felt so nervous and frightened that if she had not been ashamed before herself she would have turned back. In about twenty minutes the car stopped at the corner of Seventy-fourth Street. Shirley descended and with a quickened pulse walked towards the Ryder mansion, which she knew well by sight.

There was one other person in New York who, that same morning, had read the newspaper item regarding the Ryder-Roberts betrothal, and he did not take the matter so calmly as Shirley had done. On the contrary, it had the effect of putting him into a violent rage. This was Jefferson. He was working in his studio when he read it and five minutes later he was tearing up-town to seek the author of it. He understood its object, of course; they wanted to force his hand, to shame him into this marriage, to so entangle him with the girl that no other alternative would be possible to an honourable man. It was a despicable trick and he had no doubt that his father was at the back of it. So his mind now was fully made up. He would go away at once where they could not make his life a burden with this odious marriage which was fast becoming a nightmare to him. He would close up his studio and leave immediately for Europe. He would show his father once for all that he was a man and expected to be treated as one.

He wondered what Shirley was doing. Where had she gone, what was this mysterious work of which she had spoken? He only realized now, when she seemed entirely beyond his reach, how much he loved her and how empty his life would be without her. He would know no happiness until she was his wife. Her words on the porch did not discourage him. Under the circumstances he could not expect her to have said anything else. She could not marry into John Ryder's family with such a charge hanging over her own father's head, but, later, when the trial was over, no matter how it turned out, he would go to her again and ask her to be his wife.

On arriving home the first person he saw was the ubiquitous Mr. Bagley, who stood at the top of the first staircase giving some letters to the butler. Jefferson cornered him at once, holding out the newspaper containing the offending paragraph.

" Say, Bagley," he cried, " what does this mean? Is this any of your doing? "

The English secretary gave his employer's son a haughty stare, and then, without deigning to reply or even to glance at the newspaper, continued his instructions to the servant:

" Here, Jorkins, get stamps for all these letters and see they are mailed at once. They are very important."

" Very good, sir."

The man took the letters and disappeared, while Jefferson, impatient, repeated his question:

" My doing? " sneered Mr. Bagley. " Really, Jefferson, you go too far! Do you suppose for one instant that I would condescend to trouble myself with your affairs? "

Jefferson was in no mood to put up with insolence from anyone, especially from a man whom he heartily despised, so advancing menacingly he thundered:

" I mean—were you, in the discharge of your menial-like duties, instructed by my father to send that paragraph to the newspapers regarding my alleged betrothal to Miss Roberts? Yes or No? "

The man winced and made a step backward. There was a gleam in the Ryder eye which he knew by experience boded no good.

" Really, Jefferson," he said in a more conciliatory

tone, " I know absolutely nothing about the paragraph. This is the first I hear of it. Why not ask your father? "

" I will," replied Jefferson grimly.

He was turning to go in the direction of the library when Bagley stopped him.

" You cannot possibly see him now," he said. " Sergeant Ellison of the Secret Service is in there with him, and your father told me not to disturb him on any account. He has another appointment at three o'clock with some woman who writes books."

Seeing that the fellow was in earnest, Jefferson did not insist. He could see his father a little later or send him a message through his mother. Proceeding upstairs he found Mrs. Ryder in her room and in a few energetic words he explained the situation to his mother. They had gone too far with this match-making business, he said, his father was trying to interfere with his personal liberty and he was going to put a stop to it. He would leave at once for Europe. Mrs. Ryder had already heard of the projected trip abroad, so the news of this sudden departure was not the shock it might otherwise have been. In her heart she did not blame her son, on the contrary she admired his spirit, and if the temporary absence from home would make him happier, she would not hold him back. Yet, mother like, she wept and coaxed, but nothing would shake Jefferson in his determination and he begged his mother to make it very plain to his father that this was final and that a few days would see him on his way abroad. He would try and come back to see his father that afternoon, but otherwise she was to say good-bye for him. Mrs. Ryder promised tearfully to do what her son demanded and a few minutes later Jefferson was on his way to the front door.

As he went down stairs something white on the carpet attracted his attention. He stooped and picked it up. It was a letter. It was in Bagley's handwriting and had evidently been dropped by the man to whom the secretary had given it to post. But what interested Jefferson more than anything else was that it was addressed to Miss Kate Roberts. Under ordinary circumstances, a king's ransom would not have tempted the young man to read a letter addressed to another, but he was convinced that his father's secretary was an adventurer and if he were carrying on an intrigue in this manner it could have only one meaning. It was his duty to unveil a rascal who was using the Ryder roof and name to further his own ends and victimize a girl who, although sophisticated enough to know better, was too silly to realize the risk she ran at the hands of an unscrupulous man. Hesitating **no** longer, Jefferson tore open the envelope and read:

My dearest wife that is to be:

I have arranged everything. Next Wednesday—just a week from to-day—we will go to the house of a discreet friend of mine where a minister will marry us; then we will go to City Hall and get through the legal part of it. Afterwards, we can catch the four o'clock train for Buffalo. Meet me in the ladies' room at the Holland House Wednesday morning at 11 a.m. I will come there with a closed cab. Your devoted

FITZ.

" Phew! " Jefferson whistled. A close shave this for Senator Roberts, he thought. His first impulse was to go upstairs again to his mother and put the matter in her hands. She would immediately inform his father, who would make short work of Mr. Bagley. But, thought Jefferson, why should he spoil a good thing? He could afford to wait a day or two. There was no hurry. He could allow Bagley to think all was going swimmingly and then uncover the plot at the eleventh hour. He would even let this letter go to Kate, there was no difficulty in procuring another envelope and imitating the handwriting—and when Bagley was just preparing to go to the rendezvous he would spring the trap. Such a cad deserved no mercy. The scandal would be a knock-out blow, his father would discharge him on the spot and that would be the last they would

see of the aristocratic English secretary. Jefferson put
the letter in his pocket and left the house rejoicing.

While the foregoing incidents were happening John
Burkett Ryder was secluded in his library. The great
man had come home earlier than usual, for he had two
important callers to see by appointment that afternoon.
One was Sergeant Ellison, who had to report on his
mission to Massapequa; the other was Miss Shirley
Green, the author of " The American Octopus," who
had at last deigned to honour him with a visit. Pending
the arrival of these visitors the financier was busy with
his secretary trying to get rid as rapidly as possible of
what business and correspondence there was on hand.

The plutocrat was sitting at his desk poring over a
mass of papers. Between his teeth was the inevitable
long black cigar and when he raised his eyes to the
light a close observer might have remarked that they
were sea-green, a colour they assumed when the man
of millions was absorbed in scheming new business
deals. Every now and then he stopped reading the
papers to make quick calculations on scraps of paper.
Then if the result pleased him, a smile overspread his
saturnine features. He rose from his chair and nervously paced the floor as he always did when thinking
deeply.

"Five millions," he muttered, "not a cent more. If they won't sell we'll crush them——"

Mr. Bagley entered. Mr. Ryder looked up quickly.

"Well, Bagley?" he said interrogatively. "Has Sergeant Ellison come?"

"Yes, sir. But Mr. Herts is downstairs. He insists on seeing you about the Philadelphia gas deal. He says it is a matter of life and death."

"To him—yes," answered the financier dryly. "Let him come up. We might as well have it out now."

Mr. Bagley went out and returned almost immediately, followed by a short, fat man, rather loudly dressed and apoplectic in appearance. He looked like a prosperous brewer, while, as a matter of fact, he was president of a gas company, one of the shrewdest promoters in the country, and a big man in Wall Street. There was only one bigger man and that was John Ryder. But, to-day, Mr. Herts was not in good condition. His face was pale and his manner flustered and nervous. He was plainly worried.

"Mr. Ryder," he began with excited gesture, "the terms you offer are preposterous. It would mean disaster to the stockholders. Our gas properties are worth six times that amount. We will sell out for twenty millions—not a cent less."

Ryder shrugged his shoulders.

" Mr. Herts," he replied coolly, " I am busy to-day and in no mood for arguing. We'll either buy you out or force you out. Choose. You have our offer. Five millions for your gas property. Will you take it? "

" We'll see you in hell first! " cried his visitor exasperated.

" Very well," replied Ryder still unruffled, " all negotiations are off. You leave me free to act. We have an offer to buy cheap the old Germantown Gas Company which has charter rights to go into any of the streets of Philadelphia. We shall purchase that company, we will put ten millions new capital into it, and reduce the price of gas in Philadelphia to sixty cents a thousand. Where will you be then?

The face of the Colossus as he uttered this stand and deliver speech was calm and inscrutable. Conscious of the resistless power of his untold millions, he felt no more compunction in mercilessly crushing this business rival than he would in trampling out the life of a worm. The little man facing him looked haggard and distressed. He knew well that this was no idle threat. He was well aware that Ryder and his associates by the sheer weight of the enormous wealth they controlled could sell out or destroy any industrial corporation in the land. It was plainly illegal, but it was done every day, and his company was not the first victim nor the last. Desperate, he appealed humbly to the tyrannical Money Power:

"Don't drive us to the wall, Mr. Ryder. This forced sale will mean disaster to us all. Put yourself in our place—think what it means to scores of families whose only support is the income from their investment in our company."

"Mr. Herts," replied Ryder unmoved, "I never allow sentiment to interfere with business. You have heard my terms. I refuse to argue the matter further. What is it to be? Five millions or competition? Decide now or this interview must end!"

He took out his watch and with his other hand touched a bell. Beads of perspiration stood on his visitor's forehead. In a voice broken with suppressed emotion he said hoarsely:

"You're a hard, pitiless man, John Ryder! So be it—five millions. I don't know what they'll say. I don't dare return to them."

"Those are my terms," said Ryder coldly. "The papers," he added, "will be ready for your signature to-morrow at this time, and I'll have a cheque ready for the entire amount. Good-day."

Mr. Bagley entered. Ryder bowed to Herts, who slowly retired. When the door had closed on him

Ryder went back to his desk, a smile of triumph on his face. Then he turned to his secretary:

" Let Sergeant Ellison come up," he said.

The secretary left the room and Mr. Ryder sank comfortably in his chair, puffing silently at his long black cigar. The financier was thinking, but his thoughts concerned neither the luckless gas president he had just pitilessly crushed, nor the detective who had come to make his report. He was thinking of the book " The American Octopus," and its bold author whom he was to meet in a very few minutes. He glanced at the clock. A quarter to three. She would be here in fifteen minutes if she were punctual, but women seldom are, he reflected. What kind of a woman could she be, this Shirley Green, to dare cross swords with a man whose power was felt in two hemispheres? No ordinary woman, that was certain. He tried to imagine what she looked like, and he pictured a tall, gaunt, sexless spinster with spectacles, a sort of nightmare in the garb of a woman. A sour, discontented creature, bitter to all mankind, owing to disappointments in early life and especially vindictive towards the rich, whom her socialistic and even anarchistical tendencies prompted her to hate and attack. Yet, withal, a brainy, intelligent woman, remarkably well informed as to political and industrial conditions—a woman to make a friend of rather than an enemy. And John Ryder, who had educated himself to believe that with gold he could do everything, that none could resist its power, had no doubt that with money he could enlist this Shirley Green in his service. At least it would keep her from writing more books about him.

The door opened and Sergeant Ellison entered, followed by the secretary, who almost immediately withdrew.

"Well, sergeant," said Mr. Ryder cordially, "what have you to tell me? I can give you only a few minutes. I expect a lady friend of yours."

The plutocrat sometimes condescended to be jocular with his subordinates.

"A lady friend of mine, sir?" echoed the man, puzzled.

"Yes—Miss Shirley Green, the author," replied the financier, enjoying the detective's embarrassment. "That suggestion of yours worked out all right. She's coming here to-day."

"I'm glad you've found her, sir."

"It was a tough job," answered Ryder with a grimace. "We wrote her half a dozen times before she was satisfied with the wording of the invitation. But, finally, we landed her and I expect her at three o'clock.

Now what about that Rossmore girl? Did you go down to Massapequa?"

"Yes, sir, I have been there half a dozen times. In fact, I've just come from there. Judge Rossmore is there, all right, but his daughter has left for parts unknown."

"Gone away—where?" exclaimed the financier.

This was what he dreaded. As long as he could keep his eye on the girl there was little danger of Jefferson making a fool of himself; with her disappeared everything was possible.

"I could not find out, sir. Their neighbours don't know much about them. They say they're haughty and stuck up. The only one I could get anything out of was a parson named Deetle. He said it was a sad case, that they had reverses and a daughter who was in Paris——"

"Yes, yes," said Ryder impatiently, "we know all that. But where's the daughter now?"

"Search me, sir. I even tried to pump the Irish slavey. Gee, what a vixen! She almost flew at me. She said she didn't know and didn't care."

Ryder brought his fist down with force on his desk, a trick he had when he wished to emphasize a point.

"Sergeant, I don't like the mysterious disappearance of that girl. You must find her, do you hear, you must find her if it takes all the sleuths in the country. Had my son been seen there?"

"The parson said he saw a young fellow answering his description sitting on the porch of the Rossmore cottage the evening before the girl disappeared, but he didn't know who he was and hasn't seen him since."

"That was my son, I'll wager. He knows where the girl is. Perhaps he's with her now. Maybe he's going to marry her. That must be prevented at any cost. Sergeant, find that Rossmore girl and I'll give you $1,000."

The detective's face flushed with pleasure at the prospect of so liberal a reward. Rising he said:

"I'll find her, sir. I'll find her."

Mr. Bagley entered, wearing the solemn, important air he always affected when he had to announce a visitor of consequence. But before he could open his mouth Mr. Ryder said:

"Bagley, when did you see my son, Jefferson, last?"

"To-day, sir. He wanted to see you to say good-bye. He said he would be back."

Ryder gave a sigh of relief and addressing the detective said:

"It's not so bad as I thought." Then turning again to his secretary he asked:

"Well, Bagley, what is it?"

"There's a lady downstairs, sir—Miss Shirley Green."

The financier half sprang from his seat.

"Oh, yes. Show her up at once. Good-bye, sergeant, good-bye. Find that Rossmore woman and the $1,000 is yours."

The detective went out and a few moments later Mr. Bagley reappeared ushering in Shirley.

The mouse was in the den of the lion.

## CHAPTER XII

MR. RYDER remained at his desk and did not
even look up when his visitor entered. He
pretended to be busily preoccupied with his
papers, which was a favourite pose of his when receiving strangers. This frigid reception invariably served
its purpose, for it led visitors not to expect more than
they got, which usually was little enough. For several
minutes Shirley stood still, not knowing whether to
advance or to take a seat. She gave a little conventional cough, and Ryder looked up. What he saw so
astonished him that he at once took from his mouth
the cigar he was smoking and rose from his seat. He
had expected a gaunt old maid with spectacles, and
here was a stylish, good-looking young woman, who
could not possibly be over twenty-five. There was
surely some mistake. This slip of a girl could not
have written " The American Octopus." He advanced
to greet Shirley.

" You wish to see me, Madame? " he asked cour-
teously. There were times when even John Burkett
Ryder could be polite.

"Yes," replied Shirley, her voice trembling a little in spite of her efforts to keep cool. "I am here by appointment. Three o'clock, Mrs. Ryder's note said. I am Miss Green."

"*You*—Miss Green?" echoed the financier dubiously.

"Yes, I am Miss Green—Shirley Green, author of 'The American Octopus.' You asked me to call. Here I am."

For the first time in his life, John Ryder was nonplussed. He coughed and stammered and looked round for a place where he could throw his cigar. Shirley, who enjoyed his embarrassment, put him at his ease.

"Oh, please go on smoking," she said; "I don't mind it in the least."

Ryder threw the cigar into a receptacle and looked closely at his visitor.

"So you are Shirley Green, eh?"

"That is my *nom-de-plume*—yes," replied the girl nervously. She was already wishing herself back at Massapequa. The financier eyed her for a moment in silence as if trying to gauge the strength of the personality of this audacious young woman, who had dared to criticise his business methods in public print; then, waving her to a seat near his desk, he said:

# THE MOUSE

"Won't you sit down?"

"Thank you," murmured Shirley. She sat down, and he took his seat at the other side of the desk, which brought them face to face. Again inspecting the girl with a close scrutiny that made her cheeks burn, Ryder said:

"I rather expected—" He stopped for a moment as if uncertain what to say, then he added: "You're younger than I thought you were, Miss Green, much younger."

"Time will remedy that," smiled Shirley. Then, mischievously, she added: "I rather expected to see Mrs. Ryder."

There was the faintest suspicion of a smile playing around the corners of the plutocrat's mouth as he picked up a book lying on his desk and replied:

"Yes—she wrote you, but I—wanted to see you about this."

Shirley's pulse throbbed faster, but she tried hard to appear unconcerned as she answered:

"Oh, my book—have you read it?"

"I have," replied Ryder slowly and, fixing her with a stare that was beginning to make her uncomfortable, he went on: "No doubt your time is valuable, so I'll come right to the point. I want to ask you, Miss Green, where you got the character of your central figure—the Octopus, as you call him—John Broderick?"

"From imagination—of course," answered Shirley.

Ryder opened the book, and Shirley noticed that there were several passages marked. He turned the leaves over in silence for a minute or two and then he said:

"You've sketched a pretty big man here——"

"Yes," assented Shirley, "he has big possibilities, but I think he makes very small use of them."

Ryder appeared not to notice her commentary, and, still reading the book, he continued:

"On page 22 you call him '*the world's greatest individualized potentiality, a giant combination of materiality, mentality and money—the greatest exemplar of individual human will in existence to-day.*' And you make indomitable will and energy the keystone of his marvellous success. Am I right?" He looked at her questioningly.

"Quite right," answered Shirley.

Ryder proceeded:

"On page 26 you say '*the machinery of his money-making mind typifies the laws of perpetual unrest. It must go on, relentlessly, resistlessly, ruthlessly making money-making money and continuing to make money. It cannot stop until the machinery crumbles.*'"

# THE MOUSE

Laying the book down and turning sharply on Shirley, he asked her bluntly:

"Do you.mean to say that I couldn't stop to-morrow if I wanted to?"

She affected to not understand him.

"*You?*" she inquired in a tone of surprise.

"Well—it's a natural question," stammered Ryder, with a nervous little laugh; "every man sees himself in the hero of a novel just as every woman sees herself in the heroine. We're all heroes and heroines in our own eyes. But tell me what's your private opinion of this man. You drew the character. What do you think of him as a type, how would you classify him?"

"As the greatest criminal the world has yet produced," replied Shirley without a moment's hesitation.

The financier looked at the girl in unfeigned astonishment.

"Criminal?" he echoed.

"Yes, criminal," repeated Shirley decisively. "He is avarice, egotism, and ambition incarnate. He loves money because he loves power, and he loves power more than his fellow man."

Ryder laughed uneasily. Decidedly, this girl had opinions of her own which she was not backward to express.

"Isn't that rather strong?" he asked.

" I don't think so," replied Shirley. Then quickly she asked: " But what does it matter? No such man exists."

" No, of course not," said Ryder, and he relapsed into silence.

Yet while he said nothing, the plutocrat was watching his visitor closely from under his thick eyebrows. She seemed supremely unconscious of his scrutiny. Her aristocratic, thoughtful face gave no sign that any ulterior motive had actuated her evidently very hostile attitude against him. That he was in her mind when she drew the character of John Broderick there was no doubt possible. No matter how she might evade the identification, he was convinced he was the hero of her book. Why had she attacked him so bitterly? At first, it occurred to him that blackmail might be her object; she might be going to ask for money as the price of future silence. Yet it needed but a glance at her refined and modest demeanour to dispel that idea as absurd. Then he remembered, too, that it was not she who had sought this interview, but himself. No, she was no blackmailer. More probably she was a dreamer—one of those meddling sociologists who, under pretence of bettering the conditions of the working classes, stir up discontent and bitterness of feeling. As such, she might prove more to be feared than a mere blackmailer whom he could buy off with money. He knew he was not popular, but he was no worse than the other captains of industry. It was a cut-throat game at best. Competition was the soul of commercial life, and if he had outwitted his competitors and made himself richer than all of them, he was not a criminal for that. But all these attacks in newspapers and books did not do him any good. One day the people might take these demagogic writings seriously and then there would be the devil to pay. He took up the book again and ran over the pages. This certainly was no ordinary girl. She knew more and had a more direct way of saying things than any woman he had ever met. And as he watched her furtively across the desk he wondered how he could use her; how instead of being his enemy, he could make her his friend. If he did not, she would go away and write more such books, and literature of this kind might become a real peril to his interests. Money could do anything; it could secure the services of this woman and prevent her doing further mischief. But how could he employ her? Suddenly an inspiration came to him. For some years he had been collecting material for a history of the Empire Trading Company. She could write it. It would practically be his own biography. Would she undertake it?

Embarrassed by the long silence, Shirley finally broke it by saying:

" But you didn't ask me to call merely to find out what I thought of my own work."

" No," replied Ryder slowly, " I want you to do some work for me."

He opened a drawer at the left-hand side of his desk and took out several sheets of foolscap and a number of letters. Shirley's heart beat faster as she caught sight of the letters. Were her father's among them? She wondered what kind of work John Burkett Ryder had for her to do and if she would do it whatever it was. Some literary work probably, compiling or something of that kind. If it was well paid, why should she not accept? There would be nothing humiliating in it; it would not tie her hands in any way. She was a professional writer in the market to be employed by whoever could pay the price. Besides, such work might give her better opportunities to secure the letters of which she was in search. Gathering in one pile all the papers he had removed from the drawer, Mr. Ryder said:

" I want you to put my biography together from this material. But first," he added, taking up " The

American Octopus," " I want to know where you got the details of this man's life."

"Oh, for the most part—imagination, newspapers, magazines," replied Shirley carelessly. "You know the American millionaire is a very overworked topic just now—and naturally I've read——"

"Yes, I understand," he said, "but I refer to what you haven't read—what you couldn't have read. For example, here." He turned to a page marked in the book and read aloud: "*As an evidence of his petty vanity, when a youth he had a beautiful Indian girl tattooed just above the forearm.*" Ryder leaned eagerly forward as he asked her searchingly: "Now who told you that I had my arm tattooed when I was a boy?"

"Have you?" laughed Shirley nervously. "What a curious coincidence!"

"Let me read you another coincidence," said Ryder meaningly. He turned to another part of the book and read: "*the same eternal long black cigar always between his lips . . . .*"

"General Grant smoked, too," interrupted Shirley. "All men who think deeply along material lines seem to smoke."

"Well, we'll let that go. But how about this?" He turned back a few pages and read: "*John Broderick had loved, when a young man, a girl who lived in*"

*Vermont, but circumstances separated them."* He stopped and stared at Shirley a moment and then he said: " I loved a girl when I was a lad and she came from Vermont, and circumstances separated us. That isn't coincidence, for presently you make John Broderick marry a young woman who had money. I married a girl with money."

" Lots of men marry for money," remarked Shirley.

" I said *with* money, not for money," retorted Ryder. Then turning again to the book, he said: " Now, this is what I can't understand, for no one could have told you this but I myself. Listen." He read aloud: *"With all his physical bravery and personal courage, John Broderick was intensely afraid of death. It was on his mind constantly."* " Who told you that? " he demanded somewhat roughly. " I swear I've never mentioned it to a living soul."

" Most men who amass money are afraid of death," replied Shirley with outward composure, " for death is about the only thing that can separate them from their money."

Ryder laughed, but it was a hollow, mocking laugh, neither sincere nor hearty. It was a laugh such as the devil may have given when driven out of heaven.

" You're quite a character! " He laughed again, and Shirley, catching the infection, laughed, too.

284

"It's me and it isn't me," went on Ryder flourishing the book. "This fellow Broderick is all right; he's successful and he's great, but I don't like his finish."

"It's logical," ventured Shirley.

"It's cruel," insisted Ryder.

"So is the man who reverses the divine law and hates his neighbour instead of loving him," retorted Shirley.

She spoke more boldly, beginning to feel more sure of her ground, and it amused her to fence in this way with the man of millions. So far, she thought, he had not got the best of her. She was fast becoming used to him, and her first feeling of intimidation was passing away.

"Um!" grunted Ryder, "you're a curious girl; upon my word you interest me!" He took the mass of papers lying at his elbow and pushed them over to her. "Here," he said, "I want you to make as clever a book out of this chaos as you did out of your own imagination."

Shirley turned the papers over carelessly.

"So you think your life is a good example to follow?" she asked with a tinge of irony.

"Isn't it?" he demanded.

The girl looked him square in the face.

"Suppose," she said, "we all wanted to follow it,

suppose we all wanted to be the richest, the most powerful personage in the world?"

"Well—what then?" he demanded.

"I think it would postpone the era of the Brotherhood of man indefinitely, don't you?"

"I never thought of it from that point of view," admitted the billionaire. "Really," he added, "you're an extraordinary girl. Why, you can't be more than twenty—or so."

"I'm twenty-four—or so," smiled Shirley.

Ryder's face expanded in a broad smile. He admired this girl's pluck and ready wit. He grew more amiable and tried to gain her confidence. In a coaxing tone he said:

"Come, where did you get those details? Take me into your confidence."

"I have taken you into my confidence," laughed Shirley, pointing at her book. "It cost you $1.50!" Turning over the papers he had put before her she said presently: "I don't know about this."

"You don't think my life would make good reading?" he asked with some asperity.

"It might," she replied slowly, as if unwilling to commit herself as to its commercial or literary value. Then she said frankly: "To tell you the honest truth, I don't consider mere genius in money-making is sufficient provocation for rushing into print. You see, unless you come to a bad end, it would have no moral."

Ignoring the not very flattering insinuation contained in this last speech, the plutocrat continued to urge her:

" You can name your own price if you will do the work," he said. " Two, three or even five thousand dollars. It's only a few months' work."

" Five thousand dollars?" echoed Shirley. " That's a lot of money." Smiling, she added: " It appeals to my commercial sense. But I'm afraid the subject does not arouse my enthusiasm from an artistic standpoint."

Ryder seemed amused at the idea of any one hesitating to make five thousand dollars. He knew that writers do not run across such opportunities everyday.

" Upon my word," he said, " I don't know why I'm so anxious to get you to do the work. I suppose it's because you don't want to. You remind me of my son. Ah, he's a problem!"

Shirley started involuntarily when Ryder mentioned his son. But he did not notice it.

" Why, is he wild?" she asked, as if only mildly interested.

" Oh, no, I wish he were," said Ryder.

" Fallen in love with the wrong woman, I suppose," she said.

" Something of the sort—how did you guess?"
asked Ryder surprised.

Shirley coughed to hide her embarrassment and replied indifferently.

" So many boys do that. Besides," she added with
a mischievous twinkle in her eyes, " I can hardly imagine that any woman would be the right one unless
you selected her yourself! "

Ryder made no answer. He folded his arms and
gazed at her. Who was this woman who knew him
so well, who could read his inmost thoughts, who
never made a mistake? After a silence he said:

" Do you know you say the strangest things? "

" Truth is strange," replied Shirley carelessly. " I
don't suppose you hear it very often."

" Not in that form," admitted Ryder.

Shirley had taken on to her lap some of the letters
he had passed her, and was perusing them one after
another.

" All these letters from Washington consulting you
on politics and finance—they won't interest the world."

" My secretary picked them out," explained Ryder.
" Your artistic sense will tell you what to use."

" Does your son still love this girl? I mean the one
you object to? " inquired Shirley as she went on sorting the papers.

# THE MOUSE

"Oh, no, he does not care for her any more," answered Ryder hastily.

"Yes, he does; he still loves her," said Shirley positively.

"How do *you* know?" asked Ryder amazed.

"From the way you say he doesn't," retorted Shirley.

Ryder gave his caller a look in which admiration was mingled with astonishment.

"You are right again," he said. "The idiot does love the girl."

"Bless his heart," said Shirley to herself. Aloud she said:

"I hope they'll both outwit you."

Ryder laughed in spite of himself. This young woman certainly interested him more than any other he had ever known.

"I don't think I ever met anyone in my life quite like you," he said.

"What's the objection to the girl?" demanded Shirley.

"Every objection. I don't want her in my family."

"Anything against her character?"

To better conceal the keen interest she took in the personal turn the conversation had taken, Shirley pretended to be more busy than ever with the papers.

"Yes—that is no—not that I know of," replied Ryder. "But because a woman has a good character, that doesn't necessarily make her a desirable match, does it?"

"It's a point in her favor, isn't it?"

"Yes—but——" He hesitated as if uncertain what to say.

"You know men well, don't you, Mr. Ryder?"

"I've met enough to know them pretty well," he replied.

"Why don't you study women for a change?" she asked. "That would enable you to understand a great many things that I don't think are quite clear to you now."

Ryder laughed good humouredly. It was decidedly a novel sensation to have someone lecturing him.

"I'm studying you," he said, "but I don't seem to make much headway. A woman like you whose mind isn't spoiled by the amusement habit has great possibilities—great possibilities. Do you know you're the first woman I ever took into my confidence—I mean at sight?" Again he fixed her with that keen glance which in his business life had taught him how to read men. He continued: "I'm acting on sentiment—something I rarely do, but I can't help it. I

like you, upon my soul I do, and I'm going to introduce you to my wife—my son——"

He took the telephone from his desk as if he were
going to use it.

"What a commander-in-chief you would have made
—how natural it is for you to command," exclaimed
Shirley in a burst of admiration that was half real,
half mocking. "I suppose you always tell people what
they are to do and how they are to do it. You are
a born general. You know I've often thought that
Napoleon and Cæsar and Alexander must have been
great domestic leaders as well as imperial rulers. I'm
sure of it now."

Ryder listened to her in amazement. He was not
quite sure if she were making fun of him or not.

"Well, of all—" he began. Then interrupting himself he said amiably: "Won't you do me the honour
to meet my family?"

Shirley smiled sweetly and bowed.

"Thank you, Mr. Ryder, I will."

She rose from her seat and leaned over the manu-
scripts to conceal the satisfaction this promise of an
introduction to the family circle gave her. She was
quick to see that it meant more visits to the house, and
other and perhaps better opportunities to find the objects of her search. Ryder lifted the receiver of his

telephone and talked to his secretary in another room, while Shirley, who was still standing, continued examining the papers and letters.

" Is that you, Bagley? What's that? General Dodge? Get rid of him. I can't see him to-day. Tell him to come to-morrow. What's that? My son wants to see me? Tell him to come to the phone."

At that instant Shirley gave a little cry, which in vain she tried to suppress. Ryder looked up.

" What's the matter? " he demanded startled.

" Nothing—nothing ! " she replied in a hoarse whisper. " I pricked myself with a pin. Don't mind me."

She had just come across her father's missing letters, which had got mixed up, evidently without Ryder's knowledge, in the mass of papers he had handed her. Prepared as she was to find the letters somewhere in the house, she never dreamed that fate would put them so easily and so quickly into her hands; the suddenness of their appearance and the sight of her father's familiar signature affected her almost like a shock. Now she had them, she must not let them go again; yet how could she keep them unobserved? Could she conceal them? Would he miss them? She tried to slip them in her bosom while Ryder was busy at the 'phone, but he suddenly glanced in her direction and caught her eye. She still held the letters in her hand, which shook from nervousness, but he noticed nothing and went on speaking through the 'phone:

"Hallo, Jefferson, boy! You want to see me. Can you wait till I'm through? I've got a lady here. Going away? Nonsense! Determined, eh? Well, I can't keep you here if you've made up your mind. You want to say good-bye. Come up in about five minutes and I'll introduce you to a very interesting person."

He laughed and hung up the receiver. Shirley was all unstrung, trying to overcome the emotion which her discovery had caused her, and in a strangely altered voice, the result of the nervous strain she was under, she said:

"You want me to come here?"

She looked up from the letters she was reading across to Ryder, who was standing watching her on the other side of the desk. He caught her glance and, leaning over to take some manuscript, he said:

"Yes, I don't want these papers to get——"

His eye suddenly rested on the letters she was holding. He stopped short, and reaching forward he tried to snatch them from her.

"What have you got there?" he exclaimed.

He took the letters and she made no resistance. It

would be folly to force the issue now, she thought. Another opportunity would present itself. Ryder locked the letters up very carefully in the drawer on the left-hand side of his desk, muttering to himself rather than speaking to Shirley:

"How on earth did they get among my other papers?"

"From Judge Rossmore, were they not?" said Shirley boldly.

"How did you know it was Judge Rossmore?" demanded Ryder suspiciously. "I didn't know that his name had been mentioned."

"I saw his signature," she said simply. Then she added: "He's the father of the girl you don't like, isn't he?"

"Yes, he's the——"

A cloud came over the financier's face; his eyes darkened, his jaws snapped and he clenched his fist.

"How you must hate him!" said Shirley, who observed the change.

"Not at all," replied Ryder recovering his self-possession and suavity of manner. "I disagree with his politics and his methods, but——I know very little about him except that he is about to be removed from office."

"About to be?" echoed Shirley. "So his fate is

decided even before he is tried?" The girl laughed
bitterly. "Yes," she went on, "some of the newspapers are beginning to think he is innocent of the
things of which he is accused."

"Do they?" said Ryder indifferently.

"Yes," she persisted, "most people are on his
side."

She planted her elbows on the desk in front of her,
and looking him squarely in the face, she asked him
point blank:

"Whose side are you on—really and truly?"

Ryder winced. What right had this woman, a
stranger both to Judge Rossmore and himself, to come
here and catechise him? He restrained his impatience
with difficulty as he replied:

"Whose side am I on? Oh, I don't know that I
am on any side. I don't know that I give it much
thought. I——"

"Do you think this man deserves to be punished?"
she demanded.

She had resumed her seat at the desk and partly
regained her self-possession.

"Why do you ask? What is your interest in this
matter?"

"I don't know," she replied evasively; "his case
interests me, that's all. Its rather romantic. Your

son loves this man's daughter. He is in disgrace—
many seem to think unjustly." Her voice trembled
with emotion as she continued: "I have heard from
one source or another—you know I am acquainted
with a number of newspaper men—I have heard that
life no longer has any interest for him, that he is not
only disgraced but beggared, that he is pining away
slowly, dying of a broken heart, that his wife and
daughter are in despair. Tell me, do you think he
deserves such a fate?"

Ryder remained thoughtful a moment, and then he
replied:

"No, I do not—no——"

Thinking that she had touched his sympathies, Shirley followed up her advantage:

"Oh, then, why not come to his rescue—you, who
are so rich, so powerful; you, who can move the scales
of justice at your will—save this man from humiliation and disgrace!"

Ryder shrugged his shoulders, and his face expressed
weariness, as if the subject had begun to bore him.

"My dear girl, you don't understand. His removal
is necessary."

Shirley's face became set and hard. There was a
contemptuous ring to her words as she retorted:

"Yet you admit that he may be innocent!"

# THE MOUSE

"Even if I knew it as a fact, I couldn't move."

"Do you mean to say that if you had positive proof?" She pointed to the drawer in the desk where he had placed the letters. "If you had absolute proof in that drawer, for instance? Wouldn't you help him then?"

Ryder's face grew cold and inscrutable; he now wore his fighting mask.

"Not even if I had the absolute proof in that drawer?" he snapped viciously.

"Have you absolute proof in that drawer?" she demanded.

"I repeat that even if I had, I could not expose the men who have been my friends. Its *noblesse oblige* in politics as well as in society, you know."

He smiled again at her, as if he had recovered his good humour after their sharp passage at arms.

"Oh, it's politics—that's what the papers said. And you believe him innocent. Well, you must have some grounds for your belief."

"Not necessarily——"

"You said that even if you had the proofs, you could not produce them without sacrificing your friends, showing that your friends are interested in having this man put off the bench—" She stopped and burst into hysterical laughter. "Oh, I think you're having a joke at my expense," she went on, " just to see how far you can lead me. I daresay Judge Rossmore deserves all he gets. Oh, yes—I'm sure he deserves it." She rose and walked to the other side of the room to conceal her emotion.

Ryder watched her curiously.

" My dear young lady, how you take this matter to heart!"

" Please forgive me," laughed Shirley, and averting her face to conceal the fact that her eyes were filled with tears. " It's my artistic temperament, I suppose. It's always getting me into trouble. It appealed so strongly to my sympathies—this story of hopeless love between two young people—with the father of the girl hounded by corrupt politicians and unscrupulous financiers. It was too much for me. Ah! ah! I forgot where I was!"

She leaned against a chair, sick and faint from nervousness, her whole body trembling. At that moment there was a knock at the library door and Jefferson Ryder appeared. Not seeing Shirley, whose back was towards him, he advanced to greet his father.

" You told me to come up in five minutes," he said. " I just wanted to say——"

" Miss Green," said Ryder, Sr., addressing Shirley and ignoring whatever it was that the young man wanted to say, " this is my son Jefferson. Jeff—this is Miss Green."

Jefferson looked in the direction indicated and stood as if rooted to the floor. He was so surprised that he was struck dumb. Finally, recovering himself, he exclaimed:

" Shirley! "

" Yes, Shirley Green, the author," explained Ryder, Sr., not noticing the note of familiar recognition in his exclamation.

Shirley advanced, and holding out her hand to Jefferson, said demurely:

" I am very pleased to meet you, Mr. Ryder." Then quickly, in an undertone, she added: " Be careful; don't betray me! "

Jefferson was so astounded that he did not see the outstretched hand. All he could do was to stand and stare first at her and then at his father.

" Why don't you shake hands with her? " said Ryder, Sr. " She won't bite you." Then he added: " Miss Green is going to do some literary work for me, so we shall see a great deal of her. It's too bad you're going away! " He chuckled at his own pleasantry.

" Father! " blurted out Jefferson, " I came to say that I've changed my mind. You did not want me to go, and I feel I ought to do something to please you."

"Good boy," said Ryder pleased. "Now you're talking common sense." He turned to Shirley, who was getting ready to make her departure: "Well, Miss Green, we may consider the matter settled. You undertake the work at the price I named and finish it as soon as you can. Of course, you will have to consult me a good deal as you go along, so I think it would be better for you to come and stay here while the work is progressing. Mrs. Ryder can give you a suite of rooms to yourself, where you will be undisturbed and you will have all your material close at hand. What do you say?"

Shirley was silent for a moment. She looked first at Ryder and then at his son, and from them her glance went to the little drawer on the left-hand side of the desk. Then she said quietly:

"As you think best, Mr. Ryder. I am quite willing to do the work here."

Ryder, Sr., escorted her to the top of the landing and watched her as she passed down the grand staircase, ushered by the gorgeously uniformed flunkies, to the front door and the street.

## CHAPTER XIII

SHIRLEY entered upon her new duties in the Ryder household two days later. She had returned to her rooms the evening of her meeting with the financier in a state bordering upon hysteria. The day's events had been so extraordinary that it seemed to her they could not be real, and that she must be in a dream. The car ride to Seventy-fourth Street, the interview in the library, the discovery of her father's letters, the offer to write the biography, and, what to her was still more important, the invitation to go and live in the Ryder home—all these incidents were so remarkable and unusual that it was only with difficulty that the girl persuaded herself that they were not figments of a disordered brain.

But it was all true enough. The next morning's mail brought a letter from Mrs. Ryder, who wrote to the effect that Mr. Ryder would like the work to begin at once, and adding that a suite of rooms would be ready for her the following afternoon. Shirley did not hesitate. Everything was to be gained by making the Ryder residence her headquarters, her father's very life depended upon the successful outcome of her present mission, and this unhoped for opportunity practically ensured success. She immediately wrote to Massapequa. One letter was to her mother, saying that she was extending her visit beyond the time originally planned. The other letter was to Stott. She told him all about the interview with Ryder, informed him of the discovery of the letters, and after explaining the nature of the work offered to her, said that her address for the next few weeks would be in care of John Burkett Ryder. All was going better than she had dared to hope. Everything seemed to favour their plan. Her first step, of course, while in the Ryder home, would be to secure possession of her father's letters, and these she would dispatch at once to Massapequa, so they could be laid before the Senate without delay.

So, after settling accounts with her landlady and packing up her few belongings, Shirley lost no time in transferring herself to the more luxurious quarters provided for her in the ten-million-dollar mansion uptown.

At the Ryder house she was received cordially and with every mark of consideration. The housekeeper came down to the main hall to greet her when she arrived and escorted her to the suite of rooms, comprising a small working library, a bedroom simply but daintily furnished in pink and white and a private bathroom, which had been specially prepared for her convenience and comfort, and here presently she was joined by Mrs. Ryder.

"Dear me," exclaimed the financier's wife, staring curiously at Shirley, "what a young girl you are to have made such a stir with a book! How did you do it? I'm sure I couldn't. It's as much as I can do to write a letter, and half the time that's not legible."

"Oh, it wasn't so hard," laughed Shirley. "It was the subject that appealed rather than any special skill of mine. The trusts and their misdeeds are the favourite topics of the hour. The whole country is talking about nothing else. My book came at the right time, that's all."

Although "The American Octopus" was a direct attack on her own husband, Mrs. Ryder secretly admired this young woman, who had dared to speak a few blunt truths. It was a courage which, alas! she had always lacked herself, but there was a certain satisfaction in knowing there were women in the world not entirely cowed by the tyrant Man.

"I have always wanted a daughter," went on Mrs.

Ryder, becoming confidential, while Shirley removed her things and made herself at home; " girls of your age are so companionable." Then, abruptly, she asked: " Do your parents live in New York? "

Shirley's face flushed and she stooped over her trunk to hide her embarrassment.

" No—not at present," she answered evasively. " My mother and father are in the country."

She was afraid that more questions of a personal nature would follow, but apparently Mrs. Ryder was not in an inquisitive mood, for she asked nothing further. She only said:

" I have a son, but I don't see much of him. You must meet my Jefferson. He is such a nice boy."

Shirley tried to look unconcerned as she replied:

" I met him yesterday. Mr. Ryder introduced him to me."

" Poor lad, he has his troubles too," went on Mrs. Ryder. " He's in love with a girl, but his father wants him to marry someone else. They're quarrelling over it all the time."

" Parents shouldn't interfere in matters of the heart," said Shirley decisively." What is more serious than the choosing of a life companion, and who are better entitled to make a free selection than they who are going to spend the rest of their days together?

304

# THE MOUSE

Of course, it is a father's duty to give his son the benefit of his riper experience, but to insist on a marriage based only on business interests is little less than a crime. There are considerations more important if the union is to be a happy or a lasting one. The chief thing is that the man should feel real attachment for the woman he marries. Two people who are to live together as man and wife must be compatible in tastes and temper. You cannot mix oil and water. It is these selfish marriages which keep our divorce courts busy. Money alone won't buy happiness in marriage."

" No," sighed Mrs. Ryder, " no one knows that better than I."

The financier's wife was already most favourably impressed with her guest, and she chatted on as if she had known Shirley for years. It was rarely that she had heard so young a woman express such common-sense views, and the more she talked with her the less surprised she was that she was the author of a much-discussed book. Finally, thinking that Shirley might prefer to be alone, she rose to go, bidding her make herself thoroughly at home and to ring for anything she might wish. A maid had been assigned to look exclusively after her wants, and she could have her meals served in her room or else have them with the family as she liked. But Shirley, not caring to encounter Mr. Ryder's cold, searching stare more often than necessary, said she would prefer to take her meals alone.

Left to herself, Shirley settled down to work in earnest. Mr. Ryder had sent to her room all the material for the biography, and soon she was completely absorbed in the task of sorting and arranging letters, making extracts from records, compiling data, etc., laying the foundations for the important book she was to write. She wondered what they would call it, and she smiled as a peculiarly appropriate title flashed through her mind—" The History of a Crime." Yet she thought they could hardly infringe on Victor Hugo; perhaps the best title was the simplest " The History of the Empire Trading Company." Everyone would understand that it told the story of John Burkett Ryder's remarkable career from his earliest beginnings to the present time. She worked feverishly all that evening getting the material into shape, and the following day found her early at her desk. No one disturbed her and she wrote steadily on until noon, Mrs. Ryder only once putting her head in the door to wish her good morning.

After luncheon, Shirley decided that the weather was too glorious to remain indoors. Her health must not be jeopardized even to advance the interests of the Colossus, so she put on her hat and left the house to go for a walk. The air smelled sweet to her after being confined so long indoor, and she walked with a more elastic and buoyant step than she had since her return home. Turning down Fifth Avenue, she entered the park at Seventy-second Street, following the pathway until she came to the bend in the driveway opposite the Casino. The park was almost deserted at that hour, and there was a delightful sense of solitude and a sweet scent of new-mown hay from the freshly cut lawns. She found an empty bench, well shaded by an overspreading tree, and she sat down, grateful for the rest and quiet.

She wondered what Jefferson thought of her action in coming to his father's house practically in disguise and under an assumed name. She must see him at once, for in him lay her hope of obtaining possession of the letters. Certainly she felt no delicacy or compunction in asking Jefferson to do her this service. The letters belonged to her father and they were being wrongfully withheld with the deliberate purpose of doing him an injury. She had a moral if not a legal right to recover the letters in any way that she could.

She was so deeply engrossed in her thoughts that

she had not noticed a hansom cab which suddenly drew up with a jerk at the curb opposite her bench. A man jumped out. It was Jefferson.

"Hello, Shirley," he cried gaily; "who would have expected to find you rusticating on a bench here? I pictured you grinding away at home doing literary stunts for the governor." He grinned and then added: "Come for a drive. I want to talk to you."

Shirley demurred. No, she could not spare the time. Yet, she thought to herself, why was not this a good opportunity to explain to Jefferson how he came to find her in his father's library masquerading under another name, and also to ask him to secure the letters for her? While she pondered Jefferson insisted, and a few minutes later she found herself sitting beside him in the cab. They started off at a brisk pace, Shirley sitting with her head back, enjoying the strong breeze caused by the rapid motion.

"Now tell me," he said, "what does it all mean? I was so startled at seeing you in the library the other day that I almost betrayed you. How did you come to call on father?"

Briefly Shirley explained everything. She told him how Mr. Ryder had written to her asking her to call and see him, and how she had eagerly seized at this last straw in the hope of helping her father,

308

# THE MOUSE

She told him about the letters, explaining how necessary they were for her father's defence and how she had discovered them. Mr. Ryder, she said, had seemed to take a fancy to her and had asked her to remain in the house as his guest while she was compiling his biography, and she had accepted the offer, not so much for the amount of money involved as for the splendid opportunity it afforded her to gain possession of the letters.

" So that is the mysterious work you spoke of—to get those letters? " said Jefferson.

" Yes, that is my mission. It was a secret. I couldn't tell you; I couldn't tell anyone. Only Judge Stott knows. He is aware I have found them and is hourly expecting to receive them from me. And now," she said, " I want your help."

His only answer was to grasp tighter the hand she had laid in his. She knew that she would not have to explain the nature of the service she wanted. He understood.

" Where are the letters? " he demanded.

" In the left-hand drawer of your father's desk," she answered.

He was silent for a few moments, and then he said simply :

" I will get them."

The cab by this time had got as far as Claremont, and from the hill summit they had a splendid view of the broad sweep of the majestic Hudson and the towering walls of the blue palisades. The day was so beautiful and the air so invigorating that Jefferson suggested a ramble along the banks of the river. They could leave the cab at Claremont and drive back to the city later. Shirley was too grateful to him for his promise of coöperation to make any further opposition, and soon they were far away from beaten highways, down on the banks of the historic stream, picking flowers and laughing merrily like two truant children bent on a self-made holiday. The place they had reached was just outside the northern boundaries of Harlem, a sylvan spot still unspoiled by the rude invasion of the flat-house builder. The land, thickly wooded, sloped down sharply to the water, and the perfect quiet was broken only by the washing of the tiny surf against the river bank and the shrill notes of the birds in the trees.

Although it was late in October the day was warm, and Shirley soon tired of climbing over bramble-entangled verdure. The rich grass underfoot looked cool and inviting, and the natural slope of the ground affording an ideal resting-place, she sat there, with Jefferson stretched out at her feet, both watching idly the dancing waters of the broad Hudson, spangled with gleams of light, as they swept swiftly by on their journey to the sea.

"Shirley," said Jefferson suddenly, "I suppose you saw that ridiculous story about my alleged engagement to Miss Roberts. I hope you understood that it was done without my consent."

"If I did not guess it, Jeff," she answered, "your assurance would be sufficient. Besides," she added, "what right have I to object?"

"But I want you to have the right," he replied earnestly. "I'm going to stop this Roberts nonsense in a way my father hardly anticipates. I'm just waiting a chance to talk to him. I'll show him the absurdity of announcing me engaged to a girl who is about to elope with his private secretary!"

"Elope with the secretary?" exclaimed Shirley.

Jefferson told her all about the letter he had found on the staircase, and the Hon. Fitzroy Bagley's plans for a runaway marriage with the senator's wealthy daughter.

"It's a godsend to me," he said gleefully. "Their plan is to get married next Wednesday. I'll see my father on Tuesday; I'll put the evidence in his hands, and I don't think," he added grimly, "he'll bother me any more about Miss Roberts."

"So you're not going away now?" said Shirley, smiling down at him.

He sat up and leaned over towards her.

"I can't, Shirley, I simply can't," he replied, his voice trembling. "You are more to me than I dreamed a woman could ever be. I realize it more forcibly every day. There is no use fighting against it. Without you, my work, my life means nothing."

Shirley shook her head and averted her eyes.

"Don't let us speak of that, Jeff," she pleaded gently. "I told you I did not belong to myself while my father was in peril."

"But I must speak of it," he interrupted. "Shirley, you do yourself an injustice as well as me. You are not indifferent to me—I feel that. Then why raise this barrier between us?"

A soft light stole into the girl's eyes. Ah, it was good to feel there was someone to whom she was everything in the world!

"Don't ask me to betray my trust, Jeff," she faltered. "You know I am not indifferent to you—far from it. But I——"

He came closer until his face nearly touched hers.

"I love you—I want you," he murmured feverishly. "Give me the right to claim you before all the world as my future wife!"

# THE MOUSE

Every note of his rich, manly voice, vibrating with impetuous passion, sounded in Shirley's ear like a soft caress. She closed her eyes. A strange feeling of languor was stealing over her, a mysterious thrill passed through her whole body. The eternal, inevitable sex instinct was disturbing, for the first time, a woman whose life had been singularly free from such influences, putting to flight all the calculations and resolves her cooler judgment had made. The sensuous charm of the place—the distant splash of the water, the singing of the birds, the fragrance of the trees and grass—all these symbols of the joy of life conspired to arouse the love-hunger of the woman. Why, after all, should she not know happiness like other women? She had a sacred duty to perform, it was true; but would it be less well done because she declined to stifle the natural leanings of her womanhood? Both her soul and her body called out: "Let this man love you, give yourself to him, he is worthy of your love."

Half unconsciously, she listened to his ardent wooing, her eyes shut, as he spoke quickly, passionately, his breath warm upon her cheek:

"Shirley, I offer you all the devotion a man can give a woman. Say the one word that will make me the happiest or the most wretched of men. Yes or

313

no! Only think well before you wreck my life. I love you—I love you! I will wait for you if need be until the crack of doom. Say—say you will be my wife!"

She opened her eyes. His face was bent close over hers. Their lips almost touched.

"Yes, Jefferson," she murmured, "I do love you!"

His lips met hers in a long, passionate kiss. Her eyes closed and an ecstatic thrill seemed to convulse her entire being. The birds in the trees overhead sang in more joyful chorus in celebration of the betrothal.

## CHAPTER XIV

IT was nearly seven o'clock when Shirley got back to Seventy-fourth Street. No one saw her come in, and she went direct to her room, and after a hasty dinner, worked until late into the night on her book to make up for lost time. The events of the afternoon caused her considerable uneasiness. She reproached herself for her weakness and for having yielded so readily to the impulse of the moment. She had said only what was the truth when she admitted she loved Jefferson, but what right had she to dispose of her future while her father's fate was still uncertain? Her conscience troubled her, and when she came to reason it out calmly, the more impossible seemed their union from every point of view. How could she become the daughter-in-law of the man who had ruined her own father? The idea was preposterous, and hard as the sacrifice would be, Jefferson must be made to see it in that light. Their engagement was the greatest folly; it bound each of them when nothing but unhappiness could

possibly come of it. She was sure now that she loved
Jefferson. It would be hard to give him up, but there
are times and circumstances when duty and principle
must prevail over all other considerations, and this
she felt was one of them.

The following morning she received a letter from
Stott. He was delighted to hear the good news regarding her important discovery, and he urged her
to lose no time in securing the letters and forwarding
them to Massapequa, when he would immediately
go to Washington and lay them before the Senate.
Documentary evidence of that conclusive nature, he
went on to say, would prove of the very highest value
in clearing her father's name. He added that the
judge and her mother were as well as circumstances
would permit, and that they were not in the least worried about her protracted absence. Her Aunt Milly
had already returned to Europe, and Eudoxia was still
threatening to leave daily.

Shirley needed no urging. She quite realized the
importance of acting quickly, but it was not easy to
get at the letters. The library was usually kept locked
when the great man was away, and on the few occasions when access to it was possible, the lynx-eyed
Mr. Bagley was always on guard. Short as had
been her stay in the Ryder household, Shirley already

shared Jefferson's antipathy to the English secretary, whose manner grew more supercilious and overbearing as he drew nearer the date when he expected to run off with one of the richest catches of the season. He had not sought the acquaintance of his employer's biographer since her arrival, and, with the exception of a rude stare, had not deigned to notice her, which attitude of haughty indifference was all the more remarkable in view of the fact that the Hon. Fitzroy usually left nothing unturned to cultivate a flirtatious intimacy with every attractive female he met. The truth was that what with Mr. Ryder's demands upon his services and his own preparations for his coming matrimonial venture, in which he had so much at stake, he had neither time nor inclination to indulge his customary amorous diversions.

Miss Roberts had called at the house several times, ostensibly to see Mrs. Ryder, and when introduced to Shirley she had condescended to give the latter a supercilious nod. Her conversation was generally of the silly, vacuous sort, concerning chiefly new dresses or bonnets, and Shirley at once read her character— frivolous, amusement-loving, empty-headed, irresponsible—just the kind of girl to do something foolish without weighing the consequences. After chatting a few moments with Mrs. Ryder she would usually vanish, and one day, after one of these mysterious disappearances, Shirley happened to pass the library and caught sight of her and Mr. Bagley conversing in subdued and eager tones. It was very evident that the elopement scheme was fast maturing. If the scandal was to be prevented, Jefferson ought to see his father and acquaint him with the facts without delay. It was probable that at the same time he would make an effort to secure the letters. Meantime she must be patient. Too much hurry might spoil everything.

So the days passed, Shirley devoting almost all her time to the history she had undertaken. She saw nothing of Ryder, Sr., but a good deal of his wife, to whom she soon became much attached. She found her an amiable, good-natured woman, entirely free from that offensive arrogance and patronizing condescension which usually marks the parvenue as distinct from the thoroughbred. Mrs. Ryder had no claims to distinguished lineage; on the contrary, she was the daughter of a country grocer when the then rising oil man married her, and of educational advantages she had had little or none. It was purely by accident that she was the wife of the richest man in the world, and while she enjoyed the prestige her husband's prominence gave her, she never allowed it to turn her head. She gave away large sums for charitable purposes and, strange to say, when the gift came direct from her, the money was never returned on the plea that it was "tainted." She shared her husband's dislike for entertaining, and led practically the life of a recluse. The advent of Shirley, therefore, into her quiet and uneventful existence was as welcome as sunshine when it breaks through the clouds after days of gloom. Quite a friendship sprang up between the two women, and when tired of writing, Shirley would go into Mrs. Ryder's room and chat until the financier's wife began to look forward to these little impromptu visits, so much she enjoyed them.

Nothing more had been said concerning Jefferson and Miss Roberts. The young man had not yet seen his father, but his mother knew he was only waiting an opportunity to demand an explanation of the engagement announcements. Her husband, on the other hand, desired the match more than ever, owing to the continued importunities of Senator Roberts. As usual, Mrs. Ryder confided these little domestic troubles to Shirley.

"Jefferson," she said, "is very angry. He is determined not to marry the girl, and when he and his father do meet there'll be another scene."

" What objection has your son to Miss Roberts? " inquired Shirley innocently.

" Oh, the usual reason," sighed the mother, " and I've no doubt he knows best. He's in love with another girl—a Miss Rossmore."

" Oh, yes," answered Shirley simply. " Mr. Ryder spoke of her."

Mrs. Ryder was silent, and presently she left the girl alone with her work.

The next afternoon Shirley was in her room busy writing when there came a tap at her door. Thinking it was another visit from Mrs. Ryder, she did not look up, but cried out pleasantly :

" Come in."

John Ryder entered. He smiled cordially and, as if apologizing for the intrusion, said amiably :

" I thought I'd run up to see how you were getting along."

His coming was so unexpected that for a moment Shirley was startled, but she quickly regained her composure and asked him to take a seat. He seemed pleased to find her making such good progress, and he stopped to answer a number of questions she put to him. Shirley tried to be cordial, but when she looked well at him and noted the keen, hawk-like eyes, the cruel, vindictive lines about the mouth, the square-set, relentless jaw—Wall Street had gone wrong with the Colossus that day and he was still wearing his war paint—she recalled the wrong this man had done her father and she felt how bitterly she hated him. The more her mind dwelt upon it, the more exasperated she was to think she should be there, a guest, under his roof, and it was only with the greatest difficulty that she remained civil.

" What is the moral of your life? " she demanded bluntly.

He was quick to note the contemptuous tone in her voice, and he gave her a keen, searching look as if he were trying to read her thoughts and fathom the reason for her very evident hostility towards him.

" What do you mean? " he asked.

" I mean, What can you show as your life work? Most men whose lives are big enough to call for biographies have done something useful—they have been famous statesmen, eminent scientists, celebrated authors, great inventors. What have you done? "

The question appeared to stagger him. The audacity of any one putting such a question to a man in his own house was incredible. He squared his jaws and his clenched fist descended heavily on the table.

" What have I done? " he cried. " I have built up the greatest fortune ever accumulated by one man.

My fabulous wealth has caused my name to spread to the four corners of the earth. Is that not an achievement to relate to future generations?"

Shirley gave a little shrug of her shoulders.

"Future generations will take no interest in you or your millions," she said calmly. "Our civilization will have made such progress by that time that people will merely wonder why we, in our day, tolerated men of your class so long. Now it is different. The world is money-mad. You are a person of importance in the eyes of the unthinking multitude, but it only envies you your fortune; it does not admire you personally. When you die people will count your millions, not your good deeds."

He laughed cynically and drew up a chair near her desk. As a general thing, John Ryder never wasted words on women. He had but a poor opinion of their mentality, and considered it beneath the dignity of any man to enter into serious argument with a woman. In fact, it was seldom he condescended to argue with anyone. He gave orders and talked to people; he had no patience to be talked to. Yet he found himself listening with interest to this young woman who expressed herself so frankly. It was a decided novelty for him to hear the truth.

"Marry Jefferson yourself."—Act III.

"What do I care what the world says when I'm dead?" he asked with a forced laugh.

"You do care," replied Shirley gravely. "You may school yourself to believe that you are indifferent to the good opinion of your fellow man, but right down in your heart you do care—every man does, whether he be multi-millionaire or a sneak thief."

"You class the two together, I notice," he said bitterly.

"It is often a distinction without a difference," she rejoined promptly.

He remained silent for a moment or two toying nervously with a paper knife. Then, arrogantly, and as if anxious to impress her with his importance, he said:

"Most men would be satisfied if they had accomplished what I have. Do you realize that my wealth is so vast that I scarcely know myself what I am worth? What my fortune will be in another fifty years staggers the imagination. Yet I started with nothing. I made it all myself. Surely I should get credit for that."

"*How* did you make it?" retorted Shirley.

"In America we don't ask how a man makes his money; we ask if he has got any."

"You are mistaken," replied Shirley earnestly. "America is waking up. The conscience of the nation is being aroused. We are coming to realize that the scandals of the last few years were only the fruit of public indifference to sharp business practice. The people will soon ask the dishonest rich man where he got it, and there will have to be an accounting. What account will you be able to give?

He bit his lip and looked at her for a moment without replying. Then, with a faint suspicion of a sneer, he said:

" You are a socialist—perhaps an anarchist! "

" Only the ignorant commit the blunder of confounding the two," she retorted. " Anarchy is a disease; socialism is a science."

" Indeed! " he exclaimed mockingly, " I thought the terms were synonymous. The world regards them both as insane."

Herself an enthusiastic convert to the new political faith that was rising like a flood tide all over the world, the contemptuous tone in which this plutocrat spoke of the coming reorganization of society which was destined to destroy him and his kind spurred her on to renewed argument.

" I imagine," she said sarcastically, " that you would hardly approve any social reform which threatened to interfere with your own business methods. But no matter how you disapprove of socialism on general

324

principles, as a leader of the capitalist class you should understand what socialism is, and not confuse one of the most important movements in modern world-history with the crazy theories of irresponsible cranks. The anarchists are the natural enemies of the entire human family, and would destroy it were their dangerous doctrines permitted to prevail; the socialists, on the contrary, are seeking to save mankind from the degradation, the crime and the folly into which such men as you have driven it."

She spoke impetuously, with the inspired exaltation of a prophet delivering a message to the people. Ryder listened, concealing his impatience with uneasy little coughs.

"Yes," she went on, "I am a socialist and I am proud of it. The whole world is slowly drifting toward socialism as the only remedy for the actual intolerable conditions. It may not come in our time, but it will come as surely as the sun will rise and set to-morrow. Has not the flag of socialism waved recently from the White House? Has not a President of the United States declared that the State must eventually curb the great fortunes? What is that but socialism?"

"True," retorted Ryder grimly, "and that little speech intended for the benefit of the gallery will cost him the nomination at the next Presidential elec-

tion. We don't want in the White House a President
who stirs up class hatred. Our rich men have a right
to what is their own; that is guaranteed them by the
Constitution."

" Is it their own?" interrupted Shirley.

Ryder ignored the insinuation and proceeded:

" What of our boasted free institutions if a man
is to be restricted in what he may and may not do?
If I am clever enough to accumulate millions who can
stop me?"

" The people will stop you," said Shirley calmly.
" It is only a question of time. Their patience is about
exhausted. Put your ear to the ground and listen
to the distant rumbling of the tempest which, sooner
or later, will be unchained in this land, provoked by
the iniquitous practices of organized capital. The
people have had enough of the extortions of the
Trusts. One day they will rise in their wrath and
seize by the throat this knavish plutocracy which, confident in the power of its wealth to procure legal immunity and reckless of its danger, persists in robbing
the public daily. But retribution is at hand. The
growing discontent of the proletariat, the ever-
increasing strikes and labour disputes of all kinds, the
clamour against the Railroads and the Trusts, the evidence of collusion between both—all this is the writing

326

on the wall. The capitalistic system is doomed; socialism will succeed it."

" What is socialism?" he demanded scornfully. "What will it give the public that it has not got already?"

Shirley, who never neglected an opportunity to make a convert, no matter how hardened he might be, picked up a little pamphlet printed for propaganda purposes which she had that morning received by mail.

" Here," she said, " is one of the best and clearest definitions of socialism I have ever read:

" Socialism is common ownership of natural resources and public utilities, and the common operation of all industries for the general good. Socialism is opposed to monopoly, that is, to private ownership of land and the instruments of labor, which is indirect ownership of men; to the wages system, by which labor is legally robbed of a large part of the product of labor; to competition with its enormous waste of effort and its opportunities for the spoliation of the weak by the strong. Socialism is industrial democracy. It is the government of the people by the people and for the people, not in the present restricted sense, but as regards all the common interests of men. Socialism is opposed to oligarchy and monarchy, and therefore to the tyrannies of business cliques and money kings. Socialism is for freedom, not only from the fear of force, but from the fear of want. Socialism proposes real liberty, not merely the right to vote, but the liberty to live for something more than meat and drink.

"Socialism is righteousness in the relations of men. It is based on the fundamentals of religion, the Fatherhood of God and the Brotherhood of men. It seeks through association and equality to realize fraternity. Socialism will destroy the motives which make for cheap manufacturers, poor workmanship and adulterations; it will secure the real utility of things. Use, not exchange, will be the object of labour. Things will be made to serve, not to sell. Socialism will banish war, for private ownership is back of strife between men. Socialism will purify politics, for private capitalism is the great source of political corruption. Socialism will make for education, invention and discovery; it will stimulate the moral development of men. Crime will have lost most of its motive and pauperism will have no excuse. That," said Shirley, as she concluded, "is socialism!"

Ryder shrugged his shoulders and rose to go.

"Delightful," he said ironically, "but in my judgment wholly utopian and impracticable. It's nothing but a gigantic pipe dream. It won't come in this generation nor in ten generations if, indeed, it is ever taken seriously by a majority big enough to put its theories to the test. Socialism does not take into account two great factors that move the world—men's passions and human ambition. If you eliminate ambition you remove the strongest incentive to individual effort. From your own account a socialistic world would be a dreadfully tame place to live in—everybody depressingly good, without any of the feverish turmoil of life as we know it. Such a world would not appeal to me at all. I love the fray—the daily battle of gain and loss, the excitement of making or losing millions. That is my life!"

"Yet what good is your money to you?" insisted Shirley. "You are able to spend only an infinitesimal part of it. You cannot even give it away, for nobody will have any of it."

"Money!" he hissed rather than spoke, "I hate money. It means nothing to me. I have so much that I have lost all idea of its value. I go on accumulating it for only one purpose. It buys power. I love power —that is my passion, my ambition, to rule the world with my gold. Do you know," he went on and leaning over the desk in a dramatic attitude, "that if I chose I could start a panic in Wall Street to-morrow that would shake to their foundations every financial institution in the country? Do you know that I practically control the Congress of the United States and that no legislative measure becomes law unless it has my approval?"

"The public has long suspected as much," replied Shirley. "That is why you are looked upon as a menace to the stability and honesty of our political and commercial life."

An angry answer rose to his lips when the door opened and Mrs. Ryder entered.

"I've been looking for you, John," she said peevishly. "Mr. Bagley told me you were somewhere in the house. Senator Roberts is downstairs."

"He's come about Jefferson and his daughter, I suppose," muttered Ryder. "Well, I'll see him. Where is he?"

"In the library. Kate came with him. She's in my room."

They left Shirley to her writing, and when he had closed the door the financier turned to his wife and said impatiently:

"Now, what are we going to do about Jefferson and Kate? The senator insists on the matter of their marriage being settled one way or another. Where is Jefferson?"

"He came in about half an hour ago. He was upstairs to see me, and I thought he was looking for you," answered the wife.

"Well," replied Ryder determinedly, "he and I have got to understand each other. This can't go on. It shan't."

Mrs. Ryder put her hand on his arm, and said pleadingly:

"Don't be impatient with the boy, John. Remember he is all we have. He is so unhappy. He wants to please us, but——"

"But he insists on pleasing himself," said Ryder completing the sentence.

"I'm afraid, John, that his liking for that Miss Rossmore is more serious than you realize——"

The financier stamped his foot and replied angrily:

"Miss Rossmore! That name seems to confront me at every turn—for years the father, now the daughter! I'm sorry, my dear," he went on more calmly, "that you seem inclined to listen to Jefferson. It only encourages him in his attitude towards me. Kate would make him an excellent wife, while what do we know about the other woman? Are you willing to sacrifice your son's future to a mere boyish whim?"

Mrs. Ryder sighed.

"It's very hard," she said, "for a mother to know what to advise. Miss Green says——"

"What!" exclaimed her husband, "you have consulted Miss Green on the subject?"

"Yes," answered his wife, "I don't know how I came to tell her, but I did. I seem to tell her everything. I find her such a comfort, John. I haven't had an attack of nerves since that girl has been in the house."

"She is certainly a superior woman," admitted Ryder. "I wish she'd ward that Rossmore girl off. I wish she——" He stopped abruptly as if not venturing to give expression to his thoughts, even to his wife. Then he said: "If she were Kate Roberts she wouldn't let Jeff slip through her fingers."

"I have often wished," went on Mrs. Ryder, "that Kate were more like Shirley Green. I don't think we would have any difficulty with Jeff then."

"Kate is the daughter of Senator Roberts, and if this marriage is broken off in any way without the senator's consent, he is in a position to injure my interests materially. If you see Jefferson send him to me in the library. I'll go and keep Roberts in good humour until he comes."

He went downstairs and Mrs. Ryder proceeded to her apartments, where she found Jefferson chatting with Kate. She at once delivered Ryder Sr.'s message.

"Jeff, your father wants to see you in the library."

"Yes, I want to see him," answered the young man grimly, and after a few moments more badinage with Kate he left the room.

It was not a mere coincidence that had brought Senator Roberts and his daughter and the financier's son all together under the Ryder roof at the same time. It was part of Jefferson's well-prepared plan to expose the rascality of his father's secretary, and at the same time rid himself of the embarrassing entanglement with Kate Roberts. If the senator were confronted publicly with the fact that his daughter, while keeping up the fiction of being engaged to Ryder Jr., was really preparing to run off with the Hon. Fitzroy Bagley, he would have no alternative but to retire gracefully under fire and relinquish all idea of a marriage alliance with the house of Ryder. The critical moment had arrived. To-morrow, Wednesday, was the day fixed for the elopement. The secretary's little game had gone far enough. The time had come for action. So Jefferson had written to Senator Roberts, who was in Washington, asking him if it would be convenient for him to come at once to New York and meet himself and his father on a matter of importance. The senator naturally jumped to the conclusion that Jefferson and Ryder had reached an amicable understanding, and he immediately hurried to New York and with his daughter came round to Seventy-fourth Street.

When Ryder Sr. entered the library, Senator Roberts was striding nervously up and down the room. This, he felt, was an important day. The ambition of his life seemed on the point of being attained.

" Hello, Roberts," was Ryder's cheerful greeting. " What's brought you from Washington at a critical time like this? The Rossmore impeachment needs every friend we have."

" Just as if you didn't know," smiled the senator uneasily, " that I am here by appointment to meet you and your son ! "

" To meet me and my son ? " echoed Ryder astonished.

The senator, perplexed and beginning to feel real alarm, showed the financier Jefferson's letter. Ryder read it and he looked pleased.

" That's all right," he said, " if the lad asked you to meet us here it can mean only one thing—that at last he has made up his mind to this marriage."

" That's what I thought," replied the senator, breathing more freely. " I was sorry to leave Washington at such a time, but I'm a father, and Kate is more to me than the Rossmore impeachment. Besides, to see her married to your son Jefferson is one of the dearest wishes of my life."

"You can rest easy," said Ryder; "that is practically settled. Jefferson's sending for you proves that he is now ready to meet my wishes. He'll be here any minute. How is the Rossmore case progressing?"

"Not so well as it might," growled the senator. "There's a lot of maudlin sympathy for the judge. He's a pretty sick man by all accounts, and the newspapers seem to be taking his part. One or two of the Western senators are talking Corporate influence and Trust legislation, but when it comes to a vote the matter will be settled on party lines."

"That means that Judge Rossmore will be removed?" demanded Ryder sternly.

"Yes, with five votes to spare," answered the senator.

"That's not enough," insisted Ryder. "There must be at least twenty. Let there be no blunders, Roberts. The man is a menace to all the big commercial interests. This thing must go through."

The door opened and Jefferson appeared. On seeing the senator talking with his father, he hesitated on the threshold.

" Come in, Jeff," said his father pleasantly. " You expected to see Senator Roberts, didn't you?"

" Yes, sir. How do you do, Senator?" said the young man, advancing into the room.

" I got your letter, my boy, and here I am," said the senator smiling affably. " I suppose we can guess what the business is, eh?"

" That he's going to marry Kate, of course," chimed in Ryder Sr. " Jeff, my lad, I'm glad you are beginning to see my way of looking at things. You're doing more to please me lately, and I appreciate it. You stayed at home when I asked you to, and now you've made up your mind regarding this marriage."

Jefferson let his father finish his speech, and then he said calmly:

" I think there must be some misapprehension as to the reason for my summoning Senator Roberts to New York. It had nothing to do with my marrying Miss Roberts, but to prevent her marriage with some-one else."

" What!" exclaimed Ryder, Sr.

" Marriage with someone else?" echoed the senator. He thought he had not heard aright, yet at the same time he had grave misgivings. " What do you mean, sir?"

Taking from his pocket a copy of the letter he had

336

picked up on the staircase, Jefferson held it out to the girl's father.

"Your daughter is preparing to run away with my father's secretary. To-morrow would have been too late. That is why I summoned you. Read this."

The senator took the letter, and as he read his face grew ashen and his hand trembled violently. At one blow all his ambitious projects for his daughter had been swept away. The inconsiderate act of a silly, thoughtless girl had spoiled the carefully laid plans of a lifetime. The only consolation which remained was that the calamity might have been still more serious. This timely warning had saved his family from perhaps an even greater scandal. He passed the letter in silence to Ryder, Sr.

The financier was a man of few words when the situation called for prompt action. After he had read the letter through, there was an ominous silence. Then he rang a bell. The butler appeared.

"Tell Mr. Bagley I want him."

The man bowed and disappeared.

"Who the devil is this Bagley?" demanded the senator.

"English—blue blood—no money," was Ryder's laconic answer.

"That's the only kind we seem to get over here,"

growled the senator. "We furnish the money—they furnish the blood—damn his blue blood! I don't want any in mine." Turning to Jefferson, he said: "Jefferson, whatever the motives that actuated you, I can only thank you for this warning. I think it would have broken my heart if my girl had gone away with that scoundrel. Of course, under the circumstances, I must abandon all idea of your becoming my son-in-law. I release you from all obligations you may have felt yourself bound by."

Jefferson bowed and remained silent.

Ryder, Sr. eyed his son closely, an amused expression hovering on his face. After all, it was not so much he who had desired this match as Roberts, and as long as the senator was willing to withdraw, he could make no objection. He wondered what part, if any, his son had played in bringing about this sensational dénouement to a match which had been so distasteful to him, and it gratified his paternal vanity to think that Jefferson after all might be smarter than he had given him credit for.

At this juncture Mr. Bagley entered the room. He was a little taken aback on seeing the senator, but like most men of his class, his self-conceit made him confident of his ability to handle any emergency which might arise, and he had no reason to suspect that this hasty summons to the library had anything to do with his matrimonial plans.

"Did you ask for me, sir? he demanded, addressing his employer.

"Yes, Mr. Bagley," replied Ryder, fixing the secretary with a look that filled the latter with misgivings. "What steamers leave to-morrow for England?"

"To-morrow?" echoed Mr. Bagley.

"I said to-morrow," repeated Ryder, slightly raising his voice.

"Let me see," stammered the secretary, "there is the White Star, the North German Lloyd, the Atlantic Transport——"

"Have you any preference?" inquired the financier.

"No, sir, none at all."

"Then you'll go on board one of the ships to-night," said Ryder. "Your things will be packed and sent to you before the steamer sails to-morrow."

The Hon. Fitzroy Bagley, third son of a British peer, did not understand even yet that he was discharged as one dismisses a housemaid caught kissing the policeman. He could not think what Mr. Ryder wanted him to go abroad for unless it were on some matter of business, and it was decidedly inconvenient for him to sail at this time.

"But, sir," he stammered. "I'm afraid—I'm afraid——"

"Yes," rejoined Ryder promptly, "I notice that—your hand is shaking."

"I mean that I——"

"You mean that you have other engagements!" said Ryder sternly.

"Oh no—no but——"

"No engagement at eleven o'clock to-morrow morning?" insisted Ryder.

"With my daughter?" chimed in the senator.

Mr. Bagley now understood. He broke out in a cold perspiration and he paled visibly. In the hope that the full extent of his plans were not known, he attempted to brazen it out.

"No, certainly not, under no circumstances," he said.

Ryder, Sr. rang a bell.

"Perhaps she has an engagement with you. We'll ask her." To the butler, who entered, he said: "Tell Miss Roberts that her father would like to see her here."

The man disappeared and the senator took a hand in cross-examining the now thoroughly uncomfortable secretary.

"So you thought my daughter looked pale and that

340

a little excursion to Buffalo would be a good thing for her? Well, it won't be a good thing for you, young man, I can assure you of that!"

The English aristocrat began to wilt. His assurance of manner quite deserted him and he stammered painfully as he floundered about in excuses.

"Not with me—oh dear, no," he said.

"You never proposed to run away with my daughter?" cried the irate father.

"Run away with her?" stammered Bagley.

"And marry her?" shouted the senator, shaking his fist at him.

"Oh say—this is hardly fair—three against one—really—I'm awfully sorry, eh, what?"

The door opened and Kate Roberts bounced in. She was smiling and full of animal spirits, but on seeing the stern face of her father and the pitiable picture presented by her faithful Fitz she was intelligent enough to immediately scent danger.

"Did you want to see me, father?" she inquired boldly.

"Yes, Kate," answered the senator gravely, "we have just been having a talk with Mr. Bagley, in which you were one of the subjects of conversation. Can you guess what it was?"

The girl looked from her father to Bagley and from

him to the Ryders. Her aristocratic lover made a movement forward as if to exculpate himself, but he caught Ryder's eye and remained where he was.

" Well? " she said, with a nervous laugh.

" Is it true? " asked the senator, " that you were about to marry this man secretly? "

She cast down her eyes and answered:

" I suppose you know everything."

" Have you anything to add? " asked her father sternly.

" No," said Kate shaking her head. " It's true. We intended to run away, didn't we Fitz? "

" Never mind about Mr. Bagley," thundered her father. " Haven't you a word of shame for this disgrace you have brought upon me? "

" Oh papa, don't be so cross. Jefferson did not care for me. I couldn't be an old maid. Mr. Bagley has a lovely castle in England, and one day he'll sit in the House of Lords. He'll explain everything to you."

" He'll explain nothing," rejoined the senator grimly. " Mr. Bagley returns to England to-night. He won't have time to explain anything."

" Returns to England? " echoed Kate dismayed.

" Yes, and you go with me to Washington at once."

The senator turned to Ryder.

" Good-bye Ryder. The little domestic comedy is

ended. I'm grateful it didn't turn out a drama. The next time I pick out a son-in-law I hope I'll have better luck."

He shook hands with Jefferson, and left the room followed by his crestfallen daughter.

Ryder, who had gone to write something at his desk, strode over to where Mr. Bagley was standing and handed him a cheque.

" Here, sir, this settles everything to date. Good-day."

" But I—I—" stammered the secretary helplessly.

" Good-day, sir."

Ryder turned his back on him and conversed with his son, while Mr. Bagley slowly, and as if regretfully, made his exit.

## CHAPTER XV

IT was now December and the Senate had been in
session for over a week.   Jefferson had not forgotten his promise, and one day, about two
weeks after Mr. Bagley's spectacular dismissal from
the Ryder residence, he had brought Shirley the two
letters. She did not ask him how he got them, if he
forced the drawer or procured the key. It sufficed for
her that the precious letters—the absolute proof of her
father's innocence—were at last in her possession.
She at once sent them off by registered mail to Stott,
who immediately acknowledged receipt and at the same
time announced his departure for Washington that
night.  He promised to keep her constantly informed
of what he was doing and how her father's case was
going.  It could, he thought, be only a matter of a few
days now before the result of the proceedings would
be known.

The approach of the crisis made Shirley exceedingly
nervous, and it was only by the exercise of the greatest
self-control that she did not betray the terrible anxiety
she felt.  The Ryder biography was nearly finished

344

and her stay in Seventy-fourth Street would soon come to an end. She had a serious talk with Jefferson, who contrived to see a good deal of her, entirely unsuspected by his parents, for Mr. and Mrs. Ryder had no reason to believe that their son had any more than a mere bowing acquaintance with the clever young authoress. Now that Mr. Bagley was no longer there to spy upon their actions these clandestine interviews had been comparatively easy. Shirley brought to bear all the arguments she could think of to convince Jefferson of the hopelessness of their engagement. She insisted that she could never be his wife; circumstances over which they had no control made that dream impossible. It were better, she said, to part now rather than incur the risk of being unhappy later. But Jefferson refused to be convinced. He argued and pleaded and he even swore—strange, desperate words that Shirley had never heard before and which alarmed her not a little—and the discussion ended usually by a kiss which put Shirley completely *hors de combat.*

Meantime, John Ryder had not ceased worrying about his son. The removal of Kate Roberts as a factor in his future had not eliminated the danger of Jefferson taking the bit between his teeth one day and contracting a secret marriage with the daughter of his enemy, and when he thought of the mere possibility of such a thing happening he stormed and raved until his wife, accustomed as she was to his choleric outbursts, was thoroughly frightened. For some time after Bagley's departure, father and son got along together fairly amicably, but Ryder, Sr. was quick to see that Jefferson had something on his mind which was worrying him, and he rightly attributed it to his infatuation for Miss Rossmore. He was convinced that his son knew where the judge's daughter was, although his own efforts to discover her whereabouts had been unsuccessful. Sergeant Ellison had confessed absolute failure; Miss Rossmore, he reported, had disappeared as completely as if the earth had swallowed her, and further search was futile. Knowing well his son's impulsive, headstrong disposition, Ryder, Sr. believed him quite capable of marrying the girl secretly any time. The only thing that John Ryder did not know was that Shirley Rossmore was not the kind of a girl to allow any man to inveigle her into a secret marriage. The Colossus, who judged the world's morals by his own, was not of course aware of this, and he worried night and day thinking what he could do to prevent his son from marrying the daughter of the man he had wronged.

The more he pondered **over it, the** more he regretted that there was not some other girl with whom Jefferson could fall in love and marry. He need not seek a rich girl—there was certainly enough money in the Ryder family to provide for both. He wished they knew a girl, for example, as attractive and clever as Miss Green. Ah! he thought, there was a girl who would make a man of Jefferson—brainy, ambitious, active! And the more he thought of it the more the idea grew on him that Miss Green would be an ideal daughter-in-law, and at the same time snatch his son from the clutches of the Rossmore woman.

Jefferson, during all these weeks, was growing more and more impatient. He knew that any day now Shirley might take her departure from their house and return to Massapequa. If the impeachment proceedings went against her father it was more than likely that he would lose her forever, and if, on the contrary, the judge were acquitted, Shirley never would be willing to marry him without his father's consent; and this, he felt, he would never obtain. He resolved, therefore, to have a final interview with his father and declare boldly his intention of making Miss Rossmore his wife, regardless of the consequences.

The opportunity came one evening after dinner.

Ryder, Sr. was sitting alone in the library, reading, Mrs. Ryder had gone to the theatre with a friend, Shirley as usual was writing in her room, giving the final touches to her now completed " History of the Empire Trading Company." Jefferson took the bull by the horns and boldly accosted his redoubtable parent.

" May I have a few minutes of your time, father? "

Ryder, Sr. laid aside the paper he was reading and looked up. It was unusual for his son to come to him on any errand, and he liked to encourage it.

" Certainly, Jefferson. What is it? "

" I want to appeal to you, sir. I want you to use your influence, before it is too late, to save Judge Rossmore. A word from you at this time would do wonders in Washington."

The financier swung half-round in his chair, the smile of greeting faded out of his face, and his voice was hard as he replied coldly:

" Again? I thought we had agreed not to discuss Judge Rossmore any further? "

" I can't help it, sir," rejoined Jefferson undeterred by his sire's hostile attitude, " that poor old man is practically on trial for his life. He is as innocent of wrongdoing as a child unborn, and you know it. You could save him if you would."

348

# THE MOUSE

"Jefferson," answered Ryder, Sr., biting his lip to restrain his impatience, "I told you before that I could not interfere even if I would; and I won't, because that man is my enemy. Important business interests, which you cannot possibly know anything about, demand his dismissal from the bench."

"Surely your business interests don't demand the sacrifice of a man's life!" retorted Jefferson. "I know modern business methods are none too squeamish, but I should think you'd draw the line at deliberate murder!"

Ryder sprang to his feet and for a moment stood glaring at the young man. His lips moved, but no sound came from them. Suppressed wrath rendered him speechless. What was the world coming to when a son could talk to his father in this manner?

"How dare you presume to judge my actions or to criticise my methods?" he burst out, finally.

"You force me to do so," answered Jefferson hotly. "I want to tell you that I am heartily ashamed of this whole affair and your connection with it, and since you refuse to make reparation in the only way possible for the wrong you and your associates have done Judge Rosmore—that is by saving him in the Senate—I think it only fair to warn you that I take back my word in regard to not marrying without your consent. I want you to know that I intend to marry Miss Rossmore as soon as she will consent to become my wife, that is," he added with bitterness, "if I can succeed in overcoming her prejudices against my family——"

Ryder, Sr. laughed contemptuously.

"Prejudices against a thousand million dollars?" he exclaimed sceptically.

"Yes," replied Jefferson decisively, "prejudices against our family, against you and your business practices. Money is not everything. One day you will find that out. I tell you definitely that I intend to make Miss Rossmore my wife."

Ryder, Sr. made no reply, and as Jefferson had expected an explosion, this unnatural calm rather startled him. He was sorry he had spoken so harshly. It was his father, after all.

"You've forced me to defy you, father," he added. "I'm sorry——"

Ryder, Sr. shrugged his shoulders and resumed his seat. He lit another cigar, and with affected carelessness he said:

"All right, Jeff, my boy, we'll let it go at that. You're sorry—so am I. You've shown me your cards —I'll show you mine."

His composed unruffled manner vanished. He

suddenly threw off the mask and revealed the tempest that was raging within. He leaned across the desk, his face convulsed with uncontrollable passion, a terrifying picture of human wrath. Shaking his fist at his son he shouted:

"When I get through with Judge Rossmore at Washington, I'll start after his daughter. This time to-morrow he'll be a disgraced man. A week later she will be a notorious woman. Then we'll see if you'll be so eager to marry her!"

"Father!" cried Jefferson.

"There is sure to be something in her life that won't bear inspection," sneered Ryder. "There is in everybody's life. I'll find out what it is. Where is she to-day? She can't be found. No one knows where she is—not even her own mother. Something is wrong—the girl's no good!"

Jefferson started forward as if to resent these insults to the woman he loved, but, realizing that it was his own father, he stopped short and his hands fell powerless at his side.

"Well, is that all?" inquired Ryder, Sr. with a sneer.

"That's all," replied Jefferson, "I'm going. Good-bye."

"Good-bye," answered his father indifferently; "leave your address with your mother."

Jefferson left the room, and Ryder, Sr., as if exhausted by the violence of his own outburst, sank back limp in his chair. The crisis he dreaded had come at last. His son had openly defied his authority and was going to marry the daughter of his enemy. He must do something to prevent it; the marriage must not take place, but what could he do? The boy was of age and legally his own master. He could do nothing to restrain his actions unless they put him in an insane asylum. He would rather see his son there, he mused, than married to the Rossmore woman.

Presently there was a timid knock at the library door. Ryder rose from his seat and went to see who was there. To his surprise it was Miss Green.

"May I come in?" asked Shirley.

"Certainly, by all means. Sit down."

He drew up a chair for her, and his manner was so cordial that it was easy to see she was a welcome visitor.

"Mr. Ryder," she began in a low, tremulous voice, "I have come to see you on a very important matter. I've been waiting to see you all evening—and as I shall be here only a short time longer I—want to ask you a great favour—perhaps the greatest you were ever

asked—I want to ask you for mercy—for mercy
to——"

She stopped and glanced nervously at him, but
she saw he was paying no attention to what she
was saying. He was puffing heavily at his cigar, entirely preoccupied with his own thoughts. Her sudden silence aroused him. He apologized:

"Oh, excuse me—I didn't quite catch what you
were saying."

She said nothing, wondering what had happened to
render him so absent-minded. He read the question
in her face, for, turning towards her, he exclaimed:

"For the first time in my life I am face to face with
defeat—defeat of the most ignominious kind—in-
capacity—inability to regulate my own internal affairs.
I can rule a government, but I can't manage my own
family—my own son. I'm a failure. Tell me," he
added, appealing to her, "why can't I rule my own
household, why can't I govern my own child?"

"Why can't you govern yourself?" said Shirley
quietly.

Ryder looked keenly at her for a moment without
answering her question; then, as if prompted by a
sudden inspiration, he said:

"You can help me, but not by preaching at me.
This is the first time in my life I ever called on a

living soul for help. I'm only accustomed to deal
with men. This time there's a woman in the case—
and I need your woman's wit——"

" How can I help you? " asked Shirley.

" I don't know," he answered with suppressed excitement. " As I told you, I am up against a blank
wall. I can't see my way." He gave a nervous little
laugh and went on: " God! I'm ashamed of myself—
ashamed! Did you ever read the fable of the Lion
and the Mouse? Well, I want you to gnaw with your
sharp woman's teeth at the cords which bind the son
of John Burkett Ryder to this Rossmore woman. I
want you to be the mouse—to set me free of this disgraceful entanglement."

" How? asked Shirley calmly.

" Ah, that's just it—how? " he replied. " Can't
you think—you're a woman—you have youth, beauty
—brains." He stopped and eyed her closely until
she reddened from the embarrassing scrutiny. Then
he blurted out: " By George! marry him yourself—
force him to let go of this other woman! Why not?
Come, what do you say? "

This unexpected suggestion came upon Shirley with
all the force of a violent shock. She immediately saw
the falseness of her position. This man was asking
for her hand for his son under the impression that

she was another woman. It would be dishonorable of her to keep up the deception any longer. She passed her hand over her face to conceal her confusion.

" You—you must give me time to think," she stammered. " Suppose I don't love your son—I should want something—something to compensate."

" Something to compensate? " echoed Ryder surprised and a little disconcerted. " Why, the boy will inherit millions—I don't know how many."

" No—no, not money," rejoined Shirley; " money only compensates those who love money. It's something else—a man's honour—a man's life! It means nothing to you."

He gazed at her, not understanding. Full of his own project, he had mind for nothing else. Ignoring therefore the question of compensation, whatever she might mean by that, he continued:

" You can win him if you make up your mind to. A woman with your resources can blind him to any other woman."

" But if—he loves Judge Rossmore's daughter? " objected Shirley.

" It's for you to make him forget her—and you can," replied the financier confidently. " My desire is to separate him from this Rossmore woman at any cost. You must help me." His sternness relaxed somewhat and his eyes rested on her kindly. "Do you know, I should be glad to think you won't have to leave us. Mrs. Ryder has taken a fancy to you, and I myself shall miss you when you go."

"You ask me to be your son's wife and you know nothing of my family," said Shirley.

"I know you—that is sufficient," he replied.

"No—no you don't," returned Shirley, "nor do you know your son. He has more constancy—more strength of character than you think—and far more principle than you have."

"So much the greater the victory for you," he answered good humouredly.

"Ah," she said reproachfully, "you do not love your son."

"I do love him," replied Ryder warmly. "It's because I love him that I'm such a fool in this matter. Don't you see that if he marries this girl it would separate us, and I should lose him. I don't want to lose him. If I welcomed her to my house it would make me the laughing-stock of all my friends and business associates. Come, will you join forces with me?"

Shirley shook her head and was about to reply when

the telephone bell rang. Ryder took up the receiver and spoke to the butler downstairs:

" Who's that? Judge Stott? Tell him I'm too busy to see anyone. What's that? A man's life at stake? What's that to do with me? Tell him——"

On hearing Stott's name, Shirley nearly betrayed herself. She turned pale and half-started up from her chair. Something serious must have happened to bring her father's legal adviser to the Ryder residence at such an hour! She thought he was in Washington. Could it be that the proceedings in the Senate were ended and the result known? She could hardly conceal her anxiety, and instinctively she placed her hand on Ryder's arm.

" No, Mr. Ryder, do see Judge Stott! You must see him. I know who he is. Your son has told me. Judge Stott is one of Judge Rossmore's advisers. See him. You may find out something about the girl. You may find out where she is. If Jefferson finds out you have refused to see her father's friend at such a critical time it will only make him sympathize more deeply with the Rossmores, and you know sympathy is akin to love. That's what you want to avoid, isn't it?"

Ryder still held the telephone, hesitating what to do. What she said sounded like good sense.

'Upon my word— he said. "You may be right and yet——"

"Am I to help you or not?" demanded Shirley. "You said you wanted a woman's wit."

"Yes," said Ryder, "but still——"

"Then you had better see him," she said emphatically.

Ryder turned to the telephone.

"Hello, Jorkins, are you there? Show Judge Stott up here." He laid the receiver down and turned again to Shirley. "That's one thing I don't like about you," he said. "I allow you to decide against me and then I agree with you." She said nothing and he went on looking at her admiringly. "I predict that you'll bring that boy to your feet within a month. I don't know why, but I seem to feel that he is attracted to you already. Thank Heaven! you haven't a lot of troublesome relations. I think you said you were almost alone in the world. Don't look so serious," he added laughing. "Jeff is a fine fellow, and believe me an excellent catch as the world goes."

Shirley raised her hand as if entreating him to desist.

"Oh, don't—don't—please! My position is so false! You don't know how false it is!" she cried.

At that instant the library door was thrown open

and the butler appeared, ushering in Stott. The lawyer looked anxious, and his dishevelled appearance indicated that he had come direct from the train. Shirley scanned his face narrowly in the hope that she might read there what had happened. He walked right past her, giving no sign of recognition, and advanced direct towards Ryder, who had risen and remained standing at his desk.

"Perhaps I had better go?" ventured Shirley, although tortured by anxiety to hear the news from Washington.

"No," said Ryder quickly, "Judge Stott will detain me but a very few moments."

Having delivered himself of this delicate hint, he looked towards his visitor as if inviting him to come to the point as rapidly as possible.

"I must apologize for intruding at this unseemly hour, sir," said Stott, "but time is precious. The Senate 1 eets to-morrow to vote. If anything is to be done fo. Judge Rossmore it must be done to-night."

"I fail to see why you address yourself to me in this matter, sir," replied Ryder with asperity.

"As Judge Rossmore's friend and counsel," answered Stott, "I am impelled to ask your help at this critical moment."

"The matter is in the hands of the United States Senate, sir," replied Ryder coldly.

"They are against him!" cried Stott; "not one senator I've spoken to holds out any hope for him. If he is convicted it will mean his death. Inch by inch his life is leaving him. The only thing that can save him is the good news of the Senate's refusal to find him guilty."

Stott was talking so excitedly and loudly that neither he nor Ryder heard the low moan that came from the corner of the room where Shirley was standing listening.

"I can do nothing," repeated Ryder coldly, and he turned his back and began to examine some papers lying on his desk as if to notify the caller that the interview was ended. But Stott was not so easily discouraged. He went on:

"As I understand it, they will vote on strictly party lines, and the party in power is against him. He's a marked man. You have the power to help him." Heedless of Ryder's gesture of impatience he continued: "When I left his bedside to-night, sir, I promised to return to him with good news; I have told him that the Senate ridicules the charges against him. I must return to him with good news. He is very ill to-night, sir." He halted for a moment and glanced in Shirley's direction, and slightly raising his voice so she might hear, he added: "If he gets worse we shall send for his daughter."

"Where is his daughter?" demanded Ryder, suddenly interested.

"She is working in her father's interests," replied Stott, and, he added significantly, "I believe with some hope of success."

He gave Shirley a quick, questioning look. She nodded affirmatively. Ryder, who had seen nothing of this by-play, said with a sneer:

"Surely you didn't come here to-night to tell me this?"

"No, sir, I did not." He took from his pocket two letters—the two which Shirley had sent him—and held them out for Ryder's inspection. "These letters from Judge Rossmore to you," he said, "show you to be acquainted with the fact that he bought those shares as an investment—and did not receive them as a bribe."

When he caught sight of the letters and he realized what they were, Ryder changed colour. Instinctively his eyes sought the drawer on the left-hand side of his desk. In a voice that was unnaturally calm, he asked:

"Why don't you produce them before the Senate?"

"It was too late," explained Stott, handing them to

the financier. "I received them only two days ago. But if you come forward and declare——"

Ryder made an effort to control himself.

"I'll do nothing of the kind. I refuse to move in the matter. That is final. And now, sir," he added, raising his voice and pointing to the letters, "I wish to know how comes it that you had in your possession private correspondence addressed to me?"

"That I cannot answer," replied Stott promptly.

"From whom did you receive these letters?" demanded Ryder.

Stott was dumb, while Shirley clutched at her chair as if she would fall. The financier repeated the question.

"I must decline to answer," replied Stott finally.

Shirley left her place and came slowly forward. Addressing Ryder, she said:

"I wish to make a statement."

The financier gazed at her in astonishment. What could she know about it, he wondered, and he waited with curiosity to hear what she was going to say. But Stott instantly realized that she was about to take the blame upon herself, regardless of the consequences to the success of their cause. This must be prevented at all hazards, even if another must be sacrificed, so interrupting her he said hastily to Ryder:

362

" Judge Rossmore's life and honour are at stake and no false sense of delicacy must cause the failure of my object to save him. These letters were sent to me by—your son."

" From my son!" exclaimed Ryder, starting. For a moment he staggered as if he had received a blow; he was too much overcome to speak or act. Then recovering himself, he rang a bell, and turned to Stott with renewed fury:

" So," he cried, " this man, this judge whose honour is at stake and his daughter, who most likely has no honour at stake, between them have made a thief and a liar of my son! false to his father, false to his party; and you, sir, have the presumption to come here and ask me to intercede for him!" To the butler, who entered, he said: " See if Mr. Jefferson is still in the house. If he is, tell him I would like to see him here at once."

The man disappeared, and Ryder strode angrily up and down the room with the letters in his hand. Then, turning abruptly on Stott, he said:

" And now, sir, I think nothing more remains to be said. I shall keep these letters, as they are my property."

" As you please. Good night, sir."

" Good night," replied Ryder, not looking up.

With a significant glance at Shirley, who motioned to him that she might yet succeed where he had failed, Stott left the room. Ryder turned to Shirley. His fierceness of manner softened down as he addressed the girl:

"You see what they have done to my son——"

"Yes," replied Shirley, "it's the girl's fault. If Jefferson hadn't loved her you would have helped the judge. Ah, why did they ever meet! She has worked on his sympathy and he—he took these letters for her sake, not to injure you. Oh, you must make some allowance for him! One's sympathy gets aroused in spite of oneself; even I feel sorry for—these people."

"Don't," replied Ryder grimly, "sympathy is often weakness. Ah, there you are!" turning to Jefferson, who entered the room at that moment.

"You sent for me, father?"

"Yes," said Ryder, Sr., holding up the letters. "Have you ever seen these letters before?"

Jefferson took the letters and examined them, then he passed them back to his father and said frankly:

"Yes, I took them out of your desk and sent them to Mr. Stott in the hope they would help Judge Rossmore's case."

Ryder restrained himself from proceeding to actual

violence only with the greatest difficulty. His face
grew white as death, his lips were compressed, his
hands twitched convulsively, his eyes flashed dangerously. He took another cigar to give the impression that he had himself well under control, but
the violent trembling of his hands as he lit it betrayed
the terrific strain he was under.

"So!" he said, "you deliberately sacrificed my
interests to save this woman's father—you hear him,
Miss Green? Jefferson, my boy, I think it's time you
and I had a final accounting."

Shirley made a motion as if about to withdraw.
He stopped her with a gesture.

"Please don't go, Miss Green. As the writer of
my biography you are sufficiently well acquainted
with my family affairs to warrant your being present
at the epilogue. Besides, I want an excuse for keeping
my temper. Sit down, Miss Green."

Turning to Jefferson, he went on:

"For your mother's sake, my boy, I have overlooked your little eccentricities of character. But
now we have arrived at the parting of the ways—
you have gone too far. The one aspect of this business I cannot overlook is your willingness to sell
your own father for the sake of a woman."

"My own father," interrupted Jefferson bitterly,

" would not hesitate to sell me if his business and political interests warranted the sacrifice!"

Shirley attempted the rôle of peacemaker. Appealing to the younger man, she said:

" Please don't talk like that, Mr. Jefferson." Then
she turned to Ryder, Sr.: "I don't think your son
quite understands you, Mr. Ryder, and, if you will
pardon me, I don't think you quite understand him.
Do you realize that there is a man's life at stake—that
Judge Rossmore is almost at the point of death and
that favourable news from the Senate to-morrow is
perhaps the only thing that can save him?"

" Ah, I see," sneered Ryder, Sr. " Judge Stott's
story has aroused your sympathy."

" Yes, I—I confess my sympathy is aroused. I do
feel for this father whose life is slowly ebbing away—
whose strength is being sapped hourly by the thought
of the disgrace—the injustice that is being done him!
I do feel for the wife of this suffering man!"

" Ah, its a complete picture!" cried Ryder mockingly. The dying father, the sorrowing mother—
and the daughter, what is she supposed to be doing?"

" She is fighting for her father's life," cried Shirley, " and you, Mr. Jefferson, should have pleaded—
pleaded—not demanded. It's no use trying to combat
your father's will."

"She is quite right, father I should have implored you. I do so now. I ask you for God's sake to help us!"

Ryder was grim and silent. He rose from his seat and paced the room, puffing savagely at his cigar. Then he turned and said:

"His removal is a political necessity. If he goes back on the bench every paltry justice of the peace, every petty official will think he has a special mission to tear down the structure that hard work and capital have erected. No, this man has been especially conspicuous in his efforts to block the progress of amalgamated interests."

"And so he must be sacrificed?" cried Shirley indignantly.

"He is a meddlesome man," insisted Ryder and——"

"He is innocent of the charges brought against him," urged Jefferson.

"Mr. Ryder is not considering that point," said Shirley bitterly. "All he can see is that it is necessary to put this poor old man in the public pillory, to set him up as a warning to others of his class not to act in accordance with the principles of Truth and Justice—not to dare to obstruct the car of Juggernaut set in motion by the money gods of the country!"

"It's the survival of the fittest, my dear," said Ryder coldly.

"Oh!" cried Shirley, making a last appeal to the financier's heart of stone, "use your great influence with this governing body for good, not evil! Urge them to vote not in accordance with party policy and personal interest, but in accordance with their consciences—in accordance with Truth and Justice! Ah, for God's sake, Mr. Ryder! don't permit this foul injustice to blot the name of the highest tribunal in the Western world!"

Ryder laughed cynically.

"By Jove! Jefferson, I give you credit for having secured an eloquent advocate!"

"Suppose," went on Shirley, ignoring his taunting comments, "suppose this daughter promises that she will never—never see your son again—that she will go away to some foreign country!"

"No!" burst in Jefferson, "why should she? If my father is not man enough to do a simple act of justice without bartering a woman's happiness and his son's happiness, let him find comfort in his self-justification!"

Shirley, completely unnerved, made a move towards the door, unable longer to bear the strain she was **under**. She tottered as though she would fall. Ryder

368

made a quick movement towards his son and took him by the arm. Pointing to Shirley he said in a low tone:

" You see how that girl pleads your cause for you! She loves you, my boy!" Jefferson started. " Yes, she does," pursued Ryder, Sr. " She's worth a thousand of the Rossmore woman. Make her your wife and I'll——"

" Make her my wife!" cried Jefferson joyously. He stared at his parent as if he thought he had suddenly been bereft of his senses.

" Make her my wife?" he repeated incredulously.

" Well, what do you say?" demanded Ryder, Sr.

The young man advanced towards Shirley, hands outstretched.

" Yes, yes, Shir—Miss Green, will you?" Seeing that Shirley made no sign, he said: " Not now, father; I will speak to her later."

" No, no, to-night, at once!" insisted Ryder. Addressing Shirley, he went on: " Miss Green, my son is much affected by your disinterested appeal in his behalf. He—he—you can save him from himself— my son wishes you—he asks you to become his wife! Is it not so, Jefferson?"

" Yes, yes, my wife!" advancing again towards Shirley.

The girl shrank back in alarm.

" No, no, no, Mr. Ryder, I cannot, I cannot! " she cried.

" Why not? " demanded Ryder, Sr. appealingly. " Ah, don't—don't decide hastily——"

Shirley, her face set and drawn and keen mental distress showing in every line of it, faced the two men, pale and determined. The time had come to reveal the truth. This masquerade could go on no longer. It was not honourable either to her father or to herself. Her self-respect demanded that she inform the financier of her true identity.

" I cannot marry your son with these lies upon my lips! " she cried. " I cannot go on with this deception. I told you you did not know who I was, who my people were. My story about them, my name, everything about me is false, every word I have uttered is a lie, a fraud, a cheat! I would not tell you now, but you trusted me and are willing to entrust your son's future, your family honour in my keeping, and I can't keep back the truth from you. Mr. Ryder, I am the daughter of the man you hate. I am the woman your son loves. I am Shirley Rossmore! "

Ryder took his cigar from his lips and rose slowly to his feet.

" You? You? " he stammered.

"For God's sake, Mr. Ryder, don't permit this foul injustice."—Act III.

"Yes—yes, I am the Rossmore woman! Listen, Mr. Ryder. Don't turn away from me. Go to Washington on behalf of my father, and I promise you I will never see your son again—never, never!"

"Ah, Shirley!" cried Jefferson, "you don't love me!"

"Yes, Jeff, I do; God knows I do! But if I must break my own heart to save my father I will do it."

"Would you sacrifice my happiness and your own?"

"No happiness can be built on lies, Jeff. We must build on truth or our whole house will crumble and fall. We have deceived your father, but he will forgive that, won't you?" she said, appealing to Ryder, "and you will go to Washington, you will save my father's honour, his life, you will——?"

They stood face to face—this slim, delicate girl battling for her father's life, arrayed against a cold-blooded, heartless, unscrupulous man, deaf to every impulse of human sympathy or pity. Since this woman had deceived him, fooled him, he would deal with her as with everyone else who crossed his will. She laid her hand on his arm, pleading with him. Brutally, savagely, he thrust her aside.

"No, no, I will not!" he thundered. "You have wormed yourself into my confidence by means of lies and deceit. You have tricked me, fooled me to the very limit! Oh, it is easy to see how you have beguiled my son into the folly of loving you! And you —you have the brazen effrontery to ask me to plead for your father? No! No! No! Let the law take its course, and now Miss Rossmore—you will please leave my house to-morrow morning!"

Shirley stood listening to what he had to say, her face white, her mouth quivering. At last the crisis had come. It was a fight to the finish between this man, the incarnation of corporate greed and herself, representing the fundamental principles of right and justice. She turned on him in a fury:

"Yes, I will leave your house to-night! Do you think I would remain another hour beneath the roof of a man who is as blind to justice, as deaf to mercy, as incapable of human sympathy as you are!"

She raised her voice; and as she stood there denouncing the man of money, her eyes flashing and her head thrown back, she looked like some avenging angel defying one of the powers of Evil.

"Leave the room!" shouted Ryder, beside himself, and pointing to the door.

"Father!" cried Jefferson, starting forward to protect the girl he loved.

" You have tricked him as you have me!" thundered Ryder.

" It is your own vanity that has tricked you!" cried Shirley contemptuously. " You lay traps for yourself and walk into them. You compel everyone around you to lie to you, to cajole you, to praise you, to deceive you! At least, you cannot accuse me of flattering you. I have never fawned upon you as you compel your family and your friends and your dependents to do. I have always appealed to your better nature by telling you the truth, and in your heart you know that I am speaking the truth now."

" Go!" he commanded.

" Yes, let us go, Shirley!" said Jefferson.

" No, Jeff, I came here alone and I'm going alone!"

" You are not. I shall go with you. I intend to make you my wife!"

Ryder laughed scornfully.

" No," cried Shirley. " Do you think I'd marry a man whose father is as deep a discredit to the human race as your father is? No, I wouldn't marry the son of such a merciless tyrant! He refuses to lift his voice to save my father. I refuse to marry his son!"

She turned on Ryder with all the fury of a tiger:

" You think if you lived in the olden days you'd be a Cæsar or an Alexander. But you wouldn't! You'd be a Nero—a Nero! Sink my self-respect to the extent of marrying into your family!" she exclaimed contemptuously. "Never! I am going to Washington without your aid. I am going to save my father if I have to go on my knees to every United States Senator. I'll go to the White House; I'll tell the President what you are! Marry your son—no, thank you! No, thank you!"

Exhausted by the vehemence of her passionate outburst, Shirley hurried from the room, leaving Ryder speechless, staring at his son.

## CHAPTER XVI

WHEN Shirley reached her rooms she broke down completely, she threw herself upon a sofa and burst into a fit of violent sobbing. After all, she was only a woman and the ordeal through which she had passed would have taxed the strongest powers of endurance. She had borne up courageously while there remained the faintest chance that she might succeed in moving the financier to pity, but now that all hopes in that direction were shattered and she herself had been ordered harshly from the house like any ordinary malefactor, the reaction set in, and she gave way freely to her long pent-up anguish and distress. Nothing now could save her father—not even this journey to Washington which she determined to take nevertheless, for, according to what Stott had said, the Senate was to take a vote that very night.

She looked at the time—eleven o'clock. She had told Mr. Ryder that she would leave his house at once, but on reflection it was impossible for a girl alone to seek a room at that hour. It would be midnight before she could get her things packed. No, she would stay under this hated roof until morning and then take the first train to Washington. There was still a chance that the vote might be delayed, in which case she might yet succeed in winning over some of the senators. She began to gather her things together and was thus engaged when she heard a knock at her door.

" Who's there? " she called out.

" It's I," replied a familiar voice.

Shirley went to the door and opening it found Jefferson on the threshold. He made no attempt to enter, nor did she invite him in. He looked tired and careworn.

" Of course, you're not going to-night? " he asked anxiously. " My father did not mean to-night."

" No, Jeff," she said wearily; " not to-night. It's a little too late. I did not realize it. To-morrow morning, early."

He seemed reassured and held out his hand:

" Good-night, dearest—you're a brave girl. You made a splendid fight."

" It didn't do much good," she replied in a disheartened, listless way.

" But it set him thinking," rejoined Jefferson. " No one ever spoke to my father like that before. It did him good. He's still marching up and down the library, chewing the cud——"

Noticing Shirley's tired face and her eyes, with great black circles underneath, he stopped short.

"Now don't do any more packing to-night," he said. "Go to bed and in the morning I'll come up and help you. Good night!"

"Good night, Jeff," she smiled.

He went downstairs, and after doing some more packing she went to bed. But it was hours before she got to sleep, and then she dreamed that she was in the Senate Chamber and that she saw Ryder suddenly rise and denounce himself before the astonished senators as a perjurer and traitor to his country, while she returned to Massapequa with the glad news that her father was acquitted.

Meantime, a solitary figure remained in the library, pacing to and fro like a lost soul in Purgatory. Mrs. Ryder had returned from the play and gone to bed, serenely oblivious of the drama in real life that had been enacted at home, the servants locked the house up for the night and still John Burkett Ryder walked the floor of his sanctum, and late into the small hours of the morning the watchman going his lonely rounds, saw a light in the library and the restless figure of his employer sharply silhouetted against the white blinds.

For the first time in his life John Ryder realized that there was something in the world beyond Self. He had seen with his own eyes the sacrifice a daughter will make for the father she loves, and he asked himself what manner of a man that father could be to inspire such devotion in his child. He probed into his own heart and conscience and reviewed his past career. He had been phenomenally successful, but he had not been happy. He had more money than he knew what to do with, but the pleasures of the domestic circle, which he saw other men enjoy, had been denied to him. Was he himself to blame? Had his insensate craving for gold and power led him to neglect those other things in life which contribute more truly to man's happiness? In other words, was his life a mistake? Yes, it was true what this girl charged, he had been merciless and unscrupulous in his dealings with his fellow man. It was true that hardly a dollar of his vast fortune had been honestly earned. It was true that it had been wrung from the people by fraud and trickery. He had craved for power, yet now he had tasted it, what a hollow joy it was, after all! The public hated and despised him; even his so-called friends and business associates toadied to

378

him merely because they feared him. And this judge
—this father he had persecuted and ruined, what a
better man and citizen he was, how much more worthy
of a child's love and of the esteem of the world!
What had Judge Rossmore done, after all, to deserve
the frightful punishment the amalgamated interests
had caused him to suffer? If he had blocked their
game, he had done only what his oath, his duty commanded him to do. Such a girl as Shirley Rossmore
could not have had any other kind of a father. Ah,
if he had had such a daughter he might have been a
better man, if only to win his child's respect and affection. John Ryder pondered long and deeply and
the more he ruminated the stronger the conviction
grew upon him that the girl was right and he was
wrong. Suddenly, he looked at his watch. It was one
o'clock. Roberts had told him that it would be an all
night session and that a vote would probably not be
taken until very late. He unhooked the telephone and
calling " central " asked for " long distance " and
connection with Washington.

It was seven o'clock when the maid entered Shirley's room with her breakfast and she found its
occupant up and dressed.

" Why you haven't been to bed, Miss! " exclaimed

the girl, looking at the bed in the inner room which seemed scarcely disturbed.

" No, Theresa I—I couldn't sleep." Hastily pouring out a cup of tea she added. " I must catch that nine o'clock train to Washington. I didn't finish packing until nearly three."

" Can I do anything for you, Miss?" inquired the maid. Shirley was as popular with the servants as with the rest of the household.

" No," answered Shirley, " there are only a few things to go in my suit case. Will you please have a cab here in half an hour?"

The maid was about to go when she suddenly thought of something she had forgotten. She held out an envelope which she had left lying on the tray.

" Oh, Miss, Mr. Jorkins said to give you this and master wanted to see you as soon as you had finished your breakfast."

Shirley tore open the envelope and took out the contents. It was a cheque, payable to her order for $5,000 and signed " John Burkett Ryder."

A deep flush covered the girl's face as she saw the money—a flush of annoyance rather than of pleasure. This man who had insulted her, who had wronged her father, who had driven her from his home, thought he could throw his gold at her and insolently send her her pay as one settles haughtily with a servant discharged for impertinence. She would have none of his money—the work she had done she would make him a present of. She replaced the cheque in the envelope and passed it back to Theresa.

" Give this to Mr. Ryder and tell him I cannot see him."

" But Mr. Ryder said——" insisted the girl.

" Please deliver my message as I give it," commanded Shirley with authority. " I cannot see Mr. Ryder."

The maid withdrew, but she had barely closed the door when it was opened again and Mrs. Ryder rushed in, without knocking. She was all flustered with excitement and in such a hurry that she had not even stopped to arrange her toilet.

" My dear Miss Green," she gasped; " what's this I hear—going away suddenly without giving me warning?"

" I wasn't engaged by the month," replied Shirley drily.

" I know, dear, I know. I was thinking of myself. I've grown so used to you—how shall I get on without you—no one understands me the way you do. Dear me! The whole house is upset. Mr. Ryder never went to bed at all last night. Jefferson is going away, too—forever, he threatens. If he hadn't come and woke me up to say good-bye, I should never have known you intended to leave us. My boy's going— you're going—everyone's deserting me!"

Mrs. Ryder was not accustomed to such prolonged flights of oratory and she sank exhausted on a chair, her eyes filling with tears.

"Did they tell you who I am—the daughter of Judge Rossmore?" demanded Shirley.

It had been a shock to Mrs. Ryder that morning when Jefferson burst into his mother's room before she was up and acquainted her with the events of the previous evening. The news that the Miss Green whom she had grown to love, was really the Miss Rossmore of whose relations with Jefferson her husband stood in such dread, was far from affecting the financier's wife as it had Ryder himself. To the mother's simple and ingenuous mind, free from prejudice and ulterior motive, the girl's character was more important than her name, and certainly she could not blame her son for loving such a woman as Shirley. Of course, it was unfortunate for Jefferson that his father felt this bitterness towards Judge Rossmore, for she herself could hardly have wished for a more sympathetic daughter-in-law. She had not seen her husband since the previous evening at dinner so was

382

in complete ignorance as to what he thought of this new development, but the mother sighed as she thought how happy it would make her to see Jefferson happily married to the girl of his own choice, and in her heart she still entertained the hope that her husband would see it that way and thus prevent their son from leaving them as he threatened.

"That's not your fault, my dear," she replied answering Shirley's question. "You are yourself—that's the main thing. You mustn't mind what Mr. Ryder says? Business and worry makes him irritable at times. If you must go, of course you must—you are the best judge of that, but Jefferson wants to see you before you leave." She kissed Shirley in motherly fashion, and added: "He has told me everything, dear. Nothing would make me happier than to see you become his wife. He's downstairs now waiting for me to tell him to come up."

"It's better that I should not see him," replied Shirley slowly and gravely. "I can only tell him what I have already told him. My father comes first. I have still a duty to perform."

"That's right, dear," answered Mrs. Ryder. "You're a good, noble girl and I admire you all the more for it. I'll let Jefferson be his own advocate. You'll see him for my sake!"

She gave Shirley another affectionate embrace and left the room while the girl proceeded with her final preparations for departure. Presently there was a quick, heavy step in the corridor outside and Jefferson appeared in the doorway. He stood there waiting for her to invite him in. She looked up and greeted him cordially, yet it was hardly the kind of reception he looked for or that he considered he had a right to expect. He advanced sulkily into the room.

"Mother said she had put everything right," he began. "I guess she was mistaken."

"Your mother does not understand, neither do you," she replied seriously. "Nothing can be put right until my father is restored to honour and position."

"But why should you punish me because my father fails to regard the matter as we do?" demanded Jefferson rebelliously.

"Why should I punish myself—why should we punish those nearest and dearest?" answered Shirley gently, "the victims of human injustice always suffer where their loved ones are tortured. Why are things as they are—I don't know. I know they are—that's all."

The young man strode nervously up and down the room while she gazed listlessly out of the window, looking for the cab that was to carry her away from this house of disappointment. He pleaded with her:

"I have tried honourably and failed—you have tried honourably and failed. Isn't the sting of impotent failure enough to meet without striving against a hopeless love? He approached her and said softly: "I love you Shirley—don't drive me to desperation. Must I be punished because you have failed? It's unfair. The sins of the fathers should not be visited upon the children."

"But they are—it's the law," said Shirley with resignation.

"The law?" he echoed.

"Yes, the law," insisted the girl; "man's law, not God's, the same unjust law that punishes my father—man's law which is put into the hands of the powerful of the earth to strike at the weak."

She sank into a chair and, covering up her face, wept bitterly. Between her sobs she cried brokenly:

"I believed in the power of love to soften your father's heart, I believed that with God's help I could bring him to see the truth. I believed that Truth and Love would make him see the light, but it hasn't. I stayed on and on, hoping against hope until the time has gone by and it's too late to save him, too late! What can I do now? My going to Washington is a forlorn hope, a last, miserable, forlorn hope and in this hour, the darkest of all, you ask me to think of myself—my love, your love, your happiness, your future, my future! Ah, wouldn't it be sublime selfishness?"

Jefferson kneeled down beside the chair and taking her hand in his, tried to reason with her and comfort her:

"Listen, Shirley," he said, "do not do something you will surely regret. You are punishing me not only because I have failed but because you have failed too. It seems to me that if you believed it possible to accomplish so much, if you had so much faith— that you have lost your faith rather quickly. I believed in nothing, I had no faith and yet I have not lost hope."

She shook her head and gently withdrew her hand.

"It is useless to insist, Jefferson—until my father is cleared of this stain our lives—yours and mine— must lie apart."

Someone coughed and, startled, they both looked up. Mr. Ryder had entered the room unobserved and stood watching them. Shirley immediately rose to her feet indignant, resenting this intrusion on her privacy after she had declined to receive the financier. Yet, she reflected quickly, how could she prevent it? He was at home, free to come and go as he pleased,

"So I contaminate even good money?"—Act IV.

but she was not compelled to remain in the same room with him. She picked up the few things that lay about and with a contemptuous toss of her head, retreated into the inner apartment, leaving father and son alone together.

" Hum," grunted Ryder, Sr. " I rather thought I should find you here, but I didn't quite expect to find you on your knees—dragging our pride in the mud."

" That's where our pride ought to be," retorted Jefferson savagely. He felt in the humor to say anything, no matter what the consequences.

" So she has refused you again, eh? " said Ryder, Sr. with a grin.

" Yes," rejoined Jefferson with growing irritation, " she objects to my family. I don't blame her."

The financier smiled grimly as he answered:

" Your family in general—me in particular, eh? I gleaned that much when I came in." He looked towards the door of the room in which Shirley had taken refuge and as if talking to himself he added: " A curious girl with an inverted point of view—sees everything different to others—I want to see her before she goes."

He walked over to the door and raised his hand as if he were about to knock. Then he stopped as if he had changed his mind and turning towards his son he demanded:

"Do you mean to say that she has done with you?"

"Yes," answered Jefferson bitterly.

"Finally?"

"Yes, finally—forever!"

"Does she mean it?" asked Ryder, Sr., sceptically.

"Yes—she will not listen to me while her father is still in peril."

There was an expression of half amusement, half admiration on the financier's face as he again turned towards the door.

"It's like her, damn it, just like her!" he muttered.

He knocked boldly at the door.

"Who's there?" cried Shirley from within.

"It is I—Mr. Ryder. I wish to speak to you."

"I must beg you to excuse me," came the answer, "I cannot see you."

Jefferson interfered.

"Why do you want to add to the girl's misery? Don't you think she has suffered enough?"

"Do you know what she has done?" said Ryder with pretended indignation. "She has insulted me grossly. I never was so humiliated in my life. She has returned the cheque I sent her last night in payment for her work on my biography. I mean to make her take that money. It's hers, she needs it, her father's a beggar. She must take it back. It's only flaunting her contempt for me in my face and I won't permit it."

" I don't think her object in refusing that money was to flaunt contempt in your face, or in any way humiliate you," answered Jefferson. " She feels she has been sailing under false colours and desires to make some reparation."

" And so she sends me back my money, feeling that will pacify me, perhaps repair the injury she has done me, perhaps buy me into entering into her plan of helping her father, but it won't. It only increases my determination to see her and her——" Suddenly changing the topic he asked : " When do you leave us ? "

" Now—at once—that is—I—don't know," answered Jefferson embarrassed." The fact is my faculties are numbed—I seem to have lost my power of thinking. Father," he exclaimed, " you see what a wreck you have made of our lives ! "

" Now, don't moralize," replied his father testily, " as if your own selfishness in desiring to possess that girl wasn't the mainspring of all your actions ! " Waving his son out of the room he added : " Now leave me alone with her for a few moments. Perhaps I can make her listen to reason."

Jefferson stared at his father as if he feared he were out of his mind.

"What do you mean? Are you—?" he ejaculated.

"Go—go leave her to me," commanded the financier. "Slam the door when you go out and she'll think we've both gone. Then come up again presently."

The stratagem succeeded admirably. Jefferson gave the door a vigorous pull and John Ryder stood quiet, waiting for the girl to emerge from sanctuary. He did not have to wait long. The door soon opened and Shirley came out slowly. She had her hat on and was drawing on her gloves, for through her window she had caught a glimpse of the cab standing at the curb. She started on seeing Ryder standing there motionless, and she would have retreated had he not intercepted her.

"I wish to speak to you Miss—Rossmore," he began.

"I have nothing to say," answered Shirley frigidly.

"Why did you do this?" he asked, holding out the cheque.

"Because I do not want your money," she replied with hauteur.

"It was yours—you earned it," he said.

" No, I came here hoping to influence you to help my father. The work I did was part of the plan. It happened to fall my way. I took it as a means to get to your heart."

" But it is yours, please take it. It will be useful."

" No," she said scornfully, " I can't tell you how low I should fall in my own estimation if I took your money! Money," she added, with ringing contempt, " why, that's all there is to *you!* It's your god! Shall I make your god my god? No, thank you, Mr. Ryder!"

" Am I as bad as that?" he asked wistfully.

" You are as bad as that!" she answered decisively.

" So bad that I contaminate even good money?" He spoke lightly but she noticed that he winced.

" Money itself is nothing," replied the girl, " it's the spirit that gives it—the spirit that receives it, the spirit that earns it, the spirit that spends it. Money helps to create happiness. It also creates misery. It's an engine of destruction when not properly used, it destroys individuals as it does nations. It has destroyed you, for it has warped your soul!"

" Go on," he laughed bitterly, " I like to hear you!"

" No, you don't, Mr. Ryder, no you don't, for deep down in your heart you know that I am speaking the truth. Money and the power it gives you, has dried up the well-springs of your heart."

He affected to be highly amused at her words, but behind the mask of callous indifference the man suf¹ fered. Her words seared him as with a red hot iron. She went on :

"In the barbaric ages they fought for possession, but they fought openly. The feudal barons fought for what they stole, but it was a fair fight. They didn't strike in the dark. At least, they gave a man a chance for his life. But when you modern barons of industry don't like legislation you destroy it, when you don't like your judges you remove them, when a competitor outbids you you squeeze him out of commercial existence ! You have no hearts, you are machines, and you are cowards, for you fight unfairly."

" It is not true, it is not true," he protested.

" It is true," she insisted hotly, " a few hours ago in cold blood you doomed my father to what is certain death because you decided it was a political necessity. In other words he interfered with your personal interests—your financial interests—you, with so many millions you can't count them ! " Scornfully she added: " Come out into the light—fight in the open ! At least, let him know who his enemy is ! "

" Stop—stop—not another word," he cried impatiently, " you have diagnosed the disease. What of the remedy? Are you prepared to reconstruct human nature? "

Confronting each other, their eyes met and he regarded her without resentment, almost with tenderness. He felt strangely drawn towards this woman who had defied and accused him, and made him see the world in a new light.

" I don't deny," he admitted reluctantly, " that things seem to be as you describe them, but it is part of the process of evolution."

" No," she protested, " it is the work of God!"

" It is evolution!" he insisted.

" Ah, that's it," she retorted, " you evolve new ideas, new schemes, new tricks—you all worship different gods—gods of your own making!"

He was about to reply when there was a commotion at the door and Theresa entered, followed by a man servant to carry down the trunk.

" The cab is downstairs, Miss," said the maid.

Ryder waved them away imperiously. He had something further to say which he did not care for servants to hear. Theresa and the man precipitately withdrew, not understanding, but obeying with alacrity a master who never brooked delay in the execution of his orders. Shirley, indignant, looked to him for an explanation.

"You don't need them," he exclaimed with a quiet smile in which was a shade of embarrassment. "I—I came here to tell you that I——" He stopped as if unable to find words, while Shirley gazed at him in utter astonishment. "Ah," he went on finally, "you have made it very hard for me to speak." Again he paused and then with an effort he said slowly: "An hour ago I had Senator Roberts on the long distance telephone, and I'm going to Washington. It's all right about your father. The matter will be dropped. You've beaten me. I acknowledge it. You're the first living soul who ever has beaten John Burkett Ryder."

Shirley started forward with a cry of mingled joy and surprise. Could she believe her ears? Was it possible that the dreaded Colossus had capitulated and that she had saved her father? Had the forces of right and justice prevailed, after all? Her face transfigured, radiant she exclaimed breathlessly:

"What, Mr. Ryder, you mean that you are going to help my father?"

"Not for his sake—for yours," he answered frankly.

Shirley hung her head. In her moment of triumph,

she was sorry for all the hard things she had said to this man. She held out her hand to him.

"Forgive me," she said gently, "it was for my father. I had no faith. I thought your heart was of stone."

Impulsively Ryder drew her to him, he clasped her two hands in his and looking down at her kindly he said, awkwardly:

"So it was—so it was! You accomplished the miracle. It's the first time I've acted on pure sentiment. Let me tell you something. Good sentiment is bad business and good business is bad sentiment—that's why a rich man is generally supposed to have such a hard time getting into the Kingdom of Heaven." He laughed and went on, "I've given ten millions apiece to three universities. Do you think I'm fool enough to suppose I can buy my way? But that's another matter. I'm going to Washington on behalf of your father because I—want you to marry my son. Yes, I want you in the family, close to us. I want your respect, my girl. I want your love. I want to earn it. I know I can't buy it. There's a weak spot in every man's armour and this is mine—I always want what I can't get and I can't get your love unless I earn it."

Shirley remained pensive. Her thoughts were out

on Long Island, at Massapequa. She was thinking of their joy when they heard the news—her father, her mother and Stott. She was thinking of the future, bright and glorious with promise again, now that the dark clouds were passing away. She thought of Jefferson and a soft light came into her eyes as she foresaw a happy wifehood shared with him.

"Why so sober," demanded Ryder, "you've gained your point, your father is to be restored to you, you'll marry the man you love?"

"I'm so happy!" murmured Shirley. "I don't deserve it. I had no faith."

Ryder released her and took out his watch.

"I leave in fifteen minutes for Washington," he said. "Will you trust me to go alone?"

"I trust you gladly," she answered smiling at him. "I shall always be grateful to you for letting me convert you."

"You won me over last night," he rejoined, "when you put up that fight for your father. I made up my mind that a girl so loyal to her father would be loyal to her husband. You think," he went on, "that I do not love my son—you are mistaken. I do love him and I want him to be happy. I am capable of more affection than people think. It is Wall Street," he added bitterly, "that has crushed all sentiment out of me."

Shirley laughed nervously, almost hysterically.

"I want to laugh and I feel like crying," she cried. "What will Jefferson say—how happy he will be!"

"How are you going to tell him?" inquired Ryder uneasily.

"I shall tell him that his dear, good father has relented and——"

"No, my dear," he interrupted, "you will say nothing of the sort. I draw the line at the dear, good father act. I don't want him to think that it comes from me at all."

"But," said Shirley puzzled, "I shall have to tell him that you——"

"What?" exclaimed Ryder, "acknowledge to my son that I was in the wrong, that I've seen the error of my ways and wish to repent? Excuse me," he added grimly, "it's got to come from him. He must see the error of *his* ways."

"But the error of his way," laughed the girl, "was falling in love with me. I can never prove to him that that was wrong!"

The financier refused to be convinced. He shook his head and said stubbornly:

"Well, he must be put in the wrong somehow or

other! Why, my dear child," he went on, "that boy has been waiting all his life for an opportunity to say to me: 'Father, I knew I was in the right, and I knew you were wrong.' Can't you see," he asked, "what a false position it places me in? Just picture his triumph!"

"He'll be too happy to triumph," objected Shirley.

Feeling a little ashamed of his attitude, he said:

"I suppose you think I'm very obstinate." Then, as she made no reply, he added: "I wish I didn't care what you thought."

Shirley looked at him gravely for a moment and then she replied seriously:

"Mr. Ryder, you're a great man—you're a genius—your life is full of action, energy, achievement. But it appears to be only the good, the noble and the true that you are ashamed of. When your money triumphs over principle, when your political power defeats the ends of justice, you glory in your victory. But when you do a kindly, generous, fatherly act, when you win a grand and noble victory over yourself, you are ashamed of it. It was a kind, generous impulse that has prompted you to save my father and take your son and myself to your heart. Why are you ashamed to let him see it? Are you afraid he will love you? Are you afraid I shall love you? Open your heart wide to us—let us love you."

Ryder, completely vanquished, opened his arms and Shirley sprang forward and embraced him as she would have embraced her own father. A solitary tear coursed down the financier's cheek. In thirty years he had not felt, or been touched by, the emotion of human affection.

The door suddenly opened and Jefferson entered. He started on seeing Shirley in his father's arms.

"Jeff, my boy," said the financier, releasing Shirley and putting her hand in his son's, "I've done something you couldn't do—I've convinced Miss Green—I mean Miss Rossmore—that we are not so bad after all!"

Jefferson, beaming, grasped his father's hand.

"Father!" he exclaimed.

"That's what I say—father!" echoed Shirley.

They both embraced the financier until, overcome with emotion, Ryder, Sr., struggled to free himself and made his escape from the room crying:

"Good-bye, children—I'm off for Washington!"

**THE END**

399